The LoveLock

A ROMANTIC SUSPENSE NOVEL

Thank you for Your Support

Best Wishes

04/05/23

by

Eichin Chang-Lim

Copyright © Statement

Fiction Statement

Published by Eichin Chang-Lim
Amazon Edition

The misspelling of the title is intentional.

To all the people who are fighting the silent battles rampaging within them.

"I wanted to tell her that if only something were wrong with my body it would be fine, I would rather have anything wrong with my body than something wrong with my head, but the idea seemed so involved and wearisome that I didn't say anything. I only burrowed down further in the bed." ~Sylvia Plath

"The world wavered and quivered and threatened to burst into flames." ~Virginia Woolf

Prologue

May 2008, San Diego, California

"Hey, Cheetos," Dylan said, calling her by the nickname that always made her toes curl. "Let's get the hell out of Dodge for the day." He lounged against her dorm room doorframe in his carefree way, a roguish grin on his face.

"I'm there," she replied without hesitation. Somehow, Dylan always brought out her spontaneous side in a way no one else could. She loved feeling so liberated. He was her sense of time, her compass. And the best part? She didn't even worry about time or direction with him. They existed outside the realm of structure.

Soon they were headed south on Interstate 5, blasting "Californication" from Dylan's ancient car radio. Mission Bay Park sprawled before them, with its rippling blue waves and vivid green grass punctuated by palm trees. Then, the breathtaking view from Del Coronado Bridge. From high above the bay, Violet noted the strange contrast of navy warships and the lackadaisical sailboats that floated by with no agenda.

How strange that this bridge to our blue sanctuary is also an instrument of destruction as the third deadliest suicide bridge in the United States, seventh in the world, Violet reminded herself.

Why am I even thinking about that? she wondered, shaking her head. Her mind always managed to locate the darker shade, even in the midst of something overwhelmingly beautiful.

She forgot her thoughts as Dylan released his right hand from the wheel and laced his fingers through hers.

Violet thought she knew where they were headed: the Hotel del Coronado! They'd only been there a few times, but each time had been special. Soon, the signature three-tiered, red-pointed roof came into view, piercing the placid sky. Violet had a feeling Dylan would whisk her to their favorite spot.

She loved the old-world elegance of the hotel, not to mention its impressive Tinseltown history. Clark Gable, Charlie Chaplin, Mae West . . . they'd all stayed there. It was easy to see why: the beach was enchanting, with baby-powder-white sand and splendid views.

Getting out of the car, they blinked in the blinding May sun. The boardwalk was swarming with tourists, as usual. The wind tousled Violet's hair as she kicked off her flip-flops, and they walked hand in hand through the expanse of white sand.

Finally, they came upon a patch of shoreline that was less crowded. Violet stretched out on the sand and was able to focus on the perfection around her. The blue sky framed the scene before her, and the sight of it calmed Violet's soul. Then Dylan removed his hoodie and extracted the box from his pocket. He held it out to Violet.

"Go on, open it," he urged.

"You shouldn't have," she said in her best southern drawl. But when she opened the black box, there was no joking.

Sitting within it were two chains. A red, heart-shaped locket with a tiny keyhole in its center dangled from one. The other chain held a key about half the size of her pinky finger.

"Wow," Violet said. Then she noticed something on the key. "Is there an engraving on this?" She took a closer look. "*One heart*. The key is your part, isn't it?"

"Look at the locket," Dylan replied.

"*One love*," Violet read aloud, running her finger over the engraving. "This is beautiful." She grinned mischievously at him. "I've never seen you do something so cheesy, but I'm glad you did."

Dylan laughed. "You make me do cheesy things, Cheetos." He leaned in and draped the necklace around her neck, giving her a kiss before fastening it. The heart locket nestled comfortably in the dip of her collarbone. Dylan donned his own necklace, which hung low enough that it could easily be concealed by his T-shirt. She wrapped her arms around his neck.

"So you have the key to my heart," Violet whispered in his ear.

"Literally, now." Dylan grinned.

"In every sense."

"And I hope I always do," he whispered, his heart pounding.

"Always."

Their lips met and lingered. His mouth slowly traveled downward.

She wanted more.

"How I love you, Cheetos."

PART ONE

Chapter 1

April 1995, Suburban San Diego

Violet shushed her sister and pulled the comforter over their heads as their mother, Wanda, opened the bedroom door and peeked into the room. The girls tried unsuccessfully to stifle their giggles.

"Alright, my little criminals," their mother teased. "What mischief are you into now?"

She walked over and pulled the blanket down a little to reveal a mop of tousled chestnut hair. She gave Amber a kiss on the top of her head. Violet peeked over the blanket, her amethyst eyes twinkling.

"What are you doing in your sister's bed, you little scamp?" Wanda asked, grinning. She began tickling Violet until she was screeching, squirming, and begging for mercy.

"Stop, stop!" she cried.

Their mother finally relented. "Okay, off to your own bed." She gave Violet a playful slap on her bottom as she jumped out of the bed and raced across the room to her own bed.

"Dad and I will be back soon. Gilecia is downstairs if you need anything."

Amber reached up, wrapped her arms around her mother's swan-white neck, and murmured, "I love you, Mommy. Where are you going?"

"I love you too, sweetheart. We're going to a party. Go night-night now, girls."

She stood to go. "And *please* be nice to your sitter. Violet, that means you."

Their mother gently closed the door. As her footsteps faded, Violet sat up. Amber's bed was on the opposite wall. The room was warmly lit by the pink Disney Tinkerbell night-light on the center nightstand. In the far corner of the room was a pile of packages with dolls, new dresses, and other girlish fancies from their seventh birthday party earlier that day. The glow-in-the-dark star stickers scattered on the ceiling gave the room a whimsical mood.

Violet turned to her sister. "Hey! Amber! Let's go play." Violet jumped out of bed and tiptoed to flip on the overhead light.

"What do you wanna do?" Amber asked nervously. Although she was twenty minutes older than Violet, she tended to be the more cautious child. Amber was the sweet princess, while Violet was Little Miss Independent, as their mom affectionately put it. They looked alike. However, their parents named them after their eye colors. Amber had golden, light-brown eyes; Violet had lavender eyes.

"Look at our new stuff!" Violet said. She flopped herself down on the ground by her heap of loot. Amber shimmied out of bed and sat alongside her to examine their gifts. Their favorite was the Barbie Doll Chef set. They both jumped to play with it immediately, but Violet soon grew bored and looked about for more late-night shenanigans.

"Amber, I got an idea," Violet said. "Dad just got another clock from the store to fix. I want to fix it up for him! I know how to do it. We can play with the Barbie stuff later."

Amber frowned. "I don't know," she said. "Gilecia can hear us."

Violet rolled her eyes. Sometimes she wished Amber wasn't such a baby. "Don't worry. She's downstairs, and she always just sits there and watches TV. Besides, Mom told her we were sleeping."

Violet sprang up and stealthily exited the room. She crept past the living room, keeping her eyes on the drowsy babysitter's head bobbing back and forth as she fought sleep. Soundlessly, she made her way down the hall to her father's office, where the French brass antique alarm clock sat.

One of their father's hobbies was collecting antique clocks and refurbishing them. Violet had knelt next to him on many occasions, watching him open up the panel, remove the insides—"the guts," as he called them—and put them back together again in a superior form. She was eager to try it.

Her dad had just brought this fancy one home from an antique store that afternoon. The clock and tools were on a tray. One day it would sit proudly on the mantel, but Violet knew she could speed up the process. In only a minute, she returned to her room with the project.

The sisters beheld the clock, brassy but immaculately shined, with fancy Roman numerals on the face. *Dad will be so proud when I show him*, Violet thought.

"Are you sure you can put it back together?" Amber asked with concern.

"I know how to do it. I've seen it a zillion times. Just watch." Violet placed the clock facedown and attempted to open the back panel with a small jeweler's screwdriver while Amber watched.

"I don't want you getting into trouble, Violet," Amber said. "Why don't you wait for Dad and he can show you how?"

"No way," Violet said as she yanked the back panel open and gutted the inside components. The whole *point* was to do it herself. "I got it."

When Violet set her mind to something, she would see it through— no matter what.

* * * * *

The twins lay sprawled on the living room carpet, watching *The Lion King* video they'd seen countless times before. Wanda sat behind them, nestled on the off-white leather sofa, still in her burgundy satin robe. The aroma of coffee permeated the room as she sipped from her cup.

Violet glanced back at her mother and smiled at the way her wavy, butter-blonde hair fell over her shoulder and seemed to sparkle in the morning light. People always told Violet that she had her mother's hair, and she was proud of it.

My mother is so pretty. Violet scrambled to her feet and hurried to her mother.

"How was the party last night, Mommy?" She squeezed next to her mother on the sofa and Amber joined in.

Wanda set the coffee cup on the side table and pulled both girls into her arms. She gave them a brief account of the party. However, the events of the night before replayed in her head in detail.

* * * * *

Wanda was excited to finally get a night out with her handsome husband, Aidan. She'd been looking forward to this party for weeks.

"Here you go," Aidan said as he handed the key to their Mercedes to the valet parking attendant and turned to help Wanda from the vehicle.

He extended his hand, and Wanda reached out to him, her bejeweled fingers sparkling in the restaurant's blazing porch lights.

She kept her eyes on Aidan as she extended her right leg and stepped from the vehicle. She knew she looked great tonight in her low-cut red dress and matching onyx beaded necklace and earrings. As she expected, her husband didn't make eye contact with her; he couldn't pull his gaze away from her porcelain breasts as they threatened to spill from her dress. She smiled. He always told her that she still turned him on, even after all these years.

After graduating from Yale Law School, Aidan Swanson became a criminal defense lawyer—and a successful one at that, having won a major drug trafficking case and earning his solid reputation. He ran a successful law firm with three partners and was active in the local Lions Club charity functions. On this particular night, he and Wanda were attending the Lions Club officers' installation and new member initiation dinner at a classy Italian restaurant.

The host recognized them immediately and nodded at them. "Welcome, Mr. and Mrs. Swanson. This way." They followed his crisp white-jacketed figure as he guided them to a large private room. Aidan had one arm protectively circled around Wanda's waist.

Upon entering the reserved room, Wanda beheld the opulence of the evening. Fresh-cut flowers sprang from dual-handled Italian ceramic vases with an antique finish as the centerpiece on all nine round tables. A lion head fountain gave off a soothing, tinkling sound in the corner, while people mingled and swayed to the soft classical music floating in the air.

Wanda turned and spotted Kendra waving to her from across the room. She wore a sunbeam-yellow gown. Wanda leaned into Aidan and whispered, "It looks like her hair has grown out since last time," when fine brunette baby hairs were only just starting to sprout from her head.

"You look stunning, Kendra," shouted Wanda, grinning ear to ear. The two women embraced. The warm colors of their dresses made them appear like a single ember of fire. Aidan came forward, shook hands with Gordon, Kendra's husband, and gave him an encouraging pat on the shoulder.

The family had a friendly, professional relationship. Aidan had provided Gordon Purcell and his family legal advice for his accounting and personal financial management firm, which had earned its reputable standing and acquired some major local establishments as clients. Gordon was known for his integrity, trustworthiness, and diligence in his work. As his wife battled repeated miscarriages and ovarian cancer over the last two years, he stood by her side whenever needed, always ready to support her through the valleys. Even though his personal life was turbulent at times, his business grew steadily with a cohesive team under his leadership.

The waiter came around taking the drink orders.

"I'm feeling festive. How about a Cosmopolitan?" Wanda said, smiling like she had decided to do something mischievous.

"Merlot," Aidan said.

"Make that two," Gordon said.

All eyes moved to Kendra. "Cranberry iced tea," she replied. Gordon took her hand in his and gave it a light squeeze.

* * * * *

While the men centered their conversations on business, the two women exchanged their tales and travails of motherhood until Kendra finally brought up the elephant in the room: the subject of her ovarian cancer.

"My doctor said I was cancer free at my last checkup, and my chemotherapy worked out well for my particular case." She paused before adding, "Chemo was hell. I couldn't be happier to be done with that."

"I can only imagine," Wanda said softly. "And having a child makes it so much harder, I'm sure."

"I'm not afraid of dying. I just worry about Dylan—he's still so little. The thought of not being able to see him grow up is the hardest part." Kendra's eyes glistened with the tears.

"Oh, I'm sure. But everything will be all right. I'm sure of it." Wanda extended her arms and gave her companion a hug.

The servers delivered delicate appetizer plates to each individual. On one plate sat three large shrimp gathered around a heap of cocktail sauce. The other plate contained an array of appetizers shaped in a flower-like formation, with crab-stuffed mushrooms, prosciutto-wrapped mozzarella, creamy artichoke bruschetta, baked stuffed clams, and Italian rice balls known as *arancini*.

Lifting her fork, Wanda appeared in deep thought about which item to attack first. Kendra stared at the plate absentmindedly before continuing the conversation. "How nice that your twins will always have each other. I so wish Dylan had that."

Wanda knew Kendra felt guilty about her condition, even as illogical as that was. Wanda would hate to think she couldn't provide for her children; she needed her utmost strength so her children could lean on her. But even if she couldn't, it eased her soul to know that the children would have each other when she and their father were long gone from this world.

Poor Kendra, Wanda thought as she chewed on a juicy shrimp.

* * * * *

"Mom, what are you thinking?" The twins' voices brought her back from her reverie. She pulled them in and hugged them tightly as the soundtrack from *The Lion King* filled the room.

Chapter 2

June 1995, Honolulu, Hawaii

Along with the rest of the audience, Violet and her family watched with bated breath. The silver-haired lady in front of Aidan held up her camera, and the man wearing a baseball cap beside her reminded her in a hushed tone to "remember to switch to video, and, oh, remove the lens cap." Everyone was ready to see the courageous coconut tree climber attempt a forty-foot ascent. If he slipped, he could easily fall to his death; he had no rope around his waist, no harness, nothing. He would merely have to rely on his bare feet to push him up the slim, smooth trunk.

It was the second day of the Swanson's long-awaited family vacation in Honolulu, Hawaii. They had decided to kick off their day with a grand tour. Now, having visited the somber Pearl Harbor and North Shore, they were at the Polynesian Cultural Center. It was a lot for one day, but they enjoyed every moment. The minute they stepped off the plane, Violet noticed that the air seemed fresher. It felt like there was more oxygen somehow. Did she detect a slight pineapple scent?

Prevalent earthly troubles seemed to vanish in this slice of heaven. Only a few puffs of cotton-ball clouds floated aimlessly in the azure sky. Everything appeared verdant and fertile. As the Polynesian hula dancers sang and danced to the drums on a floating boat, Violet wondered about the everyday lives of the colorfully adorned performers. Evidently, they were the happiest people on earth. Heck, she was already happier after just a single day! Life seemed perfect.

That is, except for a few hiccups with Amber on the trip. Ever since they'd arrived, she was acting uncharacteristically clingy, whining for attention every few minutes.

"Mommy, hold me." Amber pulled her mother's arm right as the climber began his upward journey.

Violet shot Amber an annoyed look. Why was she acting like such a baby? How could she be so whiny when they were in Hawaii?

She turned back to the show. When the climber made it to the top, he jokingly pretended to fall—only to hoist himself back up. While the rest of the crowd craned their necks and applauded, Amber seemed downright disinterested.

"Honey, are you okay?" their mother asked.

"I'm tired," Amber cried. "When can we go?"

Violet rolled her eyes. They were *not* going to leave early just because Amber was tired!

"Soon, sweetie. We're just sitting here. You can rest your head on me." For the moment, Amber resigned herself to rest her head in her mother's lap and seemed content in the folds of her multicolored dress. She was asleep by the end of the show. Aidan had to carry her.

"It's been a long day," Violet heard her mother say. "We just pushed them too hard."

It wasn't too hard for me, Violet thought.

Amber became increasingly fussy as the day went on. At dinnertime, she wouldn't eat and pushed her tuna tacos around the plate with her fork. She rested her soft cheek against her fist and looked positively miserable—in spite of the fact that this was a gorgeous meal under a hut by the water.

"You don't look good. Let's just go back to the hotel," Wanda said, exchanging a worried glance with her husband, who'd already tossed his napkin on the table in preparation to leave.

"But I don't wanna miss the fire dance," Amber whined.

"I don't think so. You said you're tired, and it's been a long day for everyone."

16

"But I wanna see the fire dance too! Fire dance! Fire dance!" Violet chanted.

Their mother looked skeptical.

"I'm fine," Amber said. "I want to go. *Please?*"

Violet wondered briefly if Amber was saying that because she really did want to see the fiery spectacle or so she wouldn't hold Violet back. However, she didn't think about it too hard. She wanted to see the show.

"Yeah, pleeease?" she chimed in.

Wanda and Aidan reluctantly agreed.

The fire dance was an authentic Hawaiian experience. A line of perfectly bronzed, colorfully dressed dancers in grass skirts filed out holding lit torches. They marched to the sound of a fast-beating drum. The energy was sky high. Violet watched, enraptured.

However, the rousing island dance appeared to have the opposite effect on Amber, who seemed indifferent. Within minutes, she climbed into her mother's lap and fell asleep.

As she watched the undulating dancers, Wanda absent-mindedly stroked her daughter's forehead. She quickly withdrew her hand.

"Aidan," Wanda whispered urgently, touching his knee. "Amber's burning up."

Aidan felt Amber's forehead. "All right, let's go."

Wanda nudged an engrossed Violet as Aidan scooped up Amber and indicated it was time for them to leave. "But it's not over yet!" Violet whined. But after one glare from her father she piped down.

Once they entered their hotel suite, Violet watched as her parents gently placed Amber in bed, underneath a billowy canopy that fluttered in the breeze from their full-sized window. Her face was tomato-red from the fever, and they hoped leaving the window open would cool her down.

Wanda began undressing Amber to put on her pajamas, and she gasped. "Look at this!" she said to Aidan. Violet peeked over curiously. Amber's knee was swollen like a grapefruit.

"How'd this happen, sweetie?" Wanda murmured to her child.

Amber groaned. "I dunno."

Wanda looked up at Violet. "Do you know?"

Violet shrugged. She couldn't remember Amber falling down or hitting her knee.

"I don't like this," Wanda said to Aidan. "Let's take her to the doctor in the morning." Something in her tone gave Violet a bad feeling in the pit of her stomach. *I'm sure it'll be okay,* she told herself. *The doctors will give her some medicine, and she'll be just fine.*

* * * * *

The next morning Violet bounced out of bed, hoping Amber was back to normal and they would go to the beach as they'd planned. However, when her parents tried to rouse Amber, she was still burning up and barely seemed conscious. Quickly sensing the anxiety in the room, Violet hung back and watched from the sidelines.

Wanda dressed Amber. They trooped down to the lobby, where Aidan asked the resort's concierge where the nearest emergency room was.

Emergency? Violet thought. The bad feeling in her stomach got worse. Everyone was silent as the taxi driver drove to the hospital. In her mother's arms, Amber was pale in spite of her new Hawaiian tan. Violet stared out the window at the rolling, volcanic hills and placid blue skies. She never thought they would be taking a taxi to the ER while in paradise. Nevertheless, alas, there they were.

Everything was a blur after they entered the hospital. It wasn't until the attending physician said, "I'm going to go ahead and order blood tests," that their mother snapped back into action.

18

In her mother's arms, Amber was as pale as the hospital walls. Violet's eyes were huge and glassy, at once taking in everything and processing nothing.

After they left, Violet looked over at her father, hoping he'd give her a hug and tell her it would all be all right. Instead, he didn't seem to notice her. He had a look on his face that she had never seen before. With a jolt, it occurred to her that her big, brave daddy was as terrified as she was.

* * * * *

Violet heard many unfamiliar words in Hawaii. *Bone marrow. Biopsy. Cell counts.* All sounded frightening. Moreover, it was awful seeing her mother try to be brave. She clearly wasn't; however, she tried to be for Amber. It was so strange seeing her sister fading away. Amber could be such a worrywart, but that day she calmly accepted all the poking, prodding, and needles that came along with figuring out her condition.

All Violet knew was that she wanted to get out of the hospital and back to what they came for. If Amber could just get better, they could finish seeing the island before their trip was over.

"Dad," she said, tugging on the back of his T-shirt, "I'm hungry." Violet's stomach was rumbling; they hadn't even grabbed breakfast that morning.

"Wait just a darn minute, Violet." Her father had a rough edge to his voice. He didn't exactly snap at her, but he was on his way. She knew he must have been really worried, but it still angered her.

"But I haven't eaten today!"

Her father softened as he remembered. Then he gently reassured her. "In a few minutes, sweetie. Promise." Amber was finishing up a scan. He wanted to be there when she came back.

Once she did, he took Violet to the hospital cafeteria while Wanda stayed with Amber. Violet got a breakfast burrito and munched on it while her father sipped on black coffee and nibbled on a kolache. It was a quiet meal, but peaceful.

"When do you think Amber will be out of here?"

"I don't know," her father replied stoically.

"If she's out soon, can we go to the beach?"

"Amber will need to take it easy, sweetie."

Violet rested her cheek on her fist. "I hope she feels better soon then."

Little did the pair know that it would be one of the last blissfully ignorant meals they would have.

Chapter 3

The trip ended catastrophically.

Violet hadn't understood much of what the doctor said, but she witnessed her parents' reaction and knew it wasn't good news. The pale, drawn faces. The cursing from her normally quiet and composed father. The way her mother left the room to weep where she thought no one could hear her.

Violet had never heard her mother cry before. Each sob cut to Violet's core.

No one told Violet what was going on. She didn't want to ask.

* * * * *

Violet didn't know much, but she knew it was bad enough to fly home early. Amber was admitted to the hospital right away. All of their family began to arrive, including their grandparents on both sides. Even her father's coworkers paid a visit. The following weekend, all of them came to the house with food in tow—mostly those typical Sunday school-style casseroles made with Campbell's cream of mushroom soup, covered in foil or carried over in thermal casings to keep them warm.

"Does this have onions in it?" Violet asked her grandma. She hesitantly dipped her spoon into the cheesy mass and twisted it around.

Her Grandma Rose, a stern-faced Catholic woman who dyed her hair a wretched shade of black, scolded Violet. "Don't you turn your nose up at this, Violet! It was very nice of your parents' dear friends to make this for us to eat. We have to go up to the hospital soon."

Violet learned that Amber had something called leukemia and needed to take powerful medicine—chemotherapy—to kill off all the bad cancer cells that were making her sick.

Violet hated seeing her sister so weak and lethargic, so she tried to avoid going to the hospital. Instead, she played by herself and tried to forget everything that was going on. It wasn't like anyone cared where she was anyway. Amber was too tired to notice, and everyone else was so concerned about Amber that they didn't even seem to know she was there.

Nevertheless, one day Grandma Rose pulled her granddaughter aside. "Violet, listen carefully to me." She spoke in an uncharacteristically gentle tone that immediately struck Violet. This *had* to be important. "This situation is scary for your sister. Now, she's going to be all right, don't you worry, but you have to be there for your sister. Play with her and talk with her like usual. She needs you, Violet."

At first, it was difficult for Violet to spend time with her sister, but she was committed to keeping her promise to her grandma, even when it was hard. She made it her personal mission to entertain her sister and mother, keep their minds off everything that was happening.

Violet told long, detailed stories about what she did at school, mimicking her teachers and classmates with spot-on accuracy. When Amber's hair began to fall out, Violet got her own hair cut in a super-short pixie style. They played dress-up with fancy hairbands and their mother's scarf collection. On Amber's good days, they colored or played UNO, checkers, or Go Fish. Their mother always hovered around, fretting and unable to sit still.

"You wanna play too, Mom?" Violet asked.

"No, dear. Amber, do you need anything? A sip of water? Sprite?"

"Maybe a Sprite."

"I'll get it," Violet said quickly. Her mother barely glanced her way. As usual, it was as if Violet didn't even exist.

Her eyes filling with tears, Violet rushed out of the room and headed for the vending area. She stood on her tiptoes to drop the quarters into the machine and hit the button for the Sprite.

"Violet!" a voice called out. "Is that you?"

She looked around and saw a boy from school, Dylan Purcell. They were in the same grade but different classes, and they had never really talked. The only reason she knew him at all was that their parents knew each other. They'd been at a few social functions together.

Wide-eyed, Violet said, "Dylan? What are you doing here?"

"I'm here for my mom," he said. "She's got cancer."

As jarring as the c-word could be for most people, it actually made Violet relax. She nodded. "Yeah, my sister has cancer too. Well, kind of. Leukemia."

"I'm sorry. That's rough." That was all he said. Somehow she knew he knew. He *understood.* It was like they were part of a secret club.

"We're getting ready to play Go Fish," she said. She smiled, suddenly feeling shy. "You can join us if you want."

"That sounds good."

Violet extracted the soda from the machine. "Cool," she said. They smiled at each other.

* * * * *

"Honey, there's something we'd like to talk to you about. A way you might be able to help Amber," Violet's mother said. She had a nurse from the hospital with her.

Violet looked at her mother's haggard face and listened as she explained that the doctors wanted to give some of Violet's healthy bone marrow to Amber since it so closely matched her sister's. "But of course, it is your decision," her mother added.

"Will it hurt?" She hated asking, because she was supposed to be

23

brave.

Her mother glanced at the nurse. "You'll be under anesthesia, which means you'll be in a deep, deep sleep the whole time. When you wake up, it will all be over," her mother said.

"That's right," the nurse confirmed. "You won't feel a thing. Your body will replace the marrow that gets taken out, and soon you'll be just as good as new."

"But it's still a big thing to do," Wanda said. "And you'll have to be a brave girl. You don't have to decide now. Take some time to think about it. If you have any questions, just ask. If I don't know the answer, we'll find out from the doctors and nurses." They conversed with Violet like she was an adult. Violet was aware of the seriousness of the situation.

"I want to do it," Violet said without hesitation.

"What?" her mother said, her eyes wide. "Honey, are you sure? You don't have to make a decision right now."

"It will help Amber, right?"

"Well, we *hope* so."

"She's my sister. I want to help her get better."

"Oh honey. You're my good, sweet girl. You're Mommy's warrior princess." Wanda hugged her tight. Violet felt proud and important. *She* was the one able to do something to help Amber. For the first time since Amber got sick, Violet was the center of attention. Everyone said what a good sister she was—how brave, how strong, how loving.

The only person who didn't make a big fuss was Amber. She was so weak that she didn't say much at all. She just gave Violet a long look and squeezed her hand. But they didn't need spoken language. They were more than sisters. They were twins.

24

* * * * *

On the day before the surgery, Dylan brought Violet a bag of Hot Cheetos—her favorite—and a stuffed dog that looked a little worse for wear. "I used to sleep with Waggs every night," he said with a nonchalant shrug. "You know, when I was younger. I thought you might like him." As casual as he tried to make it seem, Violet recognized the enormity of the gift. She had given her own favorite animal—Pickles, the potbellied pig—to Amber early on in her treatment.

"Thanks," she said, accepting the scruffy, one-eared canine with the gravity a queen might show a foreign dignitary.

Before the surgery, Violet's parents kissed her and told her how proud they were of her. "You've been so strong through all this," her mother said. "I don't know what we would have done without you." Violet felt ten feet tall.

Violet was wheeled into the operating room and given the shot through the IV in her arm. Almost immediately she fell into a deep, dreamless sleep.

When Violet awoke, her grandmother was there waiting for her, working on her cross-stitching. Waggs, who hadn't been allowed in the operating room with her, had been propped up by her side. Her parents were nowhere to be seen.

"You did real good," Grandma Rose told her, noticing that she was awake. "Now it's all over." She went back to her needlework.

"Where're Mom and Dad?"

"They're with Amber. Don't worry. They'll be back."

Violet closed her eyes. *What about me?* She couldn't help but wonder, hugging Waggs tight. *It doesn't matter what I do. They're never here for me anymore.*

Chapter 4

Amber was going downhill.

The blood marrow transplants gave her a slight boost, but it was just a brief respite. Violet knew by looking at her sister that she was slowly losing her every day. Amber was sallow, and her lashless, brown-gold eyes were languid and distant.

As Amber's condition worsened, Violet didn't want to leave her side, but even that became more and more difficult. Violet was being shut out as her parents were glued to Amber, attending to her every need in a manic way—especially her mother. She didn't sleep or eat anymore. *Everything* was about Amber. Violet wasn't just watching her sister waste away; she felt like she was losing her mother too.

One day, Violet was telling Amber about their next-door neighbor's funny new cat. Amber was too weak to laugh, yet Violet could see the twinkle in her twin's eyes as she imitated the cross-eyed feline trying to chase a string.

"Shh, Violet," Wanda interrupted. "You don't want to disturb your sister."

Violet stopped short, her exuberance evaporating instantly. Lately, it seemed like her mother wanted her to behave as if they were in church—no talking above a whisper, no laughing, no music or dancing or silly games. As if Violet's youthful enthusiasm was just a painful reminder of everything Amber was missing.

I just want to make Amber feel better. Was she being selfish and insensitive? Was she only making Amber feel worse by rubbing her nose in all the things she couldn't do anymore?

Her eyes filled with tears. Violet mumbled something about getting a snack and escaped to the waiting area.

She sat alone, though the hospital hummed with life all around her: social workers talking to devastated family members; families having powwows out of earshot; and then, of course, the occasional weary spouse trying to power themselves with coffee as the madness raged around them.

Then she saw Dylan. He wore his baseball cap backward.

Violet was happy to see her new friend. He had been an oasis for her during their long days together in the hospital. Sometimes they would just sit in companionable silence, but most of the time they loved to make each other laugh and feel like normal kids again.

However, today something was different.

Violet frowned as she saw the stormy look on Dylan's face. "Dylan . . .?"

"I hate it here!" he said vehemently.

"W-what happened?"

"My dad yelled at me for changing the station in my mom's room. Why do we *always* have to have it on classical? It's not fair! I'm so sick of this stupid place!" He angrily kicked a chair leg with his Nike.

"I know what you mean," she said. "It . . . *sucks*." She felt a thrill of rebelliousness using the forbidden word.

Dylan just glowered.

"My mom won't let me play music either," continued Violet when he didn't say anything. "Like Amber cares. It's dumb."

They sat in silence for a few moments. The furrows on Dylan's brow began to relax.

"Mom's not doing good. Her blood pressure was real low today, and she almost passed out," he finally said.

"Amber's not well today either. She hasn't been to school in two

27

weeks."

"I wish we could just go home," said Dylan softly. "Go back to how it used to be."

"I know. Me too."

A tear trickled down her cheek. A second later, a warm, slightly sticky hand enclosed hers. For the first time in a long time, she felt like someone actually cared about *her* feelings for a change. It felt so good. She wished they could just stay like that forever.

* * * * *

As it turned out, Violet's stint in the hospital was nearly over. The doctors said it was time to make Amber "more comfortable."

Making Amber comfortable consisted of her sleeping in a hospital bed in the middle of the living room, where everyone sat around her on the couches. Her mother, ever the worse for wear, set up camp on the longer leather couch across from Amber. She stayed strong in front of Amber, but as soon as her daughter fell asleep, Wanda slipped away to the kitchen, where she crumpled in a heap on the floor and sobbed.

Violet felt like a ghost. She floated over to her sister, who was already drugged from multiple doses of morphine she'd received that day.

"Just relax, Amber," Violet whispered. "I got your favorite book right here."

Out from underneath her arm she extracted an illustrated book— *Frog and Toad Are Friends*. She cleared her throat and began to read to Amber. She held up the pictures even though Amber was barely there.

"Spring. Frog ran up the path to Toad's house. He knocked on the front door.

"There was no answer. 'Toad, Toad,' shouted Frog, 'wake up. It is spring!'"

Her voice carried on, strong and steady, until the book was complete. When she was done, she tucked Amber in and kissed her on the forehead. She had never done that before, but it struck her as the perfect moment right then. When she looked up, her parents stood across the room, her mother's face buried in her father's shoulder, his eyes misty and emotional. Her dad motioned for her to come over, and they embraced. The soon-to-be family of three.

* * * * *

Lilies fluttered in the wind, framing the fresh tombstone and the newly carved name. Each stone dotting the rolling green hills represented another soul, but only one mattered to the black-clad group surrounding the small casket as it was lowered into the ground.

Violet tugged on the strap of her black dress. She hadn't worn it in ages, and it was at least one size too small. She hated it. Just like she hated all the people there that she had never met before. She wanted them all to go away so they could grieve for Amber alone, as a family.

During the funeral service, Wanda had been flanked on all sides by family, friends, and coworkers—a mass of people to help her carry the burden she now bore. Her mouth was a thin, tight line, her eyes overflowing with tears, but she hadn't fallen apart.

Now, at Amber's final resting place, Violet wondered if her tortured mother had a reserve of strength to get her through this final trial. Wanda approached the grave one last time. With a trembling hand, she threw a handful of lilies onto the glossy, black wood. Tears streamed down her face, and she appeared to be struggling to breathe. Her knees shook, buckled, and all of a sudden, her mother was falling to the ground.

Violet's father was swiftly at her side. "Wanda, Wanda!" he cried, trying to revive her. She had passed out from the stress.

Watching the scene unfold had a profound impact on Violet. She felt nauseous to her core. She worried she'd have to use the bathroom.

Soon Wanda opened her eyes and, after a moment, managed to get to her feet. Everyone gathered around, clucking with concern, as Aidan supported her to the car.

No one paid any attention to the little girl standing by the grave, tears flowing down her face.

* * * * *

That night was grim. Her mother was inconsolable; her father self-medicated with whiskey. Meanwhile, Violet stayed in her room, which was deafeningly quiet. She sat on the corner of her bed and placed her hand on her chest. Her heart felt so heavy she could barely move. It was like wearing a ten-pound vest. She lifted her head, a feat taking far too much strength, and glanced at Amber's empty bed. It had been empty for weeks at that point, yet knowing Amber was in the other room had made it bearable. And now? Now she would never return.

Violet slumped onto the bed, pulled her knees to her chest. The room was spinning. Weirdly, it hadn't occurred to her until that moment to consider what life without Amber would be like. It was incomprehensible, inconceivable. Now, it was a reality, that reality was crushing her. The sick feeling in her stomach came up, erupted through body-racking sobs.

Come back, come back! How could you leave me?

Violet cried harder and harder. She worried she wouldn't stop. Somehow, at some unknown point in the wee hours of the morning, her exhausted body finally allowed sleep to overtake her.

Her slumber was fitful. Scattered scenes flitted through her dreams: the familiar blank walls of the hospital, doctors in white coats, her mother crying, a hole in the ground that went on and on and on.

Then came the golden-eyed girl herself. Her beloved sister. She had a full mop of messy hair like she used to, framing a face alight with life once more.

"Amber!" Violet said, bewildered. "What are you doing here?"

"I missed you. Wanna play awhile?"

Violet was flooded with emotions. She wanted to reach out and touch her sister but couldn't. "You're not real. You're not really here."

Her sister's eyes flashed passionately. "I am here," Amber insisted. "I'm here whenever you need me."

Violet grabbed her sister's hand and they ran, laughing, through a field of wildflowers. Violet's sadness vanished. Not only was her sister alive, but she was healthy and bursting with energy and vitality! It was so good to see her back to her old self that the pain of the past months melted away.The peace and happiness lasted until Violet woke up.

The cold realization settled on her. Amber was dead. She always would be dead. She couldn't be there for her. Yet, it felt so real. If only it were.

Chapter 5

In the days that followed, Violet's family was still reeling from losing Amber. They all felt robbed. The initial shock gave way to anger and profound devastation that seemed to course through their very veins. Each night, Violet's sleep was punctuated by strange dreams; however, none had the clarity and emotional resonance of that first night.

Her mother often didn't get out of bed at all. Violet heard stifled sobs coming from her parents' bedroom as her mother cried into her pillow.

Most mornings she was on her own for breakfast, since her father was busy hovering over her mother. There were no good days or bad days—simply bad days and worse days.

Her father finally pulled Violet aside one morning and told her, "Your mother has depression. She'll get better, but it takes time. We just have to be patient."

Violet tried not to remember all the times she'd been told that Amber, too, would get better. *This time will be different*, she assured herself.

Soon summer was over, and it was time for school to start again.

"Let's go get your uniform today," her father said. He was referring to the dress code for the new Catholic school he wanted Violet to attend.

"But I don't want to go to a new school. I want to see my friends," she said, thinking about Dylan.

"I know you're sad. So am I. But I really think a change will help." Aidan told Violet that he hoped a new environment would do her some good. It would be a "fresh start" and "clean slate."

Her father had enough on his plate, holding down a demanding profession and playing the role of both parents lately, so Violet tried to make things as easy on him as she could. Besides, she didn't have the energy to fight. What difference did it make where she went? It all felt pointless anyway.

"Whatever," she said with a shrug. "Whenever you wanna go." She pulled out the chair opposite him and slumped down.

He pushed a piece of paper toward her. It was a list of the different after-school activities the new school offered. "The school has plenty of extracurricular programs. You can choose whatever you like." He explained that being active would help her feel better, and it would help her meet new people and, with luck, new friends.

Violet knew before she even read the list that she wanted to take dance—particularly ballet. She and Amber had always played ballerina and practiced dancing on their tippy-toes. Her father nudged her to choose a second option. Recalling what fun she'd had acting out stories and doing impressions and voices to cheer Amber up, she placed her index finger on "Theater."

She pretended to be happy often enough; she figured acting would be a cinch.

* * * * *

The first day at the new school made Violet wish she'd put up more of a fight about switching schools. Sure, it would have been hard to see all their old friends and feel Amber's absence from their usual group, but somehow this was worse. None of the kids even knew Amber. They didn't know that she dreamed of being a ballet dancer or that she always tried to "shoot the moon" in hearts, regardless of what hand she was dealt, or that she brayed like a donkey when she laughed too hard. No matter what Violet ever told her new classmates about her sister, Amber would never be a flesh-and-blood person to them. Violet felt all alone in her grief.

More than anything, she missed Dylan. Not only did he know Amber, but he knew what she—what they *all*—had been through. The fear, the anger, the self-pity, the guilt, the boredom, the heartache. Only someone who'd gone through it could ever really understand.

When she got home from her first day, Violet saw that Amber's hospital bed had been removed from the living room. *It's about time.* She started up to her room and noticed that all of the family pictures that usually lined the stairway had been taken down. When she got to her room, the room she'd always shared with Amber, there was only one bed. All of Amber's clothes and toys had been removed. It was as if Amber had never existed.

Violet ran to her mother's room and knocked on the door. There was no answer. She eased opened the door just a crack.

"Mom?"

Her mother was curled up on the bed, her back to Violet.

"Mom, Dad took some, uh, stuff out of my room. Do you know where he put it? There's some that I don't want to get rid of."

Her mother didn't respond.

"Mom?" Violet said louder.

Her mother finally shifted and rolled over. "I don't know, Violet," she mumbled. "You'll have to ask your father."

"Okay," she said, "where is he?"

"He's at work," her mother replied flatly, turning away again.

Violet retreated, closing the door behind her. She went back to her room and started looking through the closet and chest of drawers to see exactly what was missing.

When her father got home later that evening, Violet met him at the door.

"Dad, where is all the stuff you took? You didn't throw it away, did you?"

"No, honey," he assured her. "I didn't throw it away. I gave it away to a good cause."

"But I wanted some of that stuff! Amber's purple fairy wings and her favorite nightie. And Paddington Bear."

"I'm sorry, honey. It's already gone."

"How could you give them away without even asking me?"

"I know it's hard now," he said. "But in the long run, it's better this way. You'll see." He gave her a too-bright smile. "So how was your first day at school?"

"I hate it! I don't want to go there. I want to go back to my old school."

Her father's smile became strained. Violet could see his patience wearing thin. "Honey," he said, "first days are always tough. You just have to give it a chance. You'll feel differently when you've been there a while. I promise. Can you give it a chance? For me? Please?"

Violet bit her lip. He looked so exhausted.

"Okay, Dad. I'll try."

* * * * *

Her father was right, sort of. In some ways, the school did get easier. Violet made friends with two girls in her class. She especially enjoyed being a part of the theater troupe, which was run by a pretty young nun named Sister Grace.

However, Violet had more difficulty with the religious aspect of her new school. Her parents had always been strictly Christmas-and-Easter Christians. They didn't even say grace before dinner. Therefore, the Bible stories and constant talk about God, Jesus, and prayer were all new. Violet listened attentively, trying to catch up on what she didn't know. However, at times it seemed like the more she learned, the more questions she had.

In Religious Education class one day, they were studying Noah and the flood. Violet looked around in horror, but the rest of her classmates seemed perfectly calm.

She raised her hand. "You're saying God was going to *kill* all the people in the entire world?" she asked in disbelief when Sister Agnes called on her. "Why would he do that?"

"They were bad people," Sister Agnes said sternly. "Sinners."

"But still, that doesn't mean they deserved to die!"

"Young lady!" Sister Agnes said, aghast. "Are you questioning *God*? The Supreme Being? He is always justified in His actions. You can be sure God doesn't kill innocent people."

Tears sprang into Violet's eyes, but the sister's stern expression squelched any rebuttal.

Afterward, though, Sister Agnes's words kept echoing over and over again. *God doesn't kill innocent people. God doesn't kill innocent people. God doesn't kill innocent people.*

Later, at mass, Violet was in line for the sacrament. The closer she got to the priest, the more agitated she became. Then it was her turn. "The Body of Christ," said the priest as he offered the host.

Violet felt like she was going to throw up.

Blinded by tears, she took off toward the back of the chapel, pushed through the doors, and ran down the stairs to the reception hall. Sobbing and gasping for breath, she sat on the steps, hugging her knees and rocking back and forth.

All of a sudden, Sister Grace was beside her, holding her close. "There, there. It's okay," she said, stroking Violet's head.

"It's not fair!" Violet moaned. "Why? Why would God let Amber die? She wasn't a bad person. She was *good*. She didn't deserve to die!"

"Of course she didn't, sweetheart!"

"B-but Sister Agnes said . . ."

"Said what?"

"She said God doesn't kill innocent people."

Sister Grace paused. "Well, I'm sure that's true, but God didn't kill Amber."

"But He could have stopped it, couldn't He? Kept her from dying?"

Sister Grace squeezed her tight. "I don't know how it all works, honey. But I believe God only wants what's best for us."

"What's best for us?" Violet snapped, suddenly angry. "How can Amber's death be best for us?"

"That's a very good question. And I don't have all the answers. Maybe there are reasons that we can't see, or maybe some bad things have to happen in order for us to be able to make free choices. I don't know. But what I *do* know is that God loves us more than we can imagine. I know that beyond all doubt."

Violet was surprised by the firm conviction in Sister Grace's voice. "H-how do you know?"

Sister Grace thought for a moment. "You know, I didn't always want to be a nun," she said. "I was engaged to be married to a wonderful man named Joseph. We were so in love!" She smiled a faraway smile.

"Then, just a couple of weeks before the wedding, we were in a terrible car accident. A truck crossed the center line and hit us head-on. One minute I was in the car, and suddenly I was outside the car, looking down on it. Up above me, there was a bright light. It was like the sun, but it was *living*. And I was drawn upward to it."

Violet listened, spellbound.

"As I got closer, a figure approached me. It was my Nana, who had died years ago. I knew it was her even though she looked younger and not stooped over like she had been. She was so happy to see me.

She embraced me and told me that she had been watching over me. She told me she was going to help Joseph—who she had never met in life—pass over, but this was as far as I could come since I would be going back. I was very upset. I told her I didn't want to go back!"

Violet's mouth dropped open. "You didn't *want* to come back?"

"No. Being in that place, in the presence of that light, was more wonderful than anything I had ever experienced. It was pure love. Love more perfect and amazing than anything I'd ever experienced." She sighed.

"But Nana said it wasn't my time, and I had to come back. The next thing I knew, I was in my body again, in the ambulance."

Violet just sat there, trying to absorb it all. "So, is that why you became a nun?" she finally asked.

Sister Grace nodded. "Nothing else on Earth seemed as real or as important as what I had experienced in those few minutes. I wanted to devote my life to honoring God and helping others who were hurting and lost." She looked down at Violet and squeezed her shoulder.

"I'm absolutely confident that Amber is truly in a better place. She's watching over you, you know."

"I had a dream about her," Violet admitted shyly. "Right afterward."

"That wasn't just a dream," Sister Grace said. "I believe that was really her, wanting to make contact and let you know she is okay. Amber is always there with you. Someday, when it's *your* time, she'll be the one to welcome you over. Just like Joseph will for me."

Chapter 6

It was Mother's Day. Violet sat up, switched off the alarm, and tiptoed to the window. She pulled open the drapes to see dawn break. The sky was shifting from a dark gray to a vivid purple that promised a beautiful day. Violet pressed her nose on the cold window and stared out at the sky. She felt hopeful about the day for the first time since Amber's death.

Everything would be perfect. The previous night, her father took her to the market to get all the necessary ingredients for breakfast in bed, along with supplies to construct her own handmade card. Her original creation said, "Dear Mommy, Happy Mother's Day! I love you. I hope I can put a smile on your face." She signed her name and added a heart.

After putting on some jeans and an old T-shirt, Violet skipped to the kitchen. From the refrigerator, she extracted a tomato and green bell pepper. When she closed the door, her father was standing there.

"Got up earlier, hmm?" he whispered.

Violet nodded excitedly and proceeded with her top-secret operation. After extracting a chef's knife from the knife set, she carefully cut the pepper in long strips, paying special attention to keep them the same length and width. She cut the tomato in the same fashion. An hour later, the kitchen was filled with the invigorating aroma of sautéed vegetables.

Now it was time for the finishing touches. The veggie-ham omelet sat folded in the center of a plate, flanked by a mug of creamy, freshly brewed coffee. Aidan offered to carry the tray, undoubtedly a little worried that his sometimes overly enthusiastic ten-year-old daughter would spill it. Violet carried a bouquet of daffodils she had picked from their yard. She was lured to the yellow flowers, thinking that no one could be unhappy looking at such a bright and cheerful color.

With everything ready, Aidan led his daughter to the master bedroom. There they saw Wanda curled in the fetal position with her back turned toward them.

"Happy Mother's Day!" Violet exclaimed.

Silence.

"Are you awake? Honey?" Aidan's voice was soft and gentle.

They waited a few moments before Wanda turned around to face them. Her dull gaze and pale face indicated her low spirits.

"Happy Mother's Day! Violet made breakfast for you," he said, reaching over and stroking her blonde hair. He spoke slowly, his voice overly cheerful, like he was speaking to a toddler who he wanted to make sure would behave.

"Sorry, guys. I didn't sleep well. I'll eat later." Then Wanda waved her arm toward the bedside table. "Just leave it there." She rolled over on the bed, away from them.

Violet felt her heart plummet. She placed the flowers beside the tray and quietly exited the room, leaving her father stroking her mother's hair.

"It's okay. She'll wake up later and feel better," Violet murmured to herself, gnawing on her thumb.

An hour later, she tiptoed back to her parents' room and cracked open the door. The food remained untouched. Her mother was in the same position, but her father was gone. She gently closed the door.

Throughout the morning, Violet wandered aimlessly around the house, her ears perked for any sign that her mother was emerging from her room.

At noon, Violet heard hushed tones and whimpers issuing from her parents' room. She crept up and put her ear to the door.

"I wish Amber were here." Her mother's voice cracked as she broke into a sob. "Mother's Day just reminds me that I'm not a mother to my baby anymore." Aidan said something unintelligible but sounded desperate to console her, clearly to no avail.

Violet didn't think the tugging feeling in her chest could get worse, but it did. A stab of sharp pain almost immobilized her. Somehow, she made it back to her room. Violet felt a flurry of emotions. She was sad, just like her mother, and upset that her hard work was for nothing. She was disappointed that she couldn't put a smile on her mother's face today.

Beyond all, she was surprised at how angry she felt. She might as well have been dead, for all her mother was concerned. Violet couldn't contain her tears.

I wish I were the dead one.

Chapter 7

The ensuing years of Violet's childhood were defined by Wanda's depression.

Her mother didn't intentionally hurt her; she knew that intellectually. Still, the jagged hole in Violet's heart grew larger, not only due to Amber's absence but her mother's too. The one bright spot was her father stepping up as he drove her around. In order to do so, he changed his specialty from criminal defense to a corporate law attorney. He encouraged Violet in her studies and hobbies. In general, Aidan was present for his daughter—even if his primary concern was his wife.

At school, Violet found solace in drama. In spite of her beloved Sister Grace leaving at the end of her second year to teach at a school on an Indian reservation in New Mexico, Violet didn't lose her love of the theater. She threw herself into every role, taking on the speech and mannerisms of each character even when she wasn't on stage. It was a welcome break to be someone else for a while, although it was just pretend.

Her dedication to the art paid off. When her high school's drama department announced they would be performing Shakespeare's *A Midsummer Night's Dream*, Violet won the part of the Fairy Queen, a meaty role for a sophomore. All the best parts always went to seniors. It was a real honor. Violet was determined to prove herself worthy of the privilege.

Knowing her father's stressful profession, Violet usually refrained from calling him at work; this time, she called him anyway. She thought she would just leave a voice message for him about the exciting news. Surprisingly, Aidan picked up the call.

"Your hard work paid off, baby!" he said warmly. "I'm so proud of you." He paused before adding, "Your mother will be too."

Violet's heart skipped a beat. "Don't tell her! I want to be the one to tell her."

"Okay, okay. I won't say anything," Aidan assured her.

When Violet hung up the phone, she felt giddy. Her mother would surely perk up at such exciting news! She hadn't given up on her mother yet.

That afternoon, Violet walked into the living room. The curtains were drawn, so it was dark aside from the blue light emanating from the TV screen. Wanda was still in her pajamas, watching an afternoon talk show.

"Hi, Mom," Violet said, trying to keep her voice steady. She was still trembling with excitement.

"Oh, hi." Wanda didn't look up from her program. Dark circles appeared like bruises under her eyes. She was haggard and thin as a skeleton.

Violet folded her hands and inched closer. "Mom, I have good news. I was cast as the Fairy Queen for the school play!" She waited to give her mother time to respond, hoping she would share the enthusiasm.

"Oh, that's good," she said in a flat tone. Wanda didn't smile, didn't even look at her. It was as if Violet merely said, "It stopped raining outside." Just a mundane, trivial announcement.

"Well, that's it. Thanks." Violet awkwardly withdrew from her mother and went to her room, feeling utterly dejected.

It's pointless to even try. Why do I keep expecting her to be any different?

Violet forced her mother's tepid reaction from her mind and focused on the immense task of memorizing her lines. The Shakespearean dialogue was exponentially more difficult than anything she'd done up to now. Moreover, there would be no ad-libbing if she got lost or forgot her lines. Violet delved into the script. She'd recite it until she could do it backward and forward, and she'd perform it flawlessly, electrifying the audience and earning her first standing ovation.

Then she'll be proud . . .

* * * * *

"Be kind and courteous to this gentleman. Hop in his walks and . . ."

Violet rehearsed her lines at the kitchen table for the umpteenth time. The previous night she had a nightmare that was still psyching her out. In it, she was alone on the stage with only one spotlight shining far too brightly into her eyes. She was fishing for a line that wouldn't surface. As she tried to spit it out, she kept getting more and more flustered.

"Take a deep breath, Violet. You're doing great." Violet didn't have to see the amber-colored eyes to know who her big cheerleader was. Violet could still feel the warmth of her love when she woke up from the nightmare.

Violet tried to channel her sister's encouragement as she practiced one last time. Finally, she pushed aside her lines at the table and released a long exhale. She felt nervous. However, she soon realized it wasn't so much about her performance as much as a certain someone's presence at it—or lack thereof.

Even though her mother had promised earlier in the week that she would try to come to the premiere performance, now that the time had come, she'd made no noticeable moves to get ready. She hadn't showered or laid out any clothes.

Violet tentatively knocked on her mother's bedroom door. "Mom, Dad's about to take me to school. But he can come back to pick you up around 6:15. You *are* coming, right?"

Her mother stared at her with languid eyes. "I'll try, Violet. I will."

"It's my first starring role," Violet said. "I'd hate for you not to be there."

Wanda got off the bed and slowly walked to her closet. "What will I wear?" she mused. "I've lost so much weight; none of my old dresses will fit."

"How about the ivory one with all the beading?" Violet had always thought it made Wanda look like a movie star.

"My flapper dress?" Wanda said with a half smile. "You always did like that one."

Heartened, Violet fairly skipped out the door, leaving her mother to get ready. *Finally,* something had gotten her mother out of bed and out of the house! Surely, this was a turning point. Getting out, being with people again . . . this would be the thing that would bring Wanda back into the land of the living.

* * * * *

Violet felt the blinding bright lights of the stage warming her to her core. She stepped onto the stage as Titania, beside the character's husband, Oberon, the Fairy King—or as Violet knew him, her cute, dark-complected friend, Eric.

She was adorned in a virginal-white gown with bell sleeves and a flower crown. The flatiron had worked perfectly on her straight, below-shoulder-length blonde hair, which appeared extra shiny as it reflected the stage lights. Eric's hand wrapped around hers as they stepped onto the stage. At that moment, Violet was fully immersed in her role. She wouldn't dare look into the audience. The name of the game at that moment was the utmost concentration.

The play went off without a hitch. Violet nailed all her lines and felt increasingly confident as the show progressed. In the last scene, she and Eric—Titania and Oberon—entered the palace and blessed the occupants and the master bed with a fairy song.

Puck closed the play by addressing the audience, telling them that if they did not like the play, the best remedy was to pretend it was all a dream.

The audience burst into laughter, applauding in response to his famous last line. He wished the audience good night.

The curtain closed. All the nerves of the evening turned into exhilaration. Violet grinned as the curtain rose once more to reveal the entire cast, their arms linked. Each character marched to the front of the stage to give a bow. Violet and Eric approached a rowdy, whistling audience. She smiled, but now she was nervous. After they took their bow, just as Violet raised her head back up, she hastily scanned the audience. Her eyes finally locked upon her father, standing and clicking the camera.

Her mother was not beside him.

Even as the audience cried, "Bravo! Bravo!" Violet felt her heart sink, and a chill permeated her stomach and spine. Wouldn't she ever learn? Hope led to nothing but crushing disappointment each and every time. *Why am I so stupid?*

She left the theater hall and saw her father waiting by himself on a bench. He wore a wide smile, but it was too big, as if trying to compensate for her mother's absence.

"You were great!" he exclaimed, embracing his daughter. Violet suddenly felt tired, beyond exhausted, and half-heartedly returned the hug.

"Thanks, Dad."

"You really shined onstage. Literally. You looked radiant." Her father began to ramble, repeating that he was "so proud" of her and that she should be proud of herself. His praises continued until they reached Aidan's Mercedes. However, once Violet and her father got situated and the car doors shut, the floodgates opened. Violet could not hold back her tears any longer.

"Honey, what's wrong?" Aidan asked.

"Doesn't Mom love me?" Violet choked out between racking sobs.

"What?" Aidan said sharply, his hands gripping the steering wheel.

"How could she just not show up? I *told* her how important this is to me!"

"Violet—"

"You always make excuses for her! I know she's depressed. Believe me, I know. But she doesn't even try! It was *one night*. How hard is that?"

Aidan stroked his brown goatee, now streaked with the occasional silver. He chewed his lip a moment before proceeding. "I know it's not easy," he said, searching for the right words. "But depression is a very serious illness. Getting out of bed and coming to your play may sound easy to us, but to her it's overwhelming. She's not doing this to hurt you. You shouldn't be so hard on her."

Violet balled her hands into fists and tried to swallow her fury. It truly felt like her mother didn't love her. It was a difficult truth she now carried with her, as much as she rejected it or suppressed it. She was sick of her father's blindness, his ability to excuse his wife no matter how much she hurt everyone. He always had blinders on when it came to her, and the years hadn't changed that.

That was the way her family worked: Wanda yearned for Amber; Aidan fixated on Wanda. Violet just wished someone, anyone, prioritized her.

Chapter 8

October 2006, UC San Diego

Violet clutched her red Solo cup and leaned into her friend as she spoke. It was difficult to hear with the boom of the subwoofer at the party. She glanced down and saw that even the rum punch shook, with the ice vibrating against the cup.

She was at an "Around the World" party put on by one of the frat houses. Each room was decorated with a different theme and offered the appropriate corresponding beverage: Ireland had Guinness aplenty; Mexico had tequila shots and piñatas filled with airplane liquor bottles; and the Japan room, conveniently located in the kitchen, had sake bombs. Each was festive, and the partygoers were energetic.

Now that Violet was at college, she was ready to escape the gloom of her childhood. It was a new beginning, and she intended to hunt down and capture the life she'd always wanted. She loved even the mundane, scholarly aspects of the school. When she wasn't reading and studying, though? Parties were definitely a nice break.

"I'm going to the kitchen," Violet told her companion, who was taking a shot off a guy's body. "I mean, I'm going to Japan. I'll be back."

Violet went to the kitchen and dumped the watered-down punch into the sink before she heard a male voice. "Violet?"

She spun around and saw a familiar face from her childhood.

"Dylan?" she sputtered. "Is that you?"

He chuckled and said, "Yeah! I can't believe you're here!" He reached around, and they shared a warm embrace. He was at least six feet tall, because Violet's head fit perfectly under his chin, and she was five foot, seven. It was one of the better hugs she'd had in recent memory.

As they pulled apart, Violet studied his face. He was a bit unshaven, yet had a youthful face and a dazzling white smile. He reminded her of a young George Clooney. It was quite the transformation from his days as a runt back in the hospital.

"How have you been?" she asked. "You're so much older. Wow." She found her eyes tracing his body. Decent-sized biceps bulged from under his black T-shirt.

"I think I'm the one who should be asking you that. You just disappeared from school without a trace."

Violet shrugged. "Yeah . . . new school—*Catholic* school. Dad thought it'd be good for me."

Dylan smirked. "That sounds . . ."

"Medieval?" Violet said with a laugh. "Mean old nuns with switches and chastity belts? Actually it wasn't so bad. A few of the nuns were strict, but others were cool. I liked the drama classes anyway. Now I'm a theater major. What about you?"

"I'm in the school of business, majoring in economics and taking classes in accounting."

They both looked at each other and laughed. "So, we're complete opposites," Dylan said.

Violet found herself loosening up, leaning against the kitchen island as she threw her head back and laughed. She was relieved that she'd straightened her blonde hair that day, and that her plaid shirt was flatteringly formfitting on her 125-pound frame.

Lubricated by ample alcohol, the small talk soon gave way to deeper discussions, including how they resumed life after their loved ones' deaths. They found themselves talking about heavy topics with an ease they had never known with anyone else. It made Violet sad that their families lost touch as they each coped with their immense losses. How different would it have been if they'd reached out to each other instead of folding in upon themselves?

"Someone once told me, 'It never gets easier; it just becomes different,'" Dylan said of grief. "It makes sense. I still have my days."

"Graduation, birthdays, holidays," Violet said, completing his sentence. She stared into her drink. "And just seeing people with their sisters . . . or mothers," she added after some thought.

"Fuck cancer," Dylan said.

Violet lifted her drink toward his. "Amen to that. Fuck cancer!"

They took a swig and stared at each other. It was as if an invisible force tugged Violet toward Dylan, and she found herself reaching over to hug him. His arms wrapped around her waist, and there they stood. The rowdiness of the party didn't exist. Maybe it was silly, but Violet felt like she belonged in those arms.

"I'm so glad we saw each other tonight," she murmured, thinking she could melt on the floor.

Dylan's chin rested on her shoulder. "It doesn't have to end now."

Violet pulled away and nodded. "Let's get out of here."

The two of them ended up going to a Waffle House, where they talked all night. Violet told Dylan all about her mother's depression, and Dylan said his father had never gotten over his mother's death either. Unlike Wanda, he functioned well in the world; however, he'd never moved on emotionally. "It's like he's frozen in time," Dylan said. "Everything's exactly how she left it. It's like a time warp."

"My dad's the opposite," said Violet. "He took every trace of Amber away. Like he wanted to forget she ever even existed."

"At first I was like that," Dylan said. "I didn't want any reminders. But now I find it comforting to do things that remind me of my mom. Can you believe I'm actually something of a classical music

50

freak now?"

"No way!" Violet laughed, remembering how much he used to hate it. "Fairy music?"

Dylan winced. "Did I really call it that?"

"You did," she said, grinning.

"Well, I'm much more mature now."

"I can see that," Violet said, raking her eyes over his body appreciatively. Violet would never have made such a suggestive comment to another boy, but with Dylan it was different. *She* was different.

By dawn, they were a couple. The relationship effortlessly slipped into place, without a word having to be spoken. They were old friends, but it was more than that. They had lived each other's sorrows. They intimately understood one another—no explanations were necessary.

Violet felt fearless, euphoric, complete. She had finally found the love she had been looking for since her sister's death. Her soulmate. Her missing half. Life had meaning again.

* * * * *

Violet called her father the next day.

"Dad, you'll never guess who I ran into at school!"

"Who, sugarplum?" Aidan said jovially.

"Dylan Purcell."

The line was dead quiet.

"You know . . . Dylan Purcell? Gordon Purcell's son?"

"Yes, yes, of course, I remember," her father finally said. "Actually, Gordon and I have been involved in the city's business affairs and some charity functions together all these years. But maybe it's better if you don't mention that to your mother, eh? She doesn't need the reminder."

She could not believe that her father had never mentioned Gordon's name in front of them, even though they were still friends at the professional level. He hid the truth so that he wouldn't possibly say anything to remind Wanda of Amber. That's how protective he was toward her mother! *Unbelievable!*

Violet finally did tell her mother about Dylan, but only after Dylan pressed her. "You'll have to tell her someday," he said with a grin. "I'm not going anywhere."

It turned out her father had worried for no reason. "That's nice, honey," Wanda said dully, with as much interest as she might have shown in the intricacies of the tax code.

She couldn't care less.

Chapter 9

New Year's Eve 2009, Palm Springs

"What do you think about spending New Year's Eve and New Year's Day in Palm Springs?" Dylan suggested.

"Absolutely!" Violet was excited. Palm Springs was one of her favorite vacation spots. The picturesque spa town sat at the corner of the desert and was framed by rugged mountains. Romantic didn't begin to describe it. It would be the perfect place to spend their final winter break in college. Violet couldn't believe how fast the years had flown by. It seemed like just yesterday they had been freshmen, and now they were staring graduation in the face.

"Great," he said, flashing his rakish grin. "I'll take care of all the details. Prepare to be impressed."

They arrived on New Year's Eve morning. The first thing they did was to take the rotating tram across the spectacular cliffs of Chino Canyon. The magnificent view of the snowcapped mountains and the arid expanse of land in all directions took Violet's breath away. The sky was as blue as blue could be, with few patches of cloud. The cute, mid-century modern homes of the town were mere specks. When they exited the tram, they inhaled deeply. The air was dry but felt invigorating and devoid of any impurity.

After lunch at a quaint hole-in-the-wall café, Dylan drove them to Sky's The Limit Observatory and Nature Center in the city of Twentynine Palms for even more scenic desert views. The dome-shaped building truly revealed the splendor of California: all the colors of gold, rust, sienna—and sky, so much sky. They had arrived at the perfect moment, right as the curtain of the afternoon sky gave way to sultry dusk. The landscape was aglow with the thermal orange of the receding sunlight, and stars were just beginning to poke through.

They could see the sheer density of the sky—the swirls of cloud, the cream curls in the great beyond, the illumination of thousands and thousands of stars, like sequins in a midnight-blue dress.

Later, they headed back to Palm Springs. Violet felt a sense of wonder and being part of something bigger than themselves. The ethereal beauty of Palm Springs manifested like another world, perhaps the nexus of this one and the next.

Dylan had made a reservation at a fancy restaurant. The got all dressed up, feeling like adults as they feasted on their dinner of salmon and risotto and watched the ball drop in New York City on the big screen, three hours ahead of California.

"Life goal: go to New York City for New Year's," claimed Dylan.

Violet smirked and pointed her fork at him. "I'd think you'd hate all the people there, pushing and shoving and getting up in your space."

"I don't know. New Year's just feels different. Like you have to be surrounded by people. Makes it more exciting. But tonight, I want it to be just us. Me and you."

Violet's heart pounded. No matter how long they'd been together— way longer than any of the other couples among their college friends—she never got inured to the fact that Dylan loved her. It still seemed like an incredible dream that she might wake up from at any time.

After dinner, they strolled down the street, listening to the cheer of the holiday music and absorbing energy from the Christmas lights over the local storefronts. The world was alight with merriment. As the night progressed, oddly, they found themselves more energetic. The temperature was crisp, but not uncomfortably cold.

Before long, a loudspeaker announced the countdown. "10, 9, 8 . . ." The crowd cheered with increasing intensity, as they got closer to the big moment. Finally, "3, 2, 1!"

Cheers rang out.

"Happy New Year, Cheetos!"

Fireworks exploded above them as the clock struck midnight. Dylan grabbed the back of Violet's head as they shared a passionate kiss. Then he gently pulled away, staring intently into her eyes.

"Violet . . . marry me. Let's get married after graduation."

He didn't drop to his knee. He held her close and kissed her all over, repeating his request like a mantra.

He bent further down and playfully nipped at the lovelock necklace around her throat. The gravity of his request hit her. Her insides melted. She fell into Dylan's arms and wrapped her arms around him for support.

"Are you serious?" she asked, gobsmacked.

"As a heart attack."

Violet buried her head in his chest. She couldn't believe it, but dear God, her heart felt like it would explode from love.

"Say you will," he pressed, kissing her neck.

She tried to ignore the sudden anxiety tightening her chest, the familiar sensation of impending doom. Why did she always do this? Why couldn't she just be happy for *once* without feeling like the world was going to come tumbling down?

She looked into Dylan's face, full of hope and anticipation. He was everything she ever dreamed of, and he wanted to spend the rest of his life with her! Of course, there was only one answer.

"Yes," she said. "Yes, yes, yes!"

Later in their hotel room, they made their own fireworks as the New Year's celebration continued out on the streets.

Every molecule around them seemed abuzz with excitement. Now that Violet knew where her life was headed, she wanted the rest of her life to begin as soon as possible. But she also wanted to live in the present. The room—that moment—was nothing short of perfection. Sure, it had only the most basic accommodations, and it was a little warm. Dylan's brown hair stuck to his glistening forehead. Still, it was paradise. They held each other, tossed around the possibilities, discussed their hopes and dreams.

Dylan's future had shape and substance.

"After the wedding, we'll move to Los Angeles, so you can become a big-time actress," he said eagerly, knowing of her dream to be a film star.

"It's a long shot," she murmured. "LA's filled with hopefuls."

"They'd have to be blind not to put you on the big screen. You're not just beautiful; you've got star power. When you walk on stage, no one has eyes for anyone else."

"Says her boyfriend who isn't at *all* biased," she teased. Still, she couldn't help but be touched by his whole-hearted confidence.

"What about you?" she asked. "What do *you* want?"

"I want a big family," Dylan announced, his arm wrapped around Violet's shoulders as she leaned on his chest, her blonde hair fanned over him. She listened to his heart as it still thumped rapidly. "I was always jealous of my friends who had siblings."

"Me too. I always saw myself having four kids."

They shared ideas about their ideal future. It materialized before them already, low-hanging fruit for the taking. They lovingly murmured to each other as Violet's eyelids became heavy. It was way past midnight, but she didn't want to sleep. She couldn't recall a more euphoric moment. Dylan began running his fingers through her hair. It proved hypnotic. She fell into a deep slumber.

PART TWO

Chapter 10

March 2012, Los Angeles, CA

I'm beautiful. I'm awesome. I'm sexy. I got this.

A broad smile spread across Violet's apple-red cheeks as she gazed at her reflection in the bathroom mirror. It looked as contrived as it felt. *Whoever said, "Fake it til you make it?"* Violet thought. *It's not like a cubic zirconia can turn into a real diamond.*

She feigned another smile and noticed dark circles liked shadows under her eyes—violet eyes that her parents once praised for their beauty, her namesake. The color was as fickle as a teenage boy, shifting from gray to blue to violet depending on her mood, makeup, and clothing. And today, the day of her audition, her under-eye circles dulled her gaze.

Should've used an extra layer of concealer. Too late now.

Violet effectively ignored the hubbub around her— including the nonstop flushing of toilets, the result of nervous, upset stomachs as other wannabe stars awaited their audition and muttered their lines.

Having critiqued her face, Violet scanned her outfit. Though her sage, spaghetti-strap sundress was slightly chilly for late March in Southern California, it revealed strong, round shoulders. The playful green print contrasted nicely with her eyes too.

My back could be more toned for the crisscrossed design, she thought, before muttering aloud, "All right, I don't think I can take any more scrutiny." Rummaging through her purse, she extracted and unwrinkled her audition note with the breakdown of her role.

*Audition: Resort & Casino

*Role Description: Woman #1: Attractive, ambitious, and fit

*Wardrobe: Upscale casual resort-wear

*Pay: $5000 + 20% for shoot and usage + travel & accommodations

Violet looked herself up and down one last time in hopes of a confidence boost. In her peripheral vision, she saw a young girl, probably about six, with an adorned headphone around her neck and pink polka-dotted leggings. The girl was captivated by her reflection, staring at herself in the full-length, illuminated mirror while her mother attempted to rehearse lines with her and touched up her daughter's makeup.

The child caught Violet's subtle glance. They exchanged the smallest of smiles.

With a nervous inhale, Violet sucked in her abdomen and exited the bathroom. She entered a cavernous room with eight casting offices. Acting hopefuls flitted around like bats. Violet double-checked the board. Room 5 is where she would meet her fate.

As she passed by Room 3, she noticed twenty to thirty kids around the same age as the girl she'd just met in the restroom. All sported headphones and let them hang around their neck.

Must be some kind of music commercial, Violet thought. She noted that the parents accompanying them were just as anxious, swinging their arms and wringing their hands as they waited. A little laugh escaped her as she wondered if it was the parents' dream or kids' dream to be cast.

With a lopsided smile still on her face, Violet arrived at her destination, outside of which was a small table with an iPad. She knew the drill. She signed in on line forty-nine and gave the assistant a friendly smile, her name, audition time, manager's name, and contact information.

"Got it," the assistant said after a quick iPad search. She smiled at

Violet, her white teeth contrasting with her bold, purple-red lips.

Uncertain whether she should sit on the long bench provided or pace around to settle her nerves, she halfheartedly sat at the end. For a time, she was alone with her thoughts and the anticipation of what was to come, and the chatter of the actors around her created a rush of white noise. She gulped. Suddenly she felt her lungs beginning to constrict. Her therapist's soft, yet commanding, voice entered her brain. *Close your eyes. Breathe in for four counts. Hold it for five. Breathe out for seven.* Violet shut her eyes, inhaling fully and deeply, trying not to draw attention to herself. Slowly, the cloud lifted. Violet's breathing steadied again.

Then the shrill voices of two girls penetrated her eardrums.

"Kaylee, you won't believe this. I was just booked for a cruise line commercial!" exclaimed a girl with wavy black hair and an annoying, high-pitched voice.

"Shut up! No way," her friend squealed.

"*Way.* My agent sent me the notice with the details yesterday. I'm basically getting paid to go on vacation."

"Where do you go?"

"So, we'll leave from Long Beach and sail to Puerto Vallarta, Mexico. We can stay on the ship and sail back to Long Beach for free. Not to brag or anything, but how solid is that?"

"That's great! I'm actually kinda-sorta jealous. I haven't had anything since I was booked for a holiday commercial with Walmart."

The first girl's voice only became more jarring as the conversation went on. Violet rolled her eyes so hard she worried she had pulled her ocular muscles. She imitated the girl in her mind. *Oh, not to brag, huh? Just shut up.*

Violet stood up and let out a sigh. Funny enough, she had auditioned for the cruise line commercial last week as well. Now the mystery of the humble victor was solved! The winner was gorgeous, too, which somehow made it worse. Was that the reason Violet didn't get the role?

When will I catch a break? she wondered, trying to avoid picking at her cuticles—a terrible nervous habit she kept reassuring herself she should quit.

Beautiful hands with manicured fingernails are a requirement for being an actress too, I'm sure.

* * * * *

It has been almost two years since Violet graduated with her theater degree. Like all her classmates, Violet dreamed about becoming the next Meryl Streep. It's a pretty cliché dream in that circle, but more cliché still was the typical actor's journey on which she now found herself. She moved to Los Angeles two months ago, attending an agent and manager showcase almost immediately. She had professional headshots done—even touched up her highlights: the blonder, the better—and got herself a stage name, Bethany Curtis. Her resume undoubtedly saw more of the city than Violet or Bethany ever would.

Nevertheless, she knew it was time to work, and work hard she did. Now she had a manager and, as of a month ago, had been relentlessly auditioning for any role, big or small. The ultimate goal was to land a gig on a popular TV sitcom or a feature film.

"Don't take background jobs," her manager told her sternly. "And we gotta do commercials strategically. Good experiences, get you the needed exposure."

"And income," Violet added. Her dusty wallet crossed her mind.

So here she was, auditioning yet again for a commercial she worried she'd fail to procure, feeling a sense of disquiet. Anxiety began to nibble at Violet's whole being.

Come on, Dr. Turner says you're doing well, Violet reassured herself. *She even tapered you off the meds.* Nevertheless, a chilling sense of detachment cast a foreboding shadow over her. She felt as if she were viewing herself from outside her own body. The two-month follow-up was past due. She had determined that she would never return to that center.

"Bethany Curtis!" The receptionist called her stage name with three other names in a tone that felt like a clap of thunder. Startled, Violet awoke from her fitful reverie and walked toward the desk.

"This is a group audition," the receptionist commented, glancing above her black-rimmed Ray-Bans like a disapproving librarian. Violet surveyed her group: there was a man around her age, a middle-aged man, and a woman.

The door opened as four actors exited the room, their expressions ambiguous. The cameraman emerged from behind them, wearing a casual white T-shirt and black slacks.

"The clients are in the room. This is it." He spoke casually, undoubtedly with no intention to provoke any tension. Regardless, everyone in the audition group tensed up.

He ushered them into the room. Once they entered, they lined up with their toes touching the bright blue tape on the floor. Violet recalled that the tape in the casting room means, KNOW YOUR PLACE: DO NOT STEP BEYOND THIS MARK. Between the tape and the camera was a forbidden space that only those who were invited may cross.

To her right was a middle-aged ersatz couple; on her left was the young man. She saw a petite lady dressed in jeans standing next to the cameraman. *She must be the casting director.* At the end of the room, three men and one woman sat chatting and laughing on a black leather sofa, their voices barely above a whisper.

They must be the clients.

"Everyone, let's start with names and profiles," the cameraman said while looking into his monitor screen.

The actors recited their names loudly and clearly, turned right 90 degrees and then left 90 degrees, and finally faced the camera. When they finished, the casting director spoke.

"There are two parts to this audition. First, we'd like you to describe to us your guilty pleasure." She emphasized *guilty pleasure*, letting the words roll off her tongue slowly as if she was savoring each of them. "This should take fifteen to thirty seconds of your time, and we'd like you to do so while facing the camera."

"Then please take a seat at the table." She pointed to a small plastic table with four disposable wine glasses and four plastic chairs around it. "Here you will discuss one of your fondest memories with your friends, as if you were having drinks after a luxurious day at a resort—and again, do so in no more than thirty seconds."

The casting director completed her instruction. The molecules in the air vibrated with excitement.

The first man spoke. He wore what Violet would classify as a dorky Hawaiian shirt and khaki shorts that were just a hair too short.

"Well," he began, "I like to read through celebrity tabloid magazines from cover to cover. The juicier, the better! It's the best cure when I'm not feeling well."

"Does that make you feel better?" one of the male clients asked, amused.

The Hawaiian-shirt man chuckled nervously. "Oh, yeah, usually does the trick."

Next was the lady on Violet's right. "I like to eat a whole gallon of ice cream, usually when the *Late Night Show* is on." She's tiny, probably no more than 120 pounds, and flighty.

"How often do you do that?" the female client inquired.

The lady laughed, jangling her huge, black-hoop earrings. "About once a week."

"Really?" The client nodded and scrawled something on her mini notepad.

Now it was Violet's turn. She swallowed hard. "I like to read erotic novels." She followed the first speaker's lead with the guilty reads. It was true, but it didn't even sound like her.

"What's your favorite book?" the female client asked.

"*Fifty Shades of Grey*," she said. It was an outright lie. She'd heard about it but had never read it herself. God only knew what the names of the books that she read were called—probably something like *Loins of Glory*. She usually bought the books for the cover art.

One of the male clients grinned.

"I like to eat sushi. Lots and lots of raw sushi, sometimes until I throw up," the young man said from her left.

No one had a response to that.

After an uncomfortable five seconds, maybe longer, the casting director finally spoke. "Let's move on to the next activity. Everyone take a seat."

This scene took place after dinner. The four strangers must engage in impromptu discussion, feigning total relaxation as if they'd shared a bottle of wine.

Violet felt her chest tighten. *Fond memory . . . fond memory. Why is this so hard for me?*

Nevertheless, she knew why. Although her memories were like paper records, categorized and compartmentalized with disciplined precision, random events triggered utter chaos from the order. These events were like earthquakes, cracking open the compartments and scattering the memories in a gust of wind. Violet needed to carefully extract one without encountering something unpleasant—something haunting.

"You wouldn't believe what can happen while on vacation," the older man began. "When I was in the Swiss Alps skiing, I found a man lying on the ground, partially covered by the snow. At first glance, I jumped back in fright. But when I looked closer, he looked unconscious. I grabbed his heavy arms and hoisted him onto my back before skiing down the hill."

"Oh, that's right," said the young man, his elbow resting on the back of his foldout chair. "You told us when you returned. It was a successful rescue, huh?"

The young man was a natural with his responses. "I took a trip to Paris last year. Man, that city is pure magic. The River Seine cruise was incredible. Have you all had dinner at the Eiffel Tower? If not, you gotta do it sometime. The night view of Paris, man, it was amazing. And I spent an entire day at Versailles—"

The casting director gestured for him to cut it short. The young man got the hint and swallowed his unfinished words. Violet wished he would go on forever. Still at an impasse, she simply nodded and smiled at all the forced conversation surrounding her. The lady beside her did the same before lifting her plastic wine glass. "Cheers to that!" After a hearty and affected sip, she added, "Last year I married my third husband. Right before I walked down the aisle, the left heel of my shoe broke. So I walked down the aisle barefoot. It was hilarious."

"Oh, yeah. I was there. That was a lovely ceremony—even though you had a few close calls tripping on your train," the young man chimed in eagerly.

"*You* try wearing a tent!"

Everybody laughed and took a bigger sip of nonexistent wine. Everyone was loosening up. After a while, all eyes landed on Violet, who felt the heat. Clearing her throat, she began. "I love to walk along the beach in front of the Hotel del Coronado at sunset." She paused and lowered her gaze, unsure how to continue. "I . . . I just love being there."

Everyone hesitated a beat before lifting their glass. "Cheers!"

Chapter 11

How I miss the ocean!

Violet had already built up a sense of longing. She drove down Ocean Park Boulevard, turned right at Lincoln Boulevard, left on Broadway. Once she reached Second Street, she parked the car and hopped in the back seat. She unzipped her duffel bag and extracted a new outfit, shimmying into blue jeans, a purple, long-sleeved tee, and a pair of ballet flats. To protect against the whipping wind, she hastily piled her hair into a messy bun at the top of her head.

She looked down and smoothed out her clothes, unable to do much to remove the wrinkles. She stopped for a second, gazing at her shirt. Every time she wore it, his face appeared in her mind. *Dylan.* He had bought it for her when they were vacationing in New Orleans the spring break after their engagement. The white print on the T-shirt said, "Drama School is Life. Life is Drama School."

An ephemeral smile flashed across her face as she recalled the memory.

She removed a snack-size bag of Hot Cheetos to nibble on while she walked; it always put her at ease after an audition. She exited the vehicle and waited for the pedestrian walking sign to turn at the intersection of Second Street and Colorado Avenue. It was busy in this corner of the world. She passed a Spanish-speaking family with four young kids and a toddler in a stroller, a young man with a turban speaking on his cell phone, a couple of women in colorful traditional Indian dress, and a man in his suit and tie carrying a messenger bag on his shoulder. A few teens tucked their skateboards under their arms.

The wind picked up, carrying with it the invigorating smell of the sea. Violet walked along Colorado Avenue toward the ocean, which she could see perfectly now that the bright sun was partially hidden behind the fluffs of cloud. Typical Southern California weather in late March.

There it was, in plain view, the vast expanse of blue. Violet passed beneath the iconic rainbowlike blue arch that ushered the entrants onto the Santa Monica Pier. The sign read, "YACHT HARBOR. SPORT FISHING. BOATING. CAFES. The crowd ignored the homeless person curled up in a yellowing windbreaker by the entrance. She went with the flow of people. The concrete sidewalk gave way to the broad wooden expanse of the pier sprawling before her, along with the many vendor carts dotting the sidelines. Violet looked to her right and saw all types of people on the vast beach, surfing, soaking up the rays, or playing volleyball.

She spotted a couple stretched out on a beach towel in the distance. The woman, wearing a coral bikini that contrasted pleasantly with her brown skin, was squeezing sunscreen into the palm of her hand. She rubbed her hands together before gliding them across the muscular back of the man lying beside her. He turned his head slightly and grinned at her.

Violet found a bench, sat and watched from afar.

Before she knew it, she was transported back to when Dylan was sitting in similar weather with her at Del Coronado beach. She reached for the lovelock and held on to it as if she could feel his existence right there with her at that moment. The longing for him hurt!

* * * * *

Violet's thoughts were interrupted by a lady wearing dark sunglasses and a lightweight jogging outfit. Her little dog sported a Hello Kitty headdress.

"May I sit here?" asked the lady.

Violet gaped at the dog's headdress. *Is this an insult to Hello Kitty or the other way around?*

"Uh . . . yes, yeah, no problem," she said to the woman.

Violet returned to her own world and opened her lunch sack. She'd prepared to soak in the scene of the ocean and the seagulls lazily flying across the sky—until she sensed something.

"Oh my goodness! No!" The lady scolded her dog as it squatted in front of the bench to do its business. Violet slanted her legs away. "I'm sorry," the lady said, frantically scooting her dog away from Violet.

"It's no problem. I've had dogs."

Feeling unnecessarily awkward as she tried to avoid the puddle near her toes, Violet packed her sandwich back into her paper bag and continued along the boardwalk.

"Hello, hello!" a voice called. Violet turned to see a woman wearing a huge floppy hat and sitting at a cart. A sign in front of it said, "PSYCHIC MEDIUM." Then, underneath, "LOVE, WORK, MONEY." The woman quickly made her pitch. "Come look at your future!"

Violet felt like a feather floating any which way the wind whisked her. In spite of her better judgment, she found herself sitting in a foldout chair across from the "psychic." She smiled a toothy grin at Violet and leaned closer.

"What's your name, dearie?"

Violet gave her stage name and stared at the woman's billowy floral blouse. She was not sure what she would hear. *If this is some bullshit psychic who reads my nonverbal cues to figure me out, she's out of luck,* Violet thought. She closed herself off in social situations anyway. *Good luck reading this open book.*

The psychic leaned into her crystal ball, which looked more like a disco ball with the mini reflective mirrors on it, in this case.

Love, Violet thought, staring at the sign in front of the woman's stand. *I'm not sure that's in my future. It's been almost two years since Dylan left so abruptly that day. He promised he would return after two years. Well, two years are up in few months. Where are you?*

"Lovely young lady," the psychic said, breaking Violet's reverie. "I can tell you are talented—a rising star!"

Violet's jaw dropped as she watched her muddled reflection in the crystal ball.

"You will make a good fortune from being a performer. This should happen in the near future." The psychic sounded pleasant, like the good witch from *The Wizard of Oz*. The more she spoke, though, the more cynical Violet became. *Yeah, half of the people in Los Angeles are involved in some kind of performance art and dream about fame. Only twenty miles away is the fabled* HOLLYWOOD *sign.*

The woman continued. "Now let's look into your love life."

Violet caught the psychic glancing at her lovelock pendant. Suddenly, Violet jumped to her feet. "Thank you so much. I learned what I needed to." She hurriedly extracted a ten from her wallet, handed it to the gaping psychic, and briskly turned away.

Bullshit or not, she did not want to hear anyone's thoughts on her love life—past or future.

The further she got from the psychic, the better she felt. She exhaled and decided to explore a nearby cotton candy stand to distract herself. The typical sounds of laughing, excited children receiving treats filled her ears. In honor of Easter, the vendor offered rows of chocolate bunnies and colorful chocolate eggs.

The eggs remind Violet of her time at Catholic school.

She shook her head. The best part of Santa Monica pier was that it pulled Violet in different directions—delightful distractions. She wandered toward the Ferris wheel and the multicolored joys around it. As she walked closer, she saw a young man in his twenties, sporting a wide-brimmed straw hat and darkly tinted sunglasses. He stood twenty feet from the entrance, his hands cupped around his mouth. Violet saw the glint of a harmonica. The hands holding the instrument were tattooed with skeletal, X-ray-like images extending to the fingertips.

She stopped to listen. He was playing "Sunrise, Sunset" from *Fiddler on the Roof,* one of the films she studied and wrote an essay on one quarter. Beside him, she saw a plastic Tupperware bowl and a cardboard sign: "BLIND AND HUNGRY. NEED $ FOR FOOD." Violet deposited five dollars into the container.

Passing by the Last-Stop-Shop at the end of the 2,448-mile stretch of US Route 66, Violet walked down to the beach and kicked off her ballet flats. She sat down and forgot the carnival-like atmosphere behind her.

She wiggled her toes in the fine sand and momentarily closed her eyes. She was transported to Del Coronado Beach, where time stood still with Dylan. Similar sand and sounds of laughter and joy scattered in the wind. She could feel his soft lips and the playful pressing of his tongue against her shoulder, her neck . . .

Dylan trailed his fingers along her curves before Violet caught them, pressing them to her lips and moving them down to her chest. Everything was yellow-splendid in the sunset, and Violet and Dylan were on fire in both mind and body.

Violet opened her eyes. Santa Monica Beach stretched before her, with surfers hurling themselves on their boards and paddling out to the deep. A young man carrying a surfboard walked past her, and her eyes homed in on his hands, tattooed to look skeletal.

That blind son of a bitch! Violet thought, remembering the musician on the pier. *Liar!*

Her gaze was glued to the bogus blind man. His wetsuit squeaked as he jogged to the water. His figure gradually sank into the sea. He reappeared with the tide a moment later, and then disappeared on a wave. Eventually, she lost sight of him.

Perhaps I'm the one who's blind.

The sky steadily became more overcast as a wall of dark clouds obscured the sun. With the gray hue of the sky came a slight chill.

A veil of fog descended upon the shore and smeared the horizon. A surge of weariness set in. She wanted to lie down on the soft sand and sleep it all away.

Perhaps I'm in a dream after all.

Chapter 12

Violet abruptly awoke at two o'clock in the morning to a persistent knocking on the door. "Go away," she murmured to herself, deciding to ignore it until he did just that. Then the knocks got louder and louder . . . and suddenly stopped.

Instead, Violet heard the muffled sound of a strong male voice through the door.

"Hello? Are you home?"

She would be peeved, but this person sounded rather intimidating as he continued to shout. *Is he desperate?*

Or, could it be . . .?

Violet stiffened at the realization before jerking herself out of bed. She hurriedly slid into her slippers on her way toward the door. All but throwing herself at the peephole, she loudly inquired, "Who is it?"

"LAPD!" She saw a badge through the fishbowl lens. Her heart sank. "We have a quick question for you. It'll be brief."

She opened the door and shyly appeared before the cops in her tank top and teeny plaid sleep shorts. Both men were broad and balding.

"We're looking for someone. Have you seen him?" A photo was thrust toward Violet's face, revealing a young man in his twenties or early thirties, clean-cut, with a delicate smile and dark hair.

"No, I've never seen him. I'm new here," she finally replied.

"Will you let us know if you see him?" The officer handed her a flyer with the man's photo and explained how to report to law enforcement. The other cop not-so-subtly peeked into the room behind Violet.

"Sure." Without further ado, she locked the door and slid the chain back in place. Now, Violet was fully awake. As she processed what had just happened, her stomach rolled and she immediately bolted for the bathroom to throw up. There wasn't much, thankfully. She'd had nothing to eat or drink since the previous afternoon. With her head in her hands, she closed her eyes and waited for the nausea to subside.

Violet shuffled out of the bathroom and noticed the flyer. She briefly looked at it before balling it up and hurling it into the trashcan.

To distract herself, she opened the laptop on her small, circular dining table. First, she logged into the Actors Access. Then she went to LA Casting, Casting Frontier, and Now Casting. She marked all the projects that matched her profile and noticed that some were redundant. Once she fixed that, she was spent. It took time to study the breakdowns before project submissions, so Violet told herself she would work on it when it was not the middle of the night.

"Time for some light reading." Her eyes burned, but in spite of that she indulged in celebrity new developments in *The Hollywood Reporter*. Taylor Swift's top ten looks for the year . . . J-Lo's top ten looks for the year . . . *Bring it on.*

Picking up the half-empty bag of hot Cheetos on the table, Violet looked around at her current living space. A 380-square-foot "efficiency" apartment. She supposed it was a small price to pay for proximity to Sunset Boulevard, which was just a block away. With her cheap furniture, she felt like she was living in an IKEA showroom. No bedroom, only one broom-closet-sized bathroom with a shower, and a miniature kitchen in the corner. It was tiny but sufficed . . . for now.

Violet glanced at her clock. 2:42 a.m. She remembered the earlier encounter with the police officers, and a wave of sickly heat washed over her. The stern, commanding voices, the stares, the guns too close for comfort . . . .

Violet's lungs constricted. She focused her eyes on the wall; the walls started to cave in. It pushed more air from Violet's tight lungs.

Weak, like a trapped animal, she crawled to the sofa bed and scrunched her eyes shut, hoping that somehow sleep would manage to find her.

* * * * *

When Violet awoke—this time, at a normal hour—she heard a commotion outside.

She grabbed a long-sleeve flannel shirt and walked to her tiny balcony. Looking down from the second floor, she spotted a police car and two bumper-to-bumper civilian cars blocking the narrow street. There didn't seem to be any serious injury, except the SUV appeared to have knocked off the small sedan's rear bumper. However, the traffic suggested otherwise. Both car owners looked on impatiently as the police officer took his time to write the report.

With all the casting offices along Sunset Boulevard and the scarcity of parking, frustrated actors and actresses made their dissatisfaction known—and the horn-honking began.

Violet heard a groan beside her. She glanced at the girl who appeared on the patio next to hers, only a few feet away. Her highlighted hair was messy; Violet figured she had just woken up as well.

"Oh, hi," the girl said, smiling. "I haven't seen you around before. Did you just move in?"

"A week ago," Violet replied.

Her neighbor smiled kindly but appeared tired, if the dark circles under her eyes and smudges of leftover mascara were any indication. She wore an oversized gray shirt that Violet suspected belonged to a boy at one point.

The neighbor began what Violet assumed must be her morning ritual. She extracted a cigarette from the pack on the patio table and rested it between her perfectly shaped pink lips before introducing herself. "My name is Chanel."

"I'm . . . Bethany." Not quite used to having double identities, Violet gave her stage name.

She watched as the girl extracted a lighter from the front pocket of her shirt and lit the cigarette. She had auburn hair, but judging by the half inch of brunette at her roots, it must be dyed.

After a long drag, Chanel replied. "Nice to meet you. Glad to see you look . . . well, normal." She laughed. "The people who lived here before you . . . well, not so much. I wasn't sorry to see them leave."

Violet laughed but remembered the face in the photo last night and suddenly stopped. She didn't know what to say next. She was grateful when Chanel resumed. "Well, Bethany, how about you give me a half hour to spruce up, and you come over? I'd like to meet my *normal* new neighbor."

Violet's stomach dropped a little. She nodded and gave a slight smile. "Sure. That sounds great. I'll see you then."

Chanel answered the door in a hot-pink tank top and short-shorts, revealing muscular legs with "monster quads," as Violet would call them. "Come on in," she said. As Violet entered, she saw that her neighbor's apartment was much larger. However, she almost couldn't tell. It was messy, with clothing strewn across the sofa and a pair of men's athletic shoes in the corner. Suddenly Violet felt fur brushing against her leg and saw a small, shaggy white dog, who quickly made her presence known with shrill barks.

"Hi there," she said, watching as the dog retreated to the sofa before bolting back to her, and then back to the sofa again.

"Coco, be quiet! It's all right! This is Bethany," Chanel said, putting her hands on her hips and staring down at the feisty ball of fur at her feet. She sighed and looked at Violet. "Don't worry about her. She'll calm down soon."

"She's cute." Violet was relieved to find a topic of conversation. "What breed is she?"

"Shih-Tzu and poodle mix. It's great. They don't shed! Nothing worse than having dog hair all over a cute outfit." Chanel walked to the kitchen and called out, "Do you want anything?"

"I'm okay."

"Cool. I'm making coffee."

Violet looked down at Coco circling around her, wagging her curly white tail. She approached Violet tentatively before giving her a gentle lick on her big toe. For a moment, as Violet looked into the tiny dark eyes beneath the coat of fur, she thought that a dog might be just what she needed.

"Oh good, she seems to be calming down," said Chanel, settling herself on a barstool by the kitchen. She gestured for Violet to sit beside her. "So, Bethany, what do you do?"

"Oh, you know, same thing every young person in L.A. does. Trying to get into the film or Hollywood industry, become the next big star, yadda yadda," Violet replied, laughing nervously.

Chanel didn't skip a beat. "Very cool. I could see that, actually. You have this aura about you. And you have those amazing lavender eyes," Chanel said, her gazed fixed on Violet's. "Anyone ever told you that you've got Elizabeth Taylor's eyes?"

Violet smiled shyly and looked away.

"Any good gigs lately?" Chanel asked.

"Ha! Still waiting for my big break. What about you?"

"I'm a dancer," Chanel said, looking at the swirl of cream in her coffee.

That explains those quads, Violet thought before replying. "Very nice. I used to be in ballet."

Chanel laughed. "Well, not *that* kind of dancer. I'll be frank with you because you seem cool. I work at a strip club."

Violet tried to conceal her shock. She wasn't sure what a stripper should look like, but she didn't expect that from Chanel. Perhaps it was judgmental of her to think that a stripper would live in a dilapidated shack with needles laying around.

"Oh come on! I'm a stripper, not a prostitute," Chanel said playfully, although Violet could detect her defense mechanisms going up. She tried to correct the wrong impression she'd obviously given.

"I don't judge. I just haven't met a . . . a stripper before. I guess I have a lot of questions about what it's actually like. I don't know anything except for what they show in movies."

"Well, it's a bit different to live it. Thankfully, it helps me stay in good shape. You'd be surprised at how much strength it takes."

"Oh, I'm sure."

Chanel deflected the attention off herself and pointed to Violet's lovelock necklace. "Hey, that's cute. "Does someone have a matching key? An old BFF, maybe?" Chanel grinned like she had a secret.

"It's, uh, it's just something from an old friend." Violet's fingers closed over the locket. "Nothing terribly special. A gift."

"Aw, darn. I was hoping for a juicy love story," Chanel teased.

Violet asked about Chanel's love life instead.

"Yeah, as you can probably tell from the dirty shoes and clothes everywhere, my boyfriend stays here sometimes. You heard of Beat Collision?"

Violet smiled and shook her head. "I'm not that cool, I guess."

"You'll have to come with me sometime. He has gigs all the time."

Violet agreed, glancing at the time on her phone. "I hate to cut this short, but I've gotta be somewhere," she announced. "We have to get to know each other better. It's nice finally knowing someone in this city."

"Sure thing, neighbs." Chanel grinned. "We'll go to a show. For real."

After Violet left her neighbor's apartment, she couldn't help but feel skeptical about her. On the other hand, maybe she was just skeptical of the idea of friends in general. It had been a while since she'd made a new friend. The thought made her excited . . . and nervous.

Chapter 13

May 2012, Los Angeles, CA

The receptionist called her name, tapping her foot in annoyance. "Bethany Curtis! Final call." Mortified, Violet grabbed her stuff and hurried toward the desk.

"Sorry!" she stammered. "I was in the zone."

"Go on in," the receptionist said, glancing at her with a deadpan expression.

Here I am, in an audition room again!

After slating her name, the casting director (CD) said, "I'm sure you understand this is a cold read for a paranormal romantic comedy titled *Never Apart*." He introduced the producer sitting next to him.

He gave the brief synopsis: "A couple, Elsie and Jake, take their wedding vows to the extreme, promising to love, honor, and cherish until death—and even beyond. When Elsie drowns during their honeymoon after their ship capsizes, a devastated Jake reluctantly moves on. He soon learns, however, that Elsie will stop at nothing to stay together. She returns to him as a jealous ghost." He'd certainly made the speech many times.

He handed her six pages over two different scenes. "The role you are auditioning for is Elsie. Ramon will be reading Jake, and she'll be Ophelia." He nodded toward a young man and a woman, most likely film students volunteering in the casting room to gain experience.

Violet looked through the script eagerly. Something about this role stood out to her. She had always been a fan of dark comedies, particularly the concept of humor in tragedy. *Isn't that life, after all?*

The first scene was one in which Elsie, as a ghost, begins to haunt her husband and his new love interest, Ophelia.

Violet took a moment to get into character. She imagined having to watch the love of her life courting someone else right under her nose.

Dylan!

The unbidden thought nearly took her breath away. Was he with someone right now? It wasn't an unlikely prospect. The idea was like a knife in her heart.

"Action!" the cameraman called out.

She cleared her throat, struggling to tamp down the swell of emotions that washed over her. She began reading through the first scene, barely able to keep the pain out of her voice. When she confronted Ophelia, she felt genuine anger and bitterness, imagining her as Dylan's new love.

She was sure she was bombing the audition. It was a comedy, after all, and here she was playing it as seriously as an Oscar-winning drama!

When she finished, she looked around, slightly embarrassed for allowing herself to get so emotional.

To her surprise, the CD and producer were nodding and smiling.

"Excellent," the producer said. "You're the first one who played it straight, not for laughs."

Violet was taken aback. Then she remembered a memorable tip her acting instructor once gave her: Less is more. Don't try too hard to be funny in a comedic role, just as you wouldn't want to overdramatize your emotions in a tragedy. *Looks like it worked.*

"Let's try the second scene," the man said. He grabbed his chin, leaning forward eagerly, much more engaged than when she first walked in.

Violet looked down at the second scene. It was a monologue in which Elsie recited her unique wedding vows. Before she started, she contemplated the young man who was reading the Jake part seriously. She gazed into his eyes, the window to his soul.

"Jake," she said, her voice soft and sweet, "from this day forward, I promise to love you no matter what comes our way. I promise to give you the remote from time to time. I will try to tolerate your game-time ritual of stomping, hollering, and generally startling me.

"If you want to join the Marines, or go to Africa, or move off the grid, I will support you in that . . . even if you get worms, in which case I'll toughen up and nurse you through it even though parasites are my biggest fear. I promise that leaving the toilet seat up won't be grounds for divorce, even if you commit this crime for sixty years straight. I promise that even if you gain 600 pounds, I'll see the skinny person underneath it all."

She progressed through the comically absurd vows, until the end. "And Jake, if you die, I'll love no one else. That I can easily promise you."

Suddenly Violet saw Dylan's face superimposed on the reader's face. It was surprisingly easy to recall every detail of his face: the strong chin, the dark hair, the hazel eyes. Her voice became thick with emotion and tears sprang to her eyes. For a moment, she couldn't continue. Finally, she croaked out the last words.

"There's no one else for me, and there will never be anyone else for me."

Violet barely noticed when the producer praised her performance. *There will never be anyone else for me.*

* * * * *

Heading east on Beverly Boulevard, passing the CBS Television City, Violet turned right onto N. Martel Avenue. After few more turns, she arrived at the La Brea Tar Pits on Wilshire Boulevard near the SAG-AFTRA building. As the tar pits advertised, one can "experience the world's only active, urban Ice Age excavation site."

Violet had just finished her audition and needed a good distraction. Not that she did poorly. In fact, she felt elated when she left the casting office. She rocked the wedding vow scene. She was in the zone.

Violet tried to suppress the feelings of longing and comforted herself with one thought. *Someday, I'll use those vows as a basis for my own. We'll have our wedding—maybe not as quickly as I'd hoped, but one day.*

Violet shook her head. Would that ever happen? Maybe not.

She walked toward the site, with its statues of prehistoric creatures poking through the palm trees: mammoths, dire wolves, short-faced bears, ground sloths, and the state fossil of California, the saber-toothed cat (*Smilodonfatalis*). Stone elephant-like creatures were artfully positioned in the pond, faces frozen in horror as they attempted to escape from the pits.

Violet strolled into the museum, which was constructed on the side of a hill. As she entered the high-ceilinged atrium, she immediately gravitated toward the actual bones of a massive, mighty creature.

"Mom, are these *real* dinosaur bones?" A little boy wearing camo shorts pointed to the wooly mammoth fossil display.

"No, sweetheart. The dinosaurs lived many, many years before this animal," his mother replied, glancing at the display plaque for reference.

"How many years?" the curious young boy asked.

"Oh, *millions* of years ago!"

Violet paused and crossed her arms. She didn't conceal her half smile and couldn't help but be enchanted by the boy's unassuming facial expression.

How could you expect a toddler to comprehend the concept of time?

Her thoughts flitted to Amber. Violet had experienced so much more than her sister, yet how brief was her twenty-four years compared to a thousand years, let alone a few million? Amber was a blip on the screen of time. She hardly existed at all. Moreover, since then,

Violet felt like a piece of her was missing. How would life have been different if Amber had survived?

Violet decided to join the excavator tour, following a trail of people as they returned to the pits outside. The guide explained how they discovered the animal fossils from over thousands of years and why the tar was bubbling from the ground. She listened and attempted to grasp the information, but she couldn't help but envision the animals trapped in the tar, struggling to escape from the slow, stinking death until their tired limbs gave out.

Violet momentarily leaned on the railing and stared at the bubbling tar before her. *It's crazy*, she mused. *What is a means of destruction is also, strangely, an opportunity for immortality.*

The group continued along the path, but Violet didn't follow them. She just stared into the dark liquid in contemplation.

* * * * *

"And from this day forward, I promise to love you no matter what comes our way. I will give you the remote from time to time. I will . . . I will . . ." Violet searched for the right words. She was lying on her stomach, staring at Coco's shaggy face, which provided no clues. "I will . . . ugh!" Violet curled her hand into a fist and tapped her forehead. "Well, Coco, I lost it."

Her furry friend stared at her with beady black eyes, whipping her tail as Violet rolled over to glance at the script. Sighing, she snatched it up and started pacing as she recited the lines to herself. Coco followed her, circling her feet with concern.

Soon after Chanel and Violet became acquainted, Violet graduated from neighbor to Coco's babysitter, or "puppy godmother," as Chanel put it. Chanel tended to spend three nights of the week or more at her boyfriend's place, and after hearing Coco bark through the walls, Violet mentioned it in passing to Chanel.

"I am so sorry! The dog disturbs band practice," Chanel explained apologetically. "I'm not, like, a bad owner or anything. But she prefers to be home rather than in such a loud space."

"I can take her in sometimes if that helps."

As it turned out, this was a loaded offer. The occasional night turned into once a week, until that increased to half the week. Maybe more. Honestly, Violet didn't mind. Coco required Violet to get outside and walk more. *And cardio is good,* she thought. *Cardio makes you fit and makes you happy.* Though they weren't the best of friends, Chanel's sincere appreciation did help Violet warm up to her more.

"Coco, you're great company, but I could use a coach right now," she mumbled to herself as she shuffled the pages of the script.

Two days earlier, she received a call from her manager that she had gotten a callback for the Elsie role. For the second audition, she had to memorize the lines for the two scenes she'd auditioned and an additional two.

"This is a great opportunity," her manager gushed. "The director is moving on up in the industry. Just last year he won the Short Film Special Jury Award for Best Direction at the Sundance Film Festival. I know the payday is the basic SAG scale, but the leading male role is well recognized, so this could be a sleeper hit. Bethany, this could be your big break!"

Violet sighed. "Once more, from the top," she told Coco.

Coco stared at the soliloquist before her and wagged her tail with enthusiasm. The pup seemed to sense the intensity in Violet's voice—or just wanted her dinner—and licked her.

"At least the dog approves. That's a good sign," Violet told herself with a smile.

She bent down to scratch Coco's ear, picked her up, and held her tight. "Coco, you are such a good girl!" Violet laughed as the little dog licked her face.

* * * * *

Chanel was at her vanity mirror blending charcoal-colored eye shadow in the corner of her eye while Violet reclined on Chanel's bed with Coco, flipping through a magazine. She felt a buzzing by her thigh, and her heart skipped a beat. Her manager was calling.

She was sure it was about the second audition she'd had the day before, which meant one thing: the producers either loved or hated her, and they figured it out quickly.

"Hello?" Violet said nervously.

"How are you? Feeling good about that second audition, girl?" her manager asked. Violet tried reading her tone. It sounded almost void of emotion. Did she detect the slightest bit of excitement underneath?

"Well, I am, but you tell me. What did they think?"

"Congratulations! You got the role!"

"Holy moly! No way."

Violet's eyes twinkled with a huge grin she couldn't suppress. She glanced at Chanel's face in her mirror, and her neighbor's jaw dropped. Chanel's reaction was so comical that Violet almost missed her manager explaining the next steps.

"I'm so excited for you!" Chanel shouted, giving her a hug when she hung up. "You're on your way to the top. Gosh, don't forget about us little people!"

Violet was in a daze. "Thanks," she said. "It doesn't seem real. It probably won't really hit me until we're actually shooting."

"When does that start?"

"We're shooting most of the indoor scenes in Atlanta first, and then we will be back here to shoot the rest of the local scenes. That isn't for a couple of months."

"Imagine that! Well, Coco will miss you."

Violet chuckled. "I wish I could say the same," she said. "I've been waiting for a solid gig for so long!"

84

Thirty minutes later, she received a confirmation email from the producers themselves to congratulate her. They offered some details about the project, and also let her know she'd obtain the entire script, shooting schedule, and rehearsal schedule shortly.

Violet set down her iPhone and inhaled deeply. Within her grasp was a real opportunity to make it big, along with a steady paycheck and the knowledge that her hard work led to something in spite of her personal setbacks. So why couldn't she feel that she deserved it?

While hanging up her laundry later that night, she couldn't help but think of sharing the news with someone who would understand how much it meant to her. Chanel was excited for her, yes, but it wasn't Chanel Violet wanted to tell.

Violet curled up in a ball on the bed and closed her eyes. She could still smell him.

God, Dylan. Where are you?

Chapter 14

August 2012, Atlanta, Georgia

Two months later, Violet arrived in Atlanta and felt like she'd stepped into a sauna. Her hair stuck to her neck. The oppressive humidity convinced her to avoid going outside if she could dodge it. As soon as she touched down at the airport, she grabbed a couple of bags of hot Cheetos and stored them in her large leather tote for safekeeping.

Violet still wasn't accustomed to the alternating anticipation and nervousness that consumed her. The day that would determine much of her success had finally come. It was time to meet the cast.

She couldn't help but feel a sense of tension. They were going to start with Scene 57, when Elsie would appear as a ghost. There was no dialogue, so it was a challenging scene where she had to use just the right facial expressions and convey emotions subtly but precisely. She hoped that when she met the other actors they'd have a good, chummy dynamic that would help her feel creative and empowered. She reassured herself that there was no need to feel intimidated. She hoped that when she met them, the feelings would melt away.

She ran through the agenda for the next few days. First, she had wardrobe fittings, and the first day of rehearsal was with the lead actor and the supporting actress. To stay in line with the projected budget, she had to bring some of her own outfits and rent costumes. It's just the name of the game for such low-budget productions like these.

Violet had chosen a couple of long, white dresses for the occasion. They were flowing and ethereal. She loved the way they cascaded down her hips. *Even in death, Elsie has a good sense of style,* Violet thought with a smile.

She hung the garment bag on the hook in the back of the rental car and hopped in. After double-checking the GPS, she saw that her destination was in a residential area. The assistant director had attached a map on the call sheet sent via email the night before. She followed the directions, driving through a winding, uphill road. She tried to ignore the groan of her small rental car and looked out at the expansive view of the perfectly manicured Georgia neighborhood. Most houses were gated and intentionally hidden behind dense, lush landscaping.

She arrived at a house that seemed slightly higher than the rest. Later she learned that the owner, who lived in Paris and New York most of the time, had inherited the house from his parents and that his dad had been a TV tycoon in the '80s. It had six bedrooms and six baths, along with an entertainment room, lighted tennis court, an Olympic-size swimming pool, and heated Jacuzzi surrounded by palm trees. Nevertheless, this was not just a luxurious getaway; it was set up as a short-term rental for TV movies or feature films. There was a separate storage facility on the property that housed an abundance of props. The patio overlooking the skyline of downtown Atlanta boasted custom-designed outdoor BBQ pits and furniture. The diverse layout of the house could easily be played up as a millionaire's mansion or scaled down as a humble, middle-class household, thanks to the cozy décor.

* * * * *

Based on the call sheet, Scene 57 would be filmed first. Violet studied the script while the hairstylist fixed her hair.

In Scene 57, Elsie, a jealous ghost, mischievously interferes during and intimate moment between Jake, the lead character, and Ophelia, a supporting character.

Violet considered this a fun scene to begin with. It was ridiculous, sure, but it eased her into the role in a lighthearted way. She would have to mentally prepare herself for future scenes when the story took a dark, heavy turn.

She reviewed her acting strategy one more time as she read the script. Meanwhile, the crew flitted around, meticulously placing the props in their respective locations and setting up the equipment. At first glance, the set appeared chaotic. However, there was a method to the madness, and soon everything was perfectly positioned for the first day of shooting.

After blocking, the director gathered the actors to read the scene and answer questions. Then he walked around the set with the director of photography, in thoughtful discussion while they fine-tuned the lighting and camera placement. The soundman prepared the mic before the cameraman and director readjusted its position. The other actors rehearsed the script and blocking with the director, and the camera and sound crews rehearsed with them to make final tweaks.

"Picture is up!" the assistant director, or AD, roared.

All chatter stopped. Violet's heart skipped a beat. *The moment is here.* She made her way onto the mark outside of the frame of camera, as instructed.

"Quiet, everyone!" the AD called out one more time. Everyone was still; true silence descended on the set.

"Scene 57, sound speed," the soundman said, extending the mic.

The AD commanded, "Roll camera."

"Speed!" shouted the cameraman.

"Scene 57, take 1." The clapper held the clapperboard in front of the camera and slapped it shut. *Crack!*

"Action!"

The director gave Violet a nod, signaling her to move forward as Jake and Ophelia undressed each other with their eyes during their drunken banter. Inhaling, she quietly glided into the scene. She was told that the special effects team would edit her to appear as a transparent, ghostlike image. Her primary focus should be her body movement and facial expression as she reacted to the scene with subtle emotion—a twinge of disgust, slight jealousy, an overall melancholic mood.

"You were really something," Jake said to Ophelia as the script came to life. "I can't believe you took champagne shots."

Violet homed in on the actor before her. Jake was grinning, staring at Ophelia. Violet looked into his eyes, as if wishing he could see her. She followed his gaze to the female figure on the bed.

Ophelia . . . in a red dress.

Something wasn't right! Violet's eyes locked on the evening gown the actress was wearing. Suddenly, she stiffened and her stomach flipped. Tendrils of darkness—darkness she had tried so hard to suppress—gripped her senses and plunged her into a mental black hole.

The red gown!

Violet flew to the bed. There was no thought, no control over her movements. Her hands curled over the actress's shoulders as she held her down. Her prey thrashed, crying out. Violet's hands moved to the actress's slim neck. She squeezed. Hard. Eyes bugged out of the purple face. The abhorrent dress! She strangled her with all her might.

"Cut!" the director screamed.

Violet was a woman possessed . . . until she felt hands gripping her arms and yanking her away. A few men from the crew ran over, and she emitted guttural sounds like those of a wild animal as they threw her down. She hit the ground, and the black tendrils in her mind shrank away. She saw the actress wailing with her face in her hands as the cameramen surrounded her. She rocked back and forth and screamed, "What the hell just happened?"

Violet processed what had just occurred. It felt like a nightmare, but it wasn't. This was real life.

No, no. Violet began to shiver violently. She fell back and stared at the crew gently leading Ophelia away. She felt the eyes of every crew member, actor, and producer staring at her.

Damn it, no.

She broke into a sob.

Chapter 15

September 2012, Los Angeles, CA

Violet approached her apartment after a walk with Coco and spotted something she'd hoped she wouldn't see.

The dreaded notice.

She snatched the envelope from the clip by her door. "Time-sensitive matter. Open Immediately."

Violet shoved her key into the lock. Once inside, she threw the envelope on the floor. Her mind was swimming. *What will I do next?*

Her life was in shambles. Since the incident on the movie set a month ago, her manager had dismissed her. She'd been banned from the SAG-AFTRA union and blacklisted in the industry as "emotionally and mentally unstable: dangerous to work with." They all thought she'd had a violent case of stage fright, and she preferred to keep it that way. What good would it do to tell them the truth? That would only lead to more questions and even more raised eyebrows.

She'd answered every want ad she was remotely qualified for, but none of them had been willing to give her a chance. She was up against a boatload of other unemployed actors and writers. Unlike most of them, she had no retail or restaurant experience.

Her bank account was empty, and she was behind on the rent. A stern phone call from the apartment office had warned her about the consequences of late payments a few weeks ago. And now? Well, she knew even without looking that in the envelope on the floor was her eviction notice.

Violet began pacing around the room. After a spell, she sat with her knees against her chest and let the time tick by without any meaningful thoughts on how to proceed. It was almost meditative but without actually succeeding in calming her down. Always loyal, Coco sat by her feet and gave her a wistful look and frequent licks.

Suddenly, a knock came at the door. Violet jumped. She wasn't ready to confront the landlord yet. However, the raps on the door continued.

"Bethany, open the door. I know you're in there. I see your car outside."

Coco barked and made a beeline for the door, her tail wagging as she ran. She scratched at the door, whimpering at the familiar voice she heard on the other side.

Violet groaned, got up, and let Chanel into her apartment. Her neighbor took one look at her and cocked a perfectly groomed brow. "What's up? Are you sick?"

"I'm all right," Violet mumbled unconvincingly. "Just tired."

"Liar. I may not have known you long, but I know you, Bethy." Chanel looked at her with genuine concern. She scanned the room and noticed all the empty Cheetos bags littering the coffee table. "It's 2 p.m. You're not even dressed. In addition, have you eaten anything but Cheetos all week? Let me get you something, and no, you can't refuse. I'll be right back." With that, Chanel turned on her heels, with Coco trotting behind her.

When Chanel returnedfrom her apartment, she waved a frozen dinner under Violet's nose.

"That does look good," Violet conceded. "I could use some real food."

Chanel scoffed. "Well, I don't know if Roasted Chicken Marsala from Healthy Choice qualifies as real food, but it's about the extent of my cooking skills." Chanel popped it in the microwave and turned to Violet with her hands in the pockets of her distressed jeans.

"So, you wanna tell me what's happening?"

Violet wordlessly handed her the unopened envelope.

"What's this?" Chanel asked while tearing it open. She unfolded the paper, and her eyes widened as she read. "Oh God. I'm sorry. What do you think you're gonna do next?"

"Find me a shopping cart. I'll load some dirty cats and my few belongings in it and sleep by the road. I'll become one of them. Sound good?"

"One of what? Don't be silly! You're crazy."

"One of the homeless." Violet paused. "Maybe I *am* crazy."

"C'mon. Don't talk like that. Isn't there anyone you can call? Can you get a loan?"

Violet's mind flashed for a couple of beats. "No," she said, shaking her head. "No one."

Chanel looked at her with sympathy but not surprise. "We can work this out, Bethany." Chanel reached out and clasped Violet's hand reassuringly. "Now listen . . . and I want you to hear me out here. The strip club where I'm working is hiring. Is this something you would be open to trying? With my help, of course."

"Are you kidding?" She spat the words out louder than she intended to, pulling her hand back. "I'm an actor and ballet dancer, not a stripper." Hearing how judgmental she sounded, she softened her tone. "I'm sorry. I didn't mean it that way. I've just never given it a thought before, and you know how taboo it is."

"It's okay. I know what you mean. I used to feel that way myself. But it's really not that bad. Promise. A stripper is not the same thing as a prostitute. It's like performance art, or dance aerobics in an erotic form. I won't pressure you to do anything. It's just a suggestion to help you get through this." Chanel spoke calmly, as if she had found peace with it a long time ago. "Give me a second. Have your lunch, and I'll be right back."

A few minutes later, Chanel returned to Violet's apartment with the

Aerobic Striptease box set by Carmen Electra. She pulled out the first disc and popped it into the DVD player. "This isn't a Striptease 101, but it does lead you through moves that give you a feel for it. I hope it'll loosen you up. Approach it as a fitness routine, like aerobics," Chanel suggested. Then she gently added, "I don't want you to feel uncomfortable. But believe me, you're not a prostitute if you don't allow yourself to be one. If you want me to help you brainstorm other options instead, that's fine. But homeless under the bridge isn't an option!"

"Thanks, Chanel," Violet said, feeling unexpectedly touched by her neighbor's concern.

"I just don't want you to wind up on the street. Skid row is getting way too crowded. You'd be dead meat in no time."

"Well, play the video then. What do I have to lose?"

In seconds, Chanel had the DVD on Violet's television. Carmen Electra and two other svelte girls appeared on the TV screen in all their toned glory.

"Welcome to aerobic striptease. This workout series will tone your body like a dancer and definitely spice up your personal life," the narrator said.

"Well, that sounds good to me," Violet said with a half-hearted grin.

Chanel nodded. "Excellent! Give the video a shot, do some research, and you know where to find me. I'm off to take a nap. I'm working later."

When the door closed, Violet picked up the remote, intending to turn off the video. However, something held her back. She let the video run. It truly wasn't crude or vulgar. In fact, it was pretty rhythmic and sensual. She was struck by how comfortable the dancers looked. Their bodies were fluid, even as they confidently strutted around, bent down, and snapped up in a relaxed, nonchalant w ay.

I can't believe I'm even considering this.

She immediately started the next DVD, "Aerobic Striptease in the Bedroom." The first half demonstrated stretches and yoga moves, which actually relaxed Violet. Then she observed the movements in the lap dance video. Violet had fun popping her hips and gyrating her body in a sexy way; however, she couldn't help but feel daunted by the idea of doing it outside of the comfort of her own room.

Chanel, ever enthusiastic, returned a few hours later with Coco. Her face was coated with a thick layer of makeup; her fiery hair was pulled into a tight bun on the top of her head—her favorite no-nonsense hairstyle for work. "So, what do you think?"

Violet bit her lip.

"Do you want me to call my manager to set up a time to speak with you?" Chanel pressed. "I bet he'd reassure you."

"No, no, I don't know if I'm ready yet."

"Would it help if we tried it together? Private lessons?"

Violet sighed. Chanel looked at her expectantly, and it reminded her of an energetic, tail-wagging Coco. She seemed so excited; Violet couldn't bear to disappoint her.

"I can't promise anything, but we can try."

"By the way," said Chanel, "don't worry about your rent this month. It's been taken care of. No strings attached. I just could not imagine you sleeping on the street and vanishing from the face of the earth." Chanel walked away without giving Violet a chance to respond.

* * * * *

After Violet gave Chanel the green light regarding stripping, her neighbor became relentless. The next day, Chanel decided to give Violet a one-on-one lesson.

"You can't say no," Chanel texted her earlier that day. "I know you don't have anything else going on."

Violet couldn't argue that.

Perhaps, I can find a server job. There are plenty of restaurants in this area. Well, I'll try this just for the time being.

However, with Chanel's insistence, Violet gave in.

She arrived in Chanel's living room wearing yoga pants and hoping she wouldn't make a fool of herself.

Violet surveyed Chanel's outfit—a pink sports bra and denim cutoff shorts. She learned that her neighbor had a pierced belly button, which she noticed after seeing a glint of light reflecting off the diamond bow dangling from her midriff.

"I'm so glad you're giving this a shot," Chanel gushed. "And trust me, with my instruction, you'll blossom."

"You'd better wait until you see me dance before you start making all these grandiose claims."

"Nonsense! You'll be great. If you can do ballet, you can do this, no problem. First things first: the hip roll is the foundation for any striptease. Follow my lead." Chanel stood with her feet shoulder-distance apart and instructed Violet to do the same. "Now, put your hands on your thighs, bend your knees and slowly dip down, and swing your butt to the right. While you're doing that, move your right hand to your right hip and make a delicious circle. Make sure your gaze follows your hand. Come on, give us a sexy look!"

Violet felt supremely silly, but she gave her best sultry gaze. "Do I look sexy, or do I look constipated?"

"Just right. It's a fine line though, for sure." She laughed. "I'm sure some smoky eyeshadow will help you too. Now, slowly stand up. Repeat on your left side." Chanel added, "This time, besides a sexy look, slightly part your lips and use the tip of your tongue to lick your upper lip. Very subtle. Sexy. Sensual."

I look ridiculous.

Chanel sensed her negative thoughts and piped up. "You need to stop caring about how you look. It shows on your face, and you get

96

stiff. Have fun with it!"

"Can we play some music or something?" Anything to drown out her thoughts.

"Good point. Let me get my iPod." Chanel hooked her iPod up to the speaker. Soon, a club beat filled the apartment. She bobbed her head in approval and smiled at Violet.

"There you go. Let the beat move you. It should help you keep count better."

The beat did help Violet get in the mood, even if electronic music wasn't her cup of tea. She focused on the music and tried to get into the rhythm.

"Yeah! There you go. Trust me, this move alone can drive anyone crazy."

Once Violet felt comfortable enough, Chanel relocated the full-length mirror from her bedroom so Violet could critique herself. Violet practiced her dip and continued to roll her hips as fluidly as possible.

"Hip thrust! Really push your hip out! You need to have a good attitude. Don't be afraid to put your personality into it."

Next came head rolls. Chanel playfully stroked Violet's hair. "You have the best honey-colored hair. Work it to your advantage."

Since her hair was her pride and joy, this move came more naturally for Violet.

"Sexy! Now, let's add hands. Don't be afraid to touch yourself. Run your fingers through your hair. Good! Now, drag your hands down your body, down to your 'pleaser,' as we call it. Don't skip your boobs. Graze your fingers down your torso. Do it like you really mean it."

When Violet hesitated, Chanel demonstrated and instructed Violet to follow her lead. "You want to caress your body. Just feel the music and be sexy."

"I never thought you'd see me touching myself," Violet joked.

"Hopefully I will when you're naked on a stage."

Violet couldn't help but marvel at Chanel. She was confident and never seemed awkward about nudity or sex. Even though she was much more private, Violet couldn't help but admire Chanel's complete comfort with her own body and sexuality.

"Now, lie on the floor in a sensual way. Keep your chest up. Spread your legs."

Violet snorted, but she did as she was told as Chanel continued her stream of commands.

"Scissor legs! Now flip over, and use your right hand to smack your right hip. Make it sexy."

"Do you have other vocabulary besides 'sensual,' 'sexy,' and 'hot'?" Violet protested. "If I hear those words one more time, I'll throw up."

"Well, you'll be doing a lot of vomiting," Chanel said, unperturbed. "Next time, I want you to put on a bikini and high heels. You'll have to do all these moves with a bikini on, at most, and tall shoes. Better get used to it now."

* * * * *

Violet had never been one for high heels. She used to think they were impractical—a modern-day version of Chinese foot binding, a way to "keep women down." Nevertheless, when she saw Chanel's closet and the rainbow of shoes within, she found herself wanting to slip some on and revel in the femininity.

There were cobalt blue shoes, striking red, leopard, and even clear ones with multicolored lights inside. Many of them were more than three inches tall. Wearing them would be quite a challenge for someone who seldom wore heels at all.

Chanel gave a sage recommendation. "Start doing housework in them. Vacuum with heels on, or take Coco on a short walk around the apartment." She said she had even heard about blow-drying shoes with one's feet still in them to break them in quicker. "Guess it makes the shoes mold to your feet easier."

The next day, Violet found herself at home with new coral heels. She pulled out her dryer, shrugged, and turned it on full blast. Her feet immediately started sweating, and her skin started to burn. Apparently, it was a job that needed to be done in spurts.

While Violet continued her shoe training, she knew she needed to go public—not at the strip club just yet, but to try a pole dancing class. Perhaps she'd feel more encouraged alongside other novices.

Therefore, Violet spent plastic money she didn't have to join a girls-only workout facility with "flirty, fun classes"—or so it was advertised. Burlesque, ballet, and yes, pole dancing, were all offered. She hoped that witnessing the voluptuous female forms at work in this setting would inspire her.

She walked in on the first day, a bona fide fish out of water. Girls with cute bubble butts and perfectly toned arms twirled around the pole as if they were weightless. It looked effortless, but Violet knew it was anything but. She had to swallow her pride and get ready for some hard work.

The first pole dancing class proved difficult. A girl with a pixie cut and many tattoos told the group to "get in touch with their inner sex goddess."

"Work it, ladies!" she shouted. "Circle those hips! Run those hands down to your 'pleaser!' Don't be shy."

Thank goodness I've moved past this part, Violet thought, relieved that she wasn't the stiffest person in the room. Moreover, her svelte form rivaled most, if not all, of the other girls'.

Hoisting herself on a pole proved tougher than it looked. Violet ended the class with more bruises on her body than she could count. Every single muscle fiber was sore, from her back to her triceps. Nevertheless, strangely enough, the pole made it easier. It gave her something to do with her hands other than touching herself, which she still couldn't imagine doing on stage to nameless faces.

A couple of weeks later, Violet checked her credit card bill and realized that she was about to hit her credit limit. She couldn't stall anymore. "It's the do-it-or-die moment," she told her neighbor. They were drinking cheap wine on Chanel's patio. With the balmy weather and a mild breeze, it almost felt like a vacation; however, Violet's stress couldn't have been higher. "I hate saying that, but it's true."

Violet swirled the cheap wine around in her glass and looked down at the busy street. Chanel nodded. "It'll be fine. What is your biggest concern at this point?"

Violet sighed. "I'm just worried I'm not ready for prime time yet. But my bank account screams at me that it's *high* time."

Chanel leaned forward and put her hand on Violet's knee. "Girl, come talk to my boss. We can work something out. You can work on weekdays or earlier on weekends."

"Before the real talents come out." Violet laughed.

"That'll be you soon. I know it. You've already come a long way. You just need to relax and *feel* it. When you're having a good time, it'll show. And don't forget, a little wine always helps." She tapped her wine glass against Violet's with a *clink*.

This is just for the time being, Violet promised herself. *I'll quit just as soon as I find a real job.*

* * * * *

Violet approached Chanel's employer with a sense of unease. The establishment was called Casablanca Gentlemen's Club. While the name suggested the exotic and expensive, it actually looked like any old dive bar.

The bouncer, a muscular Hispanic man with a goatee, nodded in greeting.

"Hello, hello, Edwin!" Chanel exclaimed. "I want to introduce you

100

to my friend Bethany."

Edwin acknowledged her with a nod. "She the new girl?"

"I sure hope so. That's the plan."

Violet waved meekly. "Nice to meet you." She smiled and felt the heaviness of her eyelids. She had applied fake eyelashes before leaving. *Just think of it as a role*, she told herself.

"Edwin is a good guy. You'll be glad he has your back," Chanel said, hoisting her Michael Kors handbag onto her shoulder.

They walked into the bar, and the smell of cigarettes assaulted Violet. It was like another planet where oxygen was replaced with nicotine smoke. It was only midafternoon on Tuesday, so the customers were sparse. They weren't nearly as bad as she'd feared. There were a couple of rough-looking characters, but there were a few clean-cut men in business suits too. She could pass them on the street and not think twice.

On the main stage, a woman wearing silver-colored pasties and a G-string was on the ground, her hips pushed toward the ceiling. Stacks of dollar bills were tucked into the elastic. The three men beside the stage were unquestionably feeling generous.

Violet looked around and saw two other mini stages on opposite ends of the room, along with some small platforms on which women could provide a dance up-close to the guests in their seats. A staircase in the back led up to the balcony that circled the room, allowing visitors a sweeping view of all the naked women on the premises.

She followed Chanel to a hidden black door in the back. A burly man with messy blonde curls and a prominent chin looked up. He glanced at Violet with his beefy arms crossed.

"Hi, Rob," Chanel said. "This is Bethany, my neighbor I was telling you about. Rob's the manager here."

Violet extended her hand and gave a firm handshake, hoping her hand wasn't too sweaty. He unabashedly looked her up and down. Violet's form was easy to see. She was wearing skinny black jeans, a simple beige tank top, and, of course, heels. Thankfully, she no longer walked like she had a "stick up her ass," as Chanel so delicately put it.

After slowly scanning Violet from head to toe, Rob spoke. "You're beautiful, sweetheart. You dance before?"

"No, this would be my first dancing gig."

"That's right, I remember Chanel telling me now. Well, wanna show me what you can do?"

Violet assumed this would happen, but her heart still skipped a beat. "Sure. Right here?"

Rob gestured for them to follow him and led them into a private room. There was a pole across from a dimly lit seating area. Violet took out her iPhone, started up her favorite tech house song, and began to dance. She closed her eyes, trying not to think about Rob watching her. Miraculously, she felt her self-consciousness slide away as she let the music take control. She rolled and gyrated and wrapped herself around the pole as if it were a long-lost lover.

Just feel the beat. Lose yourself in the music. Touch yourself. Turn yourself on, and you'll make them hot too.

When the music ended, she opened her eyes. Rob was poker-faced. Violet's confidence evaporated. She suddenly felt vulnerable, exposed.

"I'm gonna need you to pull off your shirt, sweetie. If you can just do that, I think we're set."

She hated being appraised like a prized pig, but she told herself he had to inspect "the goods." It's not *that* different from the movie industry. Physical perfection was practically a job requirement there too.

She took off her shirt.

He motioned her to spin around and she did, slowly, until she was facing him again.

He nodded approvingly. "You're toned enough. You've got a foundation to work from." Rob paused a moment as he thought of something. "By the way, do you have your picture ID with you? We need that on file before officially letting you work here."

Violet extracted her driver's license and handed it to him. "Oh, good. Bethany is not your real name. Our dancers don't use real names here." Rob repeated her name several times before finally saying, "I think Bethany is a good name to use here."

I didn't know Bethany was a good stripper name. How ironic! Violet thought.

"We can stick you in on the earlier shifts for now. Til you work your way up," Rob said. Chanel had warned Violet that he was very direct. Violet thanked him. He told her that they would figure out the specifics later—the house fees, discussing her dancer's license, and other housekeeping details.

As soon as they got outside, Chanel exploded. "You got it! You got it!" she squealed and high-fived Violet.

"Yes, it happened. Wow!" Violet marveled at the situation but was confused at the same time. In a few blinks of her heavily lashed eyes, her life changed, just like that. She was excited, but then the reality hit her: a stripper. She was a bona fide stripper! She knew something about her would change, but she didn't know what. What she did know was that life would never be the same.

How did I ever wind up here?

Violet consoled herself that night before dozing off.

"It's just acting," she said to herself. "I'll play the role of a stripper to get through my financial crisis. Then I''ll quit and find a real job."

Chapter 16

November 2012, Hollywood, CA

"Hey, you! Yeah, you."

Violet barely heard the man only a few feet behind her. She turned her head and saw a man with dark, curly hair wearing a button-up lilac shirt, his sleeves pushed up. He was sitting on a plush red couch near the bar, motioning to his lap.

She nodded to the customer and approached him. The booming bass of the music rattled Violet to the bone. Even though she always left the club feeling like her ears were stuffed with cotton balls, at least the beat pushed out her thoughts. A few shots of vodka helped with that too. Both came in handy on busy evenings like this particular night.

Violet was wearing a white bikini top with multicolored jewels in the center of her chest. Her "cheeky" style bottoms were decorated with a handful of rolled-up dollar bills. Now she knew just how dirty money was.

"How 'bout a personal dance? Show me what you got," said the client. He patted his lap and grinned boyishly like he was eyeballing the BB gun he wanted for Christmas. "What's your name?"

"Bethany," she said. She still could not get over the irony; it was like her own private joke. *It is a stripper name, after all.*

She gave him her best seductive gaze and knelt before him, ignoring the whistles around her. Maintaining eye contact, she rubbed her hands down his chest and toward his thighs. Arching her back, she moved upward again, gently pulling his face into her breasts.

Her body loosened a little more when she turned around and circled her bottom on his lap. She felt the hot gaze of his buddies but drew strength from it rather than fear. Plus, her gut was still warm from the vodka. She felt his hand graze her bottom, and he smacked it playfully. She circled his lap again, but felt her cheeky bottoms being lifted—and a finger moving toward her crack.

She whipped around. "No," she said firmly, wagging her index finger. "None of that."

The man put his hands up, caught in the act. "Okay, okay. My bad!"

Violet continued his lap dance without further complication. Not a minute after she finished and collected her cash, an onlooker asked for one as well.

She knew a good part of her tips came from the persona she put on. Never the bubbly type, Violet played the part of a mysterious seductress. She was no-nonsense and let her body do the talking. However, certain situations prevented her from acting the part she preferred. For instance, men sometimes paid her to stay by their side and laugh at their jokes. She did her best to "feel out" the personality of the customer du jour. Many wanted to be macho and showed off their wealth. Violet indulged them with copious "oohs" and "ahhs."

Others were more emotionally needy. She learned to distinguish the post-breakup customers with their set jaws as they concentrated to forget and tried too hard to misbehave. Many were just lonely. Some didn't have a significant other, while others felt "misunderstood" by their wives or girlfriends. Violet would never forget one man asking, "Do you masturbate to kill the pain?" She blinked in disbelief at the audacity of the question.

"Kill what pain?" she asked.

"Of being alone," the man said. "Aren't you? I mean, you're a . . . ."

He didn't need to say it.

Am I in pain? Violet wondered afterward. The longer she stripped, the more emotionally detached she became. As she got better at shutting down her feelings at work, she seemed to have lost the ability to sense anything outside of it.

But maybe not feeling isn't such a bad thing.

Violet completed a couple of other lap dances after her sensual stage performance. The first few dances are always the hardest; then she got in a groove.

By the end of the evening, she was a few hundred dollars richer, which she regarded as a good haul considering she was relatively new to the gig. Sighing, she shook her dirty blonde hair out of her up-do and pulled the bills from her bottoms. She was counting her fat stack of cash when she heard a knock. Before she could grant entry, a man walked in and shut the door behind him. It was the man from earlier, the one who tried to slip his fingers where they weren't allowed.

"Oh!" Violet said with a start. "Did you want another dance?"

He walked over to her and leaned in. He smelled like beer, and lots of it. He murmured, "Hmm, I'm in the mood for something else."

Violet's stomach dropped. She hoped it wasn't what she suspected. "Your own dance?" she said with a weak smile.

"More."

She stood up. "I'm sorry. Do you need directions to *another* establishment?"

He was too close. She could feel his yeasty beer-breath on her bare chest. His eyes were glazed over. "Come on. You mean to tell me you wouldn't take it? I have a lot more money, you know."

Violet sidestepped past the customer toward the door. "No," she asserted loudly. "I want you to leave."

She saw the man trying to untangle the situation in his inebriated mind. His eyes narrowed, and, indignant, he opened his mouth to speak. However, before he could protest, the door behind her opened.

Edwin stood in the entry in all his musky girth. His head was cocked to the side, and he eyed the drunkard like he was a cockroach—

which he was, in Violet's mind.

"Sir, it's time to leave," he bellowed. "Here, let me escort you out."

Half-wit, Violet thought. Edwin's hands circled the man's shoulder in a vice grip. It wasn't until they were both gone that Violet realized she was trembling. She collapsed into a chair and focused on her breathing. She pushed the dominant thought in her mind away: *What if Edwin hadn't come in?*

She stared down at her electric-blue platform heels, trying to collect herself. A few minutes later, Edwin returned. "Hey," he said gently. "You all right?"

Violet was so rattled that she dropped her guard. "No, I'm not," she said. "That was . . . wow."

Edwin sat beside her. "I spotted him heading this way as the rest of the guys were clearing outta the club. I wasn't gonna let anything happen."

"That's good. I just . . . I've heard things like this happen. I thought I was careful and prepared. But . . ." Violet failed to find words to complete her thoughts and chuckled in relief. "I'm so glad you came."

"We get a few dogs in here sometimes, unfortunately," said Edwin. "But I got your back. It's what I'm here for."

"Thank you."

Edwin thought for a second and said, "What do you think about getting some 24-Hour Burger after this? You like that place?"

"I mean . . . I did," she replied. She couldn't eat like she used to, not while she was on display four nights a week.

"Get a burger in a lettuce wrap or something," he replied with a grin. "It's on me."

Violet shrugged. While she normally didn't go out with guys, she felt safe with Edwin. He was like a big teddy bear. He didn't have an

107

agenda; she knew this. "I'm in."

Violet changed into her jeans and a cream-colored sweatshirt, while Edwin waited for her at the front. He ushered her into his black jeep. They exchanged small talk along the way. She learned he was from Argentina and had been working at the club for two years.

Once they arrived at 24-Hour Burger, Violet found herself ordering a regular cheeseburger and even some fries. "Screw it," she said with a sigh. "It was a bad night."

"I get by on fast food myself," Edwin said.

Once they got their food and were sitting in a red booth, Violet found herself asking what was weighing on her mind. "So why *do* you work at a strip club? Aside from the obvious."

Edwin stroked his goatee and leaned back. "The obvious?"

"Yeah. You know, being around naked women all the time."

Edwin laughed. "Oh, yeah. That. I couldn't care less about that."

Violet raised her eyebrow. "I don't buy that. Unless you're . . ."

"Unless I'm gay?" he said. "Yeah, well, I am."

Violet looked down at her half-eaten fries. "Oh. Crap. Sorry."

"Why be sorry? It's nothing I'm ashamed of."

"I don't mind either," she said. "Some people do, unfortunately."

"Yeah, like my dad. Ha. He's why I'm here, you know. Couldn't handle his son being a faggot."

Violet winced at his word choice. "Is he religious?"

"Very Catholic, yeah."

"That has to be extremely difficult to not have your family around." Violet felt a tug at her heart just thinking about it.

"Well, you know, it isn't the best situation. But I'm happier now than I was. And you know what? It keeps me focused on my job." Edwin slid a couple of fries through his blob of ketchup before continuing. "Not that I can't admire a fine pair of boobs."

"Everyone likes boobs," Violet replied. "It's a fact." They shared a laugh.

They continued talking for a time, ignoring the comings and goings of the mostly stoned clientele and the sizzle of fries in the kitchen. As it turned out, Edwin was not just a big tough mass of muscle; he was a lonely man, by himself in a strange new country, and trying to make his way. He told Violet about his strict father and devout mother. She'd had a couple of miscarriages and, as a result, had thrown herself into religion and bringing up her only son. With a little coaxing from her macho husband, she had disowned her son when, as a teenager, he had confessed his homosexuality.

Violet knew how it felt to deal with grief-stricken parents, to be all alone in life, and to feel like an outsider and an outcast. Ironically, in connecting with this damaged man, she felt "normal" for the first time in months.

This is my tribe now. A tribe of broken, wounded people. Perhaps someday, when the situation is right, I'll share my story with him.

PART THREE

Chapter 17

September 2012, Los Angeles, CA

The sleek new motorcycle ran like a knight's majestic steed: robust, smooth, and responsive. The aviator glasses under his helmet only added to his devil-may-care, James Dean image as he zipped in and out of traffic.

Dylan had just landed in Los Angeles after two years with the Peace Corps in a remote, rural island in Southeast Asia. As he rocketed along the highway, catching glimpses of billboards advertising luxurious, modern products, kitschy shops, and chain restaurants, he couldn't help but marvel at how strange it all seemed. It was culture shock all over again.

He remembered how foreign everything had seemed when he first got to the island. The smells, the taste of foods he had never heard of, the squatty potties (sometimes visited hastily as a result of said food), the dirt roads, primitive lifestyle, the culture. Dylan had had a panic attack on his first night at the humble abode of his host family. The hut walls were thin, so thin. He could only hope no one heard his heavy breathing.

"I don't know if I've made a huge mistake," he had written in his journal. "I've never felt so utterly alone."

As advertised, the Peace Corps was the hardest thing he had ever done; however, the difficulty turned out to be exactly what he needed. It kept him from thinking, from remembering. Just getting fluent in the local dialect was enough to occupy his mind most of the day. Moreover, the physically grueling labor required to survive in a primitive village ensured he fell into bed exhausted each night.

The rhythms of island life and the natural generosity of its inhabitants embraced him. Hard-won joys punctuated his experience; children laughed with joy when they finally reached that light-bulb moment in class. They listened with wonder, wide-eyed, as he told stories about life back home. *How unbelievable was the Californian lifestyle! How excessive, seriously!* He played guitar with the locals. As he forged connections, he found joy in simplicity: smiles, acts of service, working hard as a team. He absorbed energy from nature, the splendor of the rows and rows of rice paddies framed by hills overlooking glimmering pools of water. The mosaic of the green fields. He hiked often. Along the way, he witnessed natural wonders, like waterfalls cascading over verdant cliffs. The physical exertion hardened his body while softening his raw sense of pain.

He'd come to help others supposedly less fortunate than himself. Instead, he was the one being healed, somehow.

Despite all his forward progress, though, on occasion—often when he was least expecting it—he would be hijacked by a memory; it was as if the rug was pulled out from under his feet all over again. He felt himself falling in midair with no bearings and no one to catch him.

It was at those times that he longed for Violet. To see her, to hear her voice, to hold her.

Violet. Oh Violet! Without her he would never be whole.

He wrote her long letters, recounting his experiences and telling her how much he loved and missed her and how he was counting down the days until they would be together again.

The post came only once a month. He wasn't sure how reliable it was, so he wasn't surprised that he received no letters in the first couple of months. When the post arrived in his third month, Dylan was excited to see that he had finally received some mail. Not just one letter, but a thick packet of envelopes. However, his happiness quickly turned to shock when, on closer inspection, he discovered that they were all his letters to Violet, with a stamp saying, "Return to sender—No forwarding address."

Had Violet moved? Why hadn't she written to tell him? Why hadn't

111

she written him at all? He knew their last meeting had been intense; nevertheless, when he said they should give each other some space, he hadn't meant no contact at all. Was that what she'd thought?

He did the only thing he could think of; he wrote to a couple of their mutual friends to see if they knew where she was and then sat back to endure the excruciating wait. It took another couple of months before he received any replies. To his deep dismay, it seemed no one had heard from her since graduation. He decided to make a trek to the nearest bigger island that had internet service, a two-day journey. With every trip, either in the small fishing boat or by canoe with the villagers, his anxiety mounted. Would he be able to reach her? What if she didn't want to be found? He'd rather not know than face that unbearable prospect.

When he finally sat down in the tiny little internet café with its dinosaur computers, Dylan's stomach was twisted into a knot. First, he checked Violet's Facebook page. There wasn't a single post since he'd left. Violet had never been one for social media, even before the incident. Afterward, she'd avoided it like the plague. He conceded the circumstances; however, he could not let go of the tiny ray of hope. Next, he looked on AnyWho for an address, but there were no results in either San Diego or Los Angeles.

Finally, he tried IM'ing some of their college friends he hadn't had addresses for. Several got back to him right away, eager to know how he was and what the Peace Corps was like. Nevertheless, none of them had any idea where Violet might be. Of course, after graduation they had all scattered across the country, but Violet hadn't returned calls and had eventually disconnected her number. She apparently didn't want to be found, by any of them.

Heartbroken, Dylan gave them an address to get a message to him and made each of them promise to write him if they saw or heard from Violet.

Dylan began to beat himself up. What a fool he'd been! What had he been thinking, coming halfway around the world when things between them were so unstable? What if his stupid decision to give her some space cost him the love of his life?

The next few months were agony. All he could think about was getting back to Violet. Where was she? What was she doing? What if he couldn't find her? Or if he found her too late?

He made the long journey to the internet café two more times, but to no avail. Then, two months before his assignment was up, he got a letter from their friend Margo.

She said she heard that another classmate, Randall, told their friend Jenna that he saw someone he *thought* was Violet on Hollywood Boulevard, but she didn't respond when he called her name and disappeared into the crowd before he could catch up with her.

That tiny, insubstantial bit of information only made Dylan more frantic to get home. Now at least he had something to go on, somewhere to start. He counted down the days until he could get back to America and begin his search in earnest.

Finally, the long-awaited day arrived. Dylan said a heartfelt goodbye to the villagers who had become like family to him, but his thoughts were already across the ocean.

By the time he got off the plane at LAX after the long flights and many layovers, he was running on sheer adrenaline.

Unburdened by any luggage, since he had given away most of his few possessions to the villagers, Dylan didn't even have to go through baggage claim. He headed straight for the taxi line.

First order of business: transportation. He told the taxi driver to take him to Bartels' on Lincoln Boulevard. While he was in the village, his host family had owned an old, beat-up moped—one of the few in the village and a prized possession—and he'd developed quite a fondness for riding it.

It'll be fun to have something with a little more kick, he thought, eyeing the gorgeous 2012 Harley-Davidson FXSBSE CVO Breakout covetously. Soon he was atop the sleek bike and racing down the highway toward West Hollywood.

A jeep zoomed up beside him with windows down. The sounds of

113

Gotye's "Somebody That I Used to Know" emanated from the window.

Dylan changed lanes and found himself humming the song. *It's so appropriate, almost like a sign.*

Violet! I'm here. I'm coming to find you!

He reviewed his plan. First, he'd get a hotel. Then he'd start visiting some of the places she might be likely to go. He'd go to casting calls and acting classes, show her picture at all the restaurants and bars. Moreover, of course, he'd comb the beaches. She'd always loved the beach.

His thoughts were so consumed that he didn't notice the silver-blue convertible coming up fast behind him.

* * * * *

Groggy, he stirred in what turned out to be a hospital bed. Everything was sterile white, and machines surrounded him. Dylan's eyes darted around, but he couldn't move. Everything hurt. Especially his back. He struggled to look down and saw the hospital bracelet, casts, and what must be dozens of tubes and wires. It looked like someone rubbed a cheese grater on his arm; the skin was tattered and inflamed.

"Wh-where am I? Why am I here?" he mumbled, but the words didn't come out right.

The woman by his shoulder, a nurse of slight build and long brown hair, gave him a tender smile. "You're awake. Don't try to speak. You hit your jaw hard when you flew from your bike."

Dylan's head was spinning. "Flew from my bike?" he repeated, trying to remember the accident. His heart began to race as he wondered what kind of injuries he might have.

The nurse was alerted by the rapid beeping of the machine near him. She must have sensed his fear because she leaned in close. Her kind, brown eyes looked into his. "I'm not sure how much you remember.

But you're okay now." She paused before continuing. "You were hit hard, and you have quite a few fractures in your wrists and arms. You're immobilized from neck to toe to prevent any further damage. The doctor will be in later to explain it better, but you're lucky to be alive."

Lucky to be alive? What did that mean? Had he broken his back? Would he be able to walk again?

Before he could get the questions out, the nurse slipped out the door.

Dylan felt trapped in a dense mental fog. The silence was punctuated only by the beeps of his heart rate monitor and the IV drip of morphine. Was this really happening? This couldn't be his life. This was not how things were supposed to go.

The doctor finally arrived. He introduced himself, a name that Dylan was unable to recall. Words floated from his mouth that still failed to sink in, like "shoulder dislocation" and "ruptured discs."

"You're lucky," the doctor said grimly. "If you hadn't been wearing a helmet, you certainly wouldn't be here now."

Dylan struggled to speak. "W-w-will I be okay?"

"You've got a long road ahead," the doctor said. "Lots of physical therapy. But I have every confidence you will be able to achieve full mobility and independence in time."

The words were meant to reassure, but they had the opposite effect. Bile rose in his throat. Independence? Is that all he can look forward to?

Life flips in the blink of an eye. Life flips in the blink of an eye. Life flips in the blink of an eye. Where have I heard that before?

He was spinning through space . . . then he felt a hand on his.

"I know you're in pain. It will get better." The words cut through the void.

"Thanks . . ." Dylan glanced at the nurse's nametag. "Teresita." It

115

was a difficult name to say with his injury.

"Call me Tess," she said. "We couldn't find any contact information in your wallet or an address or anything. Is there someone we can call for you?"

A cloud passed over his face. "No, no one," he said with a finitude that invited no questions.

To his great relief, although she gave him a compassionate look, Tess didn't pry further.

"Well, then," she said with an easy smile. "I'll just have to make sure to check in on you more often."

Chapter 18

After enduring less-than-compassionate treatment from a brusque day nurse with a thick unibrow and cankles, Dylan was glad to see Tess the next evening when her shift began.

"How are you doing today?" she said cheerily.

"Surviving."

"That's the spirit," she said, checking his vitals. "Is there anything you need? Anything I can do to make you more comfortable?"

"There was a chain I was wearing. Is it still on?"

"Oh, no. They would have taken that off. It should have been put with your things. They're in a locker for safekeeping."

"Could you get it for me?"

"I can, but you won't be able to wear it until your neck heals."

"That's okay. I just want to have it. It's . . . it's important to me."

"Sure, I'll check the locker and see if it's there."

Dylan stewed while she went to check. What if it had been misplaced? It was the most tangible link he had to Violet, and, superstitious or not, he felt like it would be an ominous sign if it were gone.

"Found it," Tess said when she returned, flashing a triumphant smile as she held up the chain with the miniature key and placed it in his hand. He squeezed it and felt relief wash over him.

"Thanks. That means a lot."

"How about I hang it here where you can see it?" she said. "Until you can wear it again."

He thanked her again. He couldn't count how many times he'd said that word lately. He'd only been in the hospital a few days, and already he was tired of constantly having to have people do things for him. How long was this going to last?

His mind flitted back to his mother being in the hospital. She'd spent much longer, more grueling intervals in four sterile walls, being stuck like a pin cushion and pumped full of toxic drugs. *She never complained.*

Tess repositioned his pillow and prepared to leave. "Anything else?" she asked. "Would you like the TV on?" Or some music?"

Dylan nodded. "Music would be nice."

Tess turned on the radio, and classical music thundered out at full volume. Wrinkling her nose, Tess went to change the dial.

"No!" Dylan said sharply. "I mean, you can leave it."

Tess raised her eyebrows in surprise. "You like this stuff?" she asked, turning down the volume to a reasonable level.

"My mother did. Vivaldi was one of her favorites."

Tess responded to the *was* with a knowing look.

They listened to the music for a few moments.

"Do you believe in karma?" Dylan suddenly asked.

She looked at him with concern. "What do you mean?"

"Maybe this is my penance. For being so selfish. I was always such a pain when my mother was in the hospital." Seeing her quizzical look, he added, "Ovarian cancer."

"I'm sorry. How old were you?"

"She died when I was nine."

"You were just a child!"

118

"That doesn't mean anything. My . . . friend, she had a sister suffering too. She was always entertaining her, always by her side. Why wasn't I that good? Why didn't I care?" He fondly remembered Violet fluffing her sister's pillows, inventing card game after card game to pass the time.

"You did care," Tess said. "You just cared so much that you didn't know how to cope. It's why you acted out."

"I never thought of it that way." Dylan felt the sting of tears. "How I wish I could go back and do it over again. Show her how much I cared."

Tess took his hand and squeezed it. "She knows."

Unable to speak, Dylan squeezed back.

* * * * *

Dylan's recovery felt never-ending, and the pain only worsened, spreading throughout his limbs down to his toes and fingertips. However, most unsettling was that his chest was beginning to burn—cause for grave concern, in his mind.

He told the brisk, middle-aged nurse with him. "My chest. It burns. Is this normal?"

"Is it just in your chest?"

Dylan explained that he felt it in his shoulder and back too.

Is this what a heart attack feels like? The thought put him in a tailspin; he found it harder to breathe. Did he bring it on himself? Could he really not get enough oxygen?

"I'm having trouble breathing."

The nurse put in a call. Shortly, a doctor was in the room, listening to his heart and trying to elicit information from him. Dylan was in agony as he struggled to breathe, utterly paralyzed by the fear of the pain in his shoulder and chest.

In no time, he had adhesive pads stuck all over his body, stickers attached to wires that flowed into a mysterious machine. Dylan was afraid of what he'd hear. Did he get a blood clot from being bedridden? What was next?

His doctor, a thoughtful Indian man named Dr. Sharad who had been overseeing his recovery, said, "Your oxygen level is sky-high. Take a long inhale and exhale—this is a panic attack."

It took a few moments for the news to sink in, but it lifted a weight off his chest, although the pain still remained.

"Then . . . what's the pain?"

Dylan learned that his ruptured discs were causing cervical radiculopathy, a result of the disc changes prompting pressure on his nerves. This was causing the numbness, tingling, and pain he felt. Dr. Sharad explained he might need a steroid to help the pain since the NSAIDs were not enough.

As the nurse prepared him for the epidural steroid injections, she handled him roughly, not making any attempt to soothe him, and laid him back down with only a, "There you go." Dylan couldn't help but wish Tess were there.

* * * * *

True to her word, Tess went out of her way to tend to her new patient. Even though ICU nurses spend a lot of time with their patients anyway, Tess went above and beyond. Unlike some of the other nurses, she was ultra-attentive to Dylan's physical pain and had pain medication ready with a cup of chilled water on the spot whenever it was time. As Dylan lay miserably restrained in bed, unable to move, she fluffed his pillows and tucked him in. She made ample conversation to help speed along his days and always ensured the TV was turned to something he enjoyed when she left.

"You look miserable. What can I do for you?" Tess asked him one day.

Dylan sighed. "Nothing. I've had my meds, and I've got *House*

Hunters on. What more could I want?"

Tess leaned in and spoke gently. "Look, I'm serious. It's no fun being here, I know. I want to help. As a friend."

Dylan laughed and looked at the ceiling. "There's nothing you can do. I only want one person to be here, but it's impossible."

Tess looked at him sharply and scooted closer on her rolling stool. "Why is that?"

Dylan began to clam up; the details of his relationship with Violet were like a precious gem. "It's nothing." Then he added, "I don't see her anymore."

Tess looked at him earnestly. "Do you want to talk about it?"

Dylan shook his head but found himself doing just that. "I don't even know where she is. That's why I came to LA . . . to try to find her. But even if I do find her, I don't know if she even wants me around. She didn't last time we saw each other. She told me it was over. It's complicated.".

Tess bit her lip. She stared at him for a long time, as if trying to make up her mind. Finally, she came to a decision. "This girl. She doesn't have really unusual lavender eyes, does she?"

"What?" Dylan practically shouted.

"I didn't know whether to tell you this. I still don't. But while you were unconscious, a girl came to visit you. She stayed in the waiting room until you were stabilized."

Dylan was thunderstruck. "Violet was *here*? But how did she know I was in the hospital?"

Tess shrugged. "I don't know. She must have heard about it on the news, I guess. It got a little press since it was a hit and run."

"So, did she leave her number? Some way to reach her?" Dylan asked eagerly, over the moon that his search was over.

Tess suddenly avoided eye contact. "She didn't give me a name, just said she was an old friend of yours. We aren't supposed to give nonfamily members information, but it was obvious she cared about you. Since you didn't have any other visitors, I kept her updated on your progress. When you finally got out of the ER and I told her you were out of the woods, she said she was leaving now that she knew you were going to be okay. She asked me not to tell you she had been there. She said she still cared about you, but she couldn't be with you and didn't want to complicate the situation."

Tess finally looked at him. "Dylan, I'm so sorry. I hope I did the right thing by telling you."

It felt like a fishhook jerked his heart out of his chest, leaving nothing but emptiness behind. Dylan licked his lips before speaking. "I . . . I'm glad you did. Thanks. Now I know."

"Maybe you can move on now? Get some closure?"

"Maybe," he mumbled. "I think I'd like to be alone for a while, if you don't mind."

"Of course, of course. I'll check on you later." Tess's tan, slender fingers wrapped around Dylan's hand for a brief moment. She squeezed it encouragingly before leaving the room.

I guess she really meant it when she told me to go away.

He tried to unscramble the mess of negativity in his brain and find a silver lining, but he couldn't. The emotional pain was overwhelming, far more severe than any of the physical pain he was still grappling with. There was no agony worse than a broken heart.

Chapter 19

Over the next weeks, Dylan descended into a dark abyss of depression.

Tess repeatedly apologized for telling him about Violet. "I shouldn't have told you," she said vehemently. "It was a mistake."

"Stop beating yourself up," Dylan said. "I'm glad you did. As painful as it is, not knowing would have been worse."

Nevertheless, despite his assurances, his emotional state was unquestionably precarious. Tess couldn't seem to stop blaming herself for his sudden downward spiral. She was at his side whenever she could be. They talked about anything and everything—the weather, how Tess decided to pursue nursing, Dylan's time in the Peace Corps, Tess's uncanny ability to pick losers for boyfriends, politics, sports—but certain topics remained off-limits. Tess didn't pry, though, so that was a relief.

Whenever Tess wasn't there, Dylan's loneliness crept in. He appreciated her presence and the way she always kept him distracted from his pain—both emotional and physical. Often it felt like it was only her friendship that kept him going.

A couple of months later, Dylan's casts were removed, but he didn't feel that he was mended at all. His pain persisted, and he was unable to move his fingers at will in spite of the injection to treat the cervical radiculopathy caused by his ruptured disc. He would need surgery.

"I'll be with you every step of the way," Tess assured him. He was surprised at how much he had come to depend on her.

After recovering from the surgery, Dylan was transferred to the Physical Rehabilitation Center adjacent to the main hospital to undergo physical therapy. He was no longer under Tess's care.

However, she came to visit him daily after her shift and on her days off, helping him to exercise and regain his strength.

They played a game of checkers one afternoon. Tess wasn't wearing her scrubs; instead, she had on distressed jeans and a black tank top, showing off toned arms that were just strong enough that Dylan wouldn't want to meet her in a dark alley.

"So you're almost outta here. What are you gonna do?" she asked, sliding her red piece diagonally.

"Get a job, when I'm well enough," he said.

"What would you do?" she asked.

"My dad was an accountant. I guess I'll try my hand at wearing a tie every day too."

Tess's eyes widened. "Wow. That'll be a big change. A rude awakening after being a professional adventurer." She grinned.

Dylan skipped two of Tess's pieces—clumsily, at that—and told her to king him. She seemed undisturbed as they continued talking.

"You know," she said slowly, eyeing his black pieces encroaching on hers on the checkerboard. "I could help you with rehab. I mean, as a private nurse kind of hitch.If nothing else, I could help you around the house as you get back into real life."

"No," Dylan said without missing a beat. He'd begun to suspect Tess felt more for him than friendship, and he wouldn't take advantage of feelings he couldn't reciprocate. "I appreciate everything you've done for me, but you've done more than enough already. I need to start doing things on my own."

She scoffed. "You're a nice guy—maybe too nice. No need to act strong around me. You *need* help. Take it!"

One thing that was quickly becoming apparent to Dylan was that Tess was not only a helpful person, but aggressively helpful. She wouldn't take no for an answer. "You need to make sure you heal properly. You can't do too much too soon."

Dylan began to tune her out. He felt weary, both mentally and physically. He didn't have the energy to resist. "Alright, alright," he reluctantly said. "You win. I could use your help."

Chapter 20

August 2013, Orange County, CA

Dylan slowly picked up the pieces of his life. To stay away from the congestion of Los Angeles, he moved to Orange County on the outskirts of LA. Tess continued to work with him on his physical therapy exercises until he was well enough to start looking for a job.

He worked with a recruiter and almost immediately landed an entry-level accounting position. He knew it came with long hours; however, that sounded like a welcome escape. His method of dealing with heartache had always been to immerse himself in activity. He hoped it would work for him again.

Tess suggested they take a weekend trip to Las Vegas. She marketed it as "celebrating his recovery and a new job." She added, "I get the gambling bug every now and again." Even though Dylan wasn't a gambler, flights were only an hour and a half. A weekend trip sounded wonderful, truth be told.

However, Dylan had reservations. Somewhere along the way, he and Tess had crossed the line from nurse/patient to close friends. Nevertheless, going away together? Was he sending the wrong message? Tess was helpful and kind and not bad looking. She was no Violet, but she was attractive in her own way.

But, still no Violet. Dylan sighed and shook his head. *Enough!* he told himself. *Violet isn't an option. You've got to move on.*

With that, Dylan agreed to the weekend in Vegas. It was time for him to have a little fun for once.

* * * * *

"I think I have epilepsy," Dylan joked. The lights of the slot machines paired with the glittering lights of the Las Vegas strip made colorful splotches appear in his line of vision. The whole city assaulted the senses: playful, almost schizophrenic lights; loud music; the electronic buzzing, bells, and alarms of the machines; and the excited shouts and exaggerated groans of lots and lots of drunken people.

Dylan loved people-watching in the casinos. While Tess was glued to the blackjack table and knocking back rum and cokes, he wryly observed the older gentlemen with women half their age on their arms. *Or maybe a third.* At one table, there was a pack of men wearing cowboy hats and huge belt buckles, their suits as loud as their laughter.

Dylan rooted Tess on for a while before meandering over to the slot machines. The cherries didn't align on the slots, and in less than five minutes Dylan was down eighty bucks. He cursed and vowed not to give the house any more of his dollars. Instead, he recouped some of his money by taking advantage of a few more glasses of the free-flowing alcohol before returning to the blackjack table, where Tess banged her hand on the table in triumph.

"Five hundred dollars, baby!" she yelled.

Grinning, Dylan high-fived her. "You're killing 'em."

"Shhh, it's not over yet!" she cried.

Whether or not Dylan's jinx was to blame, Tess lost her gains before the night was up. It looked like she might have wanted to continue, but when she saw Dylan with his hand in the pocket of his taupe slacks, she said, "You know what? I have time to make it back tomorrow. No worries."

At night, they slept on opposite ends of the bed. Although Dylan offered to sleep on the sofa, they decided not to make a fuss over it and just enjoyed the comforts of the king-sized bed.

In the morning, they walked the Las Vegas strip. Tess grabbed Dylan's arm, pulling him this way and that. "Let's get a picture here!" she said, leading him to the magnificent fountains in front of the Bellagio. She seemed to want a selfie in front of every fake international landmark: the Eiffel Tower, the Sphinx, the Statue of Liberty, the Venetian gondolas. "Why travel abroad when you can get everything all in one place?" She laughed.

That night they went to a popular hipster bar that was dominated by trendy twenty-somethings. Men and women were intermingling at the bar and intertwined on the dance floor. Multicolored lights pulsated with the beat and flashed in different directions. Dylan felt Tess's hand on the small of his back as she led him toward the bar.

"First drink is on me," Dylan found himself offering. "What'll ya have?"

"Just a tequila shot, please. You get this round, and I'll get the next."

"Tequila shots? I haven't had those since college. I hope I'm not too old for this," he joked.

"This is our last night in Vegas. Gotta go big! Get the top-shelf liquor if you're worried."

Without thinking, Dylan did as she suggested. A surly bartender pushed two shots their way. They raised the tiny glasses, hit them with a *clink*, and knocked them back. Dylan felt the fiery liquid burning all the way down to his small intestine like a splash of gasoline. A floating sensation followed. Tess barely blinked; the trip had proven that she was obviously a veteran.

"My turn," Tess announced, dropping her credit card on the bar. Another round arrived, which flowed down easier than the first. Dylan felt himself smiling more. Tess had clearly warmed up too, as evidenced by her frequent touching. "Do you dance?" she shouted above the music.

"No, not really," Dylan said with a chuckle.

"Isn't it time you start?"

Dylan preferred talking, but the club was not very conducive to discussion. Tess grabbed his hand and led him to the floor. She began to gyrate her hips in his direction. The alcohol lowered

Dylan's inhibitions, and soon he was tearing it up on the dance floor.

After ten or so minutes, Tess pushed him toward the bar again. "Another drink!"

"Don't you think you've had enough?" he asked. "I don't know if it's you or me, but you're looking kind of wobbly."

"I'm fine," Tess scoffed, rolling her eyes. "I play better blackjack this way, and I have money to win back!"

However, they didn't make it back to the casino. Before Dylan knew it, his world was fluid. He was striking up conversations with strangers. Shots didn't taste as strong anymore; he was buying them like they were going out of fashion. With that, he began to "blow out." Later, he remembered only bits and pieces of the evening, punctuated by blackouts.

His memories were a nonsensical montage: talking to random girls; talking to Tess; Tess speaking very closely to him as they stumbled through the street; and then a strange taxi ride to nowhere with someone he didn't know. Soon they tumbled out onto the street.

Dylan's world was spinning and floating as they meandered drunkenly through the streets. Then a blinking neon sign came into focus on the horizon: "24/7 Wedding Chapel. Simple wedding, $99 and up." They stumbled up to the unassuming chapel that reminded Dylan of a fast-food joint, with couples coming in and out just about as quickly.

"Wanna get hitched?" he joked.

Tess turned serious for a moment before she abruptly began jumping up and down in excitement. "Are you kidding?"

Dylan's world was still unsteady, thanks to the alcohol. Maybe he hadn't heard her correctly. He laughed out loud.

Tess grabbed his arm and looked into his face. "I'm serious, Dylan. Haven't you had so much fun? I've loved every second with you. I mean, shit . . . we *belong* together."

Dylan swallowed the lump in his throat. He didn't know how to process this unexpected proposal. The alcohol fogging his brain didn't help.

Just then, a rowdy bachelor party cavorted around the chapel, quoting from the movie *The Hangover*. Dylan stared at them while searching for the right words.

Violet was gone, out of his life. He had to accept that. He was never going to find that kind of love again. So what did it really matter who he ended up with? Tess loved him; she'd been so good to him. If he couldn't be happy, couldn't he at least make someone else happy? Warmth flooded his body at the hazy thought of a new beginning with someone.

"You've been my anchor since the accident," he said, clumsily grabbing her hand. "And I can't thank you enough."

Tess's hands were on his shoulders. "Dylan, I know it's been hard to be alone, all by yourself through all that trauma. But I'm here for you now. I'm going to take care of you." She caressed his face with her hands and pulled his head close to hers. He could smell the booze on her breath. "No more worrying about being alone. We can be there for each other forever. We'll be a family."

This is absurdly quick. This is insane. This is . . . not the worst thing in the world.

Elvis's crooning voice emanated from the chapel, floating on the air around them. Tess rubbed his arm. "Dylan, I love you. I did everything for you. And imagine all the fun we'll have together. This is just the beginning of something wonderful. We've been here for each other for so long. It's perfect."

Tess had taken good care of him; she had fun with him. She was someone he could rely on. "You're a man now," she said as if reading his mind. "Forget about teenage romances. Take a woman who is strong, who loves you, who would move mountains for you."

The more she talked, the more it made sense. However, a tiny voice persisted in the dark corners of his drunken brain. Dylan tried to give that worry a voice. "You're sure you're okay with doing this here, now?" Dylan said. "No frills, no family?"

"It'll be spontaneous and romantic!"

Dylan was learning that Tess was always impulsive and never strayed from her whims once they struck her. Her pleading eyes were filled with yearning, searching his face hopefully.

Tess isn't Violet . . . but she's great. She was healing his heart. He couldn't bear to disappoint her after all she had done for him. He loved her in some ways. Perhaps once he completely eradicated Violet from his mind, he could give himself to Tess fully.

He looked down at the short, perky woman and smiled. "What the hell. Let's do it."

Tess squealed and kissed him, and he pulled her in, his hands sprawled across the small of her back. Her arms wrapped around his neck. It felt incredible to hold someone again. *Maybe it'll work out after all,* he thought as they followed Elvis's crooning into the merry light of the chapel.

* * * * *

The next morning, Dylan woke up, his head pounding. Tess was in his arms wearing only a pink bra. *What happened last night?* He looked around the room, trying to get his bearings. He saw their club clothes and shoes scattered on the floor.

Feeling him move, Tess stirred. She rubbed her leg against his. "So glad to be with you," she murmured, nuzzling into the crook of his arm. "Can't wait to start our future together."

Suddenly everything flooded back to Dylan. The realization of what he had done hit him like a body blow, but almost instantly he squelched his feelings. He was surprised at how quickly he was able to rationalize away the panic.

Yeah, he got married. To a wonderful woman who was crazy about him. So what? He could do a lot worse.

Chapter 21

October 2013, Orange County, CA

Immersing himself in Mozart's *Symphony No. 41*, "Jupiter," Dylan sat in a tranquil state in the study. He was always intrigued by how composers could brilliantly coordinate an array of diverse instruments into a cohesive piece of enchanting music. Music, especially classical, continued to be his solace.

Tess walked in with her hair all a mess. "Aren't you studying for the CPA exam? How can you study with this on?"

"I just can. It sets the mood." Dylan leaned back and dropped his highlighter beside his mountain of index cards.

"I just don't get it. It's dead people's music. The guy who wrote this has been deep in the ground for *centuries*." Tess pushed the power button on the Bluetooth speaker and exited the room as abruptly as she'd entered.

Dylan felt hurt. Tess's antagonistic attitude toward classical music had grown from subtle to abundantly evident. That was just one of an ever-growing list of their differences. Regret was starting to creep in, but he tried swatting it away like a fly.

Maybe he was just too easily offended. After all, his love of classical music was a gift from his mother.

"Close your eyes," his mother would say when he was young. "What do you see? Here's a hint. The title is *Trout*." Schubert's *Trout Quintet* was playing.

"I see a trout jumping in and out of a stream," he said.

"How many?"

Dylan's face contorted as he described his vision. "Two. Oh, no,

132

three. One is chasing the others."

During Beethoven's *Symphony No. 6,* "The Pastoral Symphony,*"* his mother would ask, "Do you hear the thunder?"

Moreover, during Vivaldi's *Four Seasons* she'd question him about which season each movement was in.

His mother also introduced the love of opera to him. Once he found his mother crying with all her heart as she watched Verdi's *La Traviata* led by Teresa Stratas and Placido Domingo. The rich voices sang of the untimely demise of Violetta as she succumbed to tuberculosis.

His zeal for music was the best inheritance his mother could have left him—a precious gift that he could reach for no matter what life threw at him. There was music to fit any emotion: happiness, sadness, anger, romance, tenderness . . . .

Even at the very end, there was music to express the grief that no words could touch. As his mother requested, Mozart's *Requiem* played at her funeral.

For years afterward, he couldn't bear to listen to music that reminded him of her. Now he had rekindled his love of music, and it felt like a special—almost sacred—connection.

He got up and paced around the room.. *How can Tess dismiss and even ridicule the music that's so close to my heart?* Resentment toward his wife whipped up around him like the beginning of a sandstorm.

He looked at the picture of them on their wedding night in Vegas. It was just a couple of months ago. Tess's arms were wrapped around him, their faces ruddy with the drink. Nevertheless, they both had huge, goofy smiles, like they were laughing. *Was that the last time they laughed?* he wondered. It sure seemed like it.

The cracks in their marriage were already showing. Tess was a hard worker, and she had a good heart. But she had also proven to have a surprisingly limited capacity for handling any kind of emotional pain. If something threatened to disturb her peace of mind, she utterly ignored, rejected, or dismissed it. This compartmentalization made for a great nurse; however, it did not make for a sensitive wife.

There was still so much she didn't know. Dylan shuddered at the thought of telling her why he and Violet never got married. She could never understand the gulf of pain within him. She did not understand . . . and worse, she had made it clear she didn't even want to. On the few occasions he'd tried to tell her something painful from his past, she'd shut him down in no uncertain terms. He felt more alone than he ever had.

The truth fell on him like an anvil.

What a fool I am! What a terrible mistake I've made!

* * * * *

"Let's go," Tess said as she waved a flyer around. "A brand-new nightclub just opened in Newport Beach, and the grand opening is tonight."

Dylan didn't look up from the television. "Not interested." He forced himself to maintain a calm voice, though he wanted to grimace like she did with him.

"Oh, come on! We haven't been out in ages, and the hospital is working me like a mule. I need to unwind." Tess flopped down beside Dylan and held the flyer under his nose. "Look at this: 'state-of-the-art sound system, dance hits from the '90s, new millennium, and today . . . a party atmosphere of scintillating entertainment.' Doesn't this sound fun? Let's go!"

Knowing Tess's strong personality, he decided it was easier to throw in the towel immediately since he'd probably wind up giving in in the end. "Fine," he said with a sigh before getting up and walking to their bedroom, alone.

An hour later, Dylan was standing at a tall bar table beside the dance floor. He shoved his hands in his pockets and watched Tess under the flashing lights as she bobbed her head to the music and sipped on her Mojito. She was in high spirits from liquor-mixed drinks and already losing her balance. Dylan just hoped she didn't fall; her little black dress was so short it would reveal everything. He couldn't help but feel protective, but Tess's sense of independence kept her from appreciating anything she interpreted as possessive behavior.

Another electronic number reverberated across the dance floor. "Let's get out there! The music is too good!" Tess grabbed Dylan's arm and pushed through the mass of people to get closer to the DJ stage.

Even with the air-conditioner blasting, it was stuffy on the dance floor. The air hung heavy around them, and the cloying mixture of odors—perfume, alcohol, deodorant, sweat—nearly suffocated Dylan. The only way he could bear these events was to drink himself into oblivion—and that came with its own problems.

In the dim, multicolored lighting, Dylan suddenly noticed a girl that looked like Violet from the back. She had the same build, the same cascade of honey-butter-colored hair. He turned away, not wanting to get caught staring, and fixated on Tess as she gyrated beside him. Still, his eyes were drawn to the other woman like a magnet. Dylan had tried to stop himself from thinking about Violet since he got married. However, that didn't mean she didn't show up in his mind, uninvited.

He imagined what he'd do if it were Violet. What would he say? *Does her hair feel the way it used to?*

He was yanked back to reality by the sound of shrieks. Horrified, he saw Tess vomiting all over the floor. The people around them scattered like cockroaches, backing away and covering their nostrils. A couple of them rushed to the restroom to clean themselves off.

Tess wobbled and collapsed in a pool of her own vomit.

Dylan immediately bent down to help her up, but she was dead weight, completely unresponsive. Panic rose in his throat as he shook her more forcefully, to no avail. The manager on duty raced over to them. "Let me call 911," he said, whipping out his mobile phone.

Minutes later, the paramedics were loading Tess into the ambulance. Dylan followed behind in their vehicle. He was worried and scared. Above all, he was angry. *Why can't she control her drinking?*

In the hospital, Tess was revived . . . and mortified. Dylan stroked her arm as the attending ER physician asked her a few questions. Tess admitted to feeling tired and having slept poorly lately but assured him that she was just under a lot of pressure at work. *Or at home*, Dylan thought. *Maybe I'm not the only one who's miserable.*

"It's probably heat exhaustion. Go home, drink plenty of water, and take a cool shower," the doctor said, discharging her.

Dylan and Tess drove home in silence. He avoided looking at his disheveled wife, but he could smell her stench.

The night, previously loud and hectic, suddenly felt still. Dead.

They retired that night without a word.

* * * * *

The day felt comfortably warm in Southern California. The brilliant sunshine delighted Dylan's spirits as he stepped out of the attorney's office. He was relieved and elated about the decision he had made. The marriage was heading nowhere fast, lacking passion, respect, love. All that remained was regret and anguish.

And now? Now the image of Violet's face illuminated his path forward. He had to find her.

She may reject me as a lover. But at least I can be close to her, even if it is just as friends.

The episode at the nightclub was the straw that broke the camel's back. What a disaster!

What was worse, Tess hadn't pulled herself together since then. She had been calling in sick and lounging in bed for two weeks. Dylan asked why she was still not well.

"I'm exhausted!" she claimed.

136

Dylan suspected she was guzzling alcohol when he was out of sight. He should have been angry, but he only felt disappointment.

When she's wasn't isolating herself, Tess was an unquestionable mess. The night before, she'd dropped a dish in the kitchen, causing beef tenderloin and shards of the plate to fly in every direction.

"Are you drunk?" Dylan asked, dejected. She was there physically but hardly present. Her gaze was distant, as if fixed on something that wasn't there.

She pouted. "Sorry. I don't know what happened."

Dylan sighed, tired of her manipulative behavior—an obvious ploy for his attention. As he reluctantly helped clean up the mess she'd made, picking up each jagged piece of plate with caution, he reflected on how much more difficult it would be to pick up the pieces of their marriage.

We're on life support, and it's time to pull the plug.

With that, he'd decided to pursue a clean slate.

* * * * *

The next day, the world seemed to bless his decision. The gleaming blue sky and brilliant sunlight injected optimistic energy, which eradicated the very last bit of his hesitation. This was the right move!

He told himself it would even be good for Tess. She probably realized how he felt about her—or didn't feel—and that was leading to her depression and drinking. *She'll be better off without me. No one deserves to be trapped in a loveless marriage.*

However, as much as he hoped Tess would benefit from divorce, his main thoughts were for his own future. He would be *free* again!

Then if he could just find Violet and speak to her, explain everything, he could convince her to give them another shot. Just the prospect of seeing her again filled him with exhilaration.

Chapter 22

Sitting still in the night, Dylan could barely see the outline of his hands. The illumination from his computer monitor had gone dark. The phrase, "If you want to make God laugh, tell him about your plans," circulated through his mind like a bitter marquee. Undoubtedly, God was laughing right then. He could almost hear it.

* * * * *

Dylan thought about how Tess broke the news. They sat opposite one another while eating Chinese takeout. They were buried in their own thoughts. Speaking little, as usual. The aroma of peanut oil and chili peppers from the Kung Pao Chicken didn't seem to arouse their appetite like it used to. Dylan stared at the soaked takeout container holding the Chinese broccoli with oyster sauce and fried garlic—far too greasy, as usual.

Finally, Tess placed the chopsticks down in a deliberate motion, stood up, and walked toward the kitchen. Dylan noticed her moves seemed tentative, somehow. Intentional.

She returned with a fork and sat back down. "I have something to tell you," she said, dragging the words out before pausing a few moments.

"I've had a battery of tests trying to figure out what's been wrong with me." Tess recounted her doctors' visits and diagnosis in detail.

Earlier that week, Tess sat in the exam room at the optometrist's office, looking at the complex anatomy and the many ocular diseases depicted on the posters. She felt wigged-out, sitting there as a patient. How different it was to be on the receiving end instead of working there. She wished she were there for just another harmless checkup. Dr. Tanmura had been her optometrist for the past decade, and typically they only discussed her contact lenses prescription. As a healthcare professional herself, she practiced removing herself from emotional situations and the anxiety a patient must feel at getting an unfavorable diagnosis. It sounded messed up, but she frankly had to.

She was pulling on her hair when Dr. Tanmura entered the room with all the good-naturedness she remembered from him.

"I notice you're not wearing your contact lenses today. Running out of your supply, or is something else wrong?" Dr. Tanmura's inquisitive look revealed genuine concern.

Tess described the situation. She was having episodes of blurred vision, with a persistent black spot in her left eye. To make matters worse, her eyes hurt when she moved them. She recounted the blackout in the nightclub and the persistent fatigue that was ruining her life.

Dr. Tanmura listened intently as he entered the case history into the computer. Tess tried to read his face for a hint, but he remained stoic as he performed a comprehensive eye examination followed by the retinal scan.

Once that was complete, Dr. Tanmura faced Tess and spoke with discretion. "Tess, let me show you something," he said as he revealed the image on the screen. "You have a condition called optic neuritis. The scan of OCT (optical coherence tomography) shows the thinning of your retinal layer. More precisely, the optic nerve fiber layer—"

"MS?" Tess blurted out.

Again, Dr. Tanmura carefully chose his words as he proceeded. "It could be, but let's not jump to conclusions. I'd like to refer you to a neurologist to have a complete checkup first. An MRI will be ordered."

Tess had her neurological workup by a physician, independent from the hospital at which she worked.

The results came in.

"Dylan, I was diagnosed with MS."

Dylan looked at her in disbelief. Although the news didn't register, he tried to engage. "What's MS?"

"Multiple sclerosis. I . . . I might become disabled. My neurologist couldn't give a clear prognosis yet." Tess stared at Dylan as if trying to read his face.

Dylan lowered his gaze and felt the weight of the folded envelope in his pocket. His plan of presenting her with the divorce papers after dinner? Not happening.

"I'm sorry," was all he could manage. It was insufficient. What does one say in a moment like that?

The silence returned, an invisible wall erected between them. The meal became tasteless cement, tough to swallow.

After dinner, Dylan helped clean up. His movements were robotic and his face emotionless. Unable to utter a single word, he walked to his study and closed the door.

There he remained, unsure of how to proceed.

Divorce! He could not bring the subject up to her. It would not have been an issue if she were healthy and able to go her own way. Now, her disease made things complex. She took care of him while he was going through his physical setbacks and recovery from the injury and surgery. How could he leave her alone now? Tess was almost as alone in the world as he was. Her parents divorced when she was a toddler after her father walked out of their life. For all she knew he was dead; she hadn't seen him since. She was raised by her mother, but they had a contentious relationship. Tess had moved out when she was just a teenager. Dylan had never met the woman; he didn't think Tess could count on any support in that quarter.

He remembered how his father tended to his mother while she was going through her chemo treatments. His mother would stay in bed for days. Housework fell on his father's shoulders after a long day of stressful work at his accounting firm. His father cleaned up his wife's vomit from the chemo. He never complained, not once.

During Dylan's two years in the Peace Corps, he'd conditioned himself to ask, "What's my duty? What's my responsibility?"—instead of asking, "Am I happy?"

Is happiness elusive?

If he wanted to stay in this marriage, he needed to let go of Violet. Nevertheless, her name was stuck in his consciousness like a bug on flypaper.

The mind is such a funny thing. Can you turn off the need to think about someone like a light switch?

His jumbled mind was running in super-hyper speed and crashed in all directions.

Divorce was not an option, at least not for now. His whole being rebelled.

He was *so* close! So close to freedom!

Didn't he deserve a shot at happiness after everything he'd been through?

It's unfair!

Chapter 23

November 2013, Los Angeles, CA

It was a brisk early morning in LA as Violet walked along the beach. The skies were feathery streaks of soft gray, and the pale white light from a sleepy sun crept on the horizon. Violet couldn't sleep, as was often the case. There was something calming about walking in solitude before the city stirred, the beach empty except for the occasional jogger or silver-haired power walker. The smell of salt consoled her. She gazed at the shoreline, taking comfort from the constant crashing and receding of waves. She pulled her brown leather jacket closer and crossed her arms. When she looked up, she saw a golden retriever/poodle mix on a purple leash . . . a leash that connected to an owner who looked awfully familiar.

The owner's freckled face broke into a smile. "Oh my gosh. Wow! Violet?"

"Sarah!"

Sarah was a mutual friend of Violet and Dylan. They used to hang out in college.

Sarah ran over and gave Violet a tight hug. She pulled away and laughed. "Of course the first time I see you in years I look terrible, wearing an old T-shirt and workout shorts."

Violet looked at Sarah's knobby knees and smiled fondly. "It's fine! You're being active. That's good."

"Well, how are you?" Sarah asked. "We have some catching up to do. Feel free to join in the walk with Lou and me." She gestured to her ginger-colored, curly haired pet.

Violet said that she was doing okay. Sarah asked about her job; Violet told her she was currently on the lookout for a new one. In some ways, that was semi-true. She reminded herself to look for a "real" job and leave the club every so often, although it had been ages since she seriously applied for another job.

"Oh, I've been there," Sarah said. "I hope you find something soon."

"What about you?" Violet asked, eager to change the subject.

"Blake and I got engaged last month," Sarah said, beaming

"It will be a long engagement though. We're waiting for Blake to finish graduate school first." Sarah added, "I've been wanting to get ahold of you, but no one knew how to reach you. I'd love for you to come to the wedding."

"And I'd love to," Violet said with a hint of a smile. "Congratulations, Sarah. I can't believe you and *Blake*."

Sarah nodded. "Yeah, I know. Who thought we'd ever end up together?"

"I guess you never can tell."

"Tell me about it! I was so sure you and Dylan would get back together. I couldn't believe it when he got married!"

Violet's stomach dropped to the pavement. Did she hear correctly? "Wait, what?"

The smile disappeared from Sarah's face. She rubbed her head. "Oh, crap. You didn't know?"

It wasn't a joke. Sarah's face was serious, apologetic. *Dear God* . . . .

"No. No, I didn't." She realized she had forgotten to breathe and exhaled deeply. "I'm happy for him."

They walked only a little while—though it felt excruciatingly long—before Violet broke away, claiming another appointment. "I'll be in touch soon."

They exchanged phone numbers, but Violet deliberately gave Sarah the wrong number.

* * * * *

Violet returned home, her brain swimming. She bit her lip so hard that it bled. She told herself, "You're okay. You're all right. Life moves on. You've been alone this long." As she thought more about the situation, she told herself she was relieved. No one could hurt her anymore. It was the worst-case scenario, right? She had emerged from worse tragedies.

Violet curled on the couch with a bag of hot Cheetos and let the spicy bite of the crunchy snack fill her mouth. She let it dissolve on her tongue, and she began to calm down. She told herself she'd go to work, and it would be okay; she'd get over it. That afternoon she tried perfecting her cat-eye makeup routine, applied blush a little too vigorously, and practiced a new lap dance. She didn't have much, but she had work, and she was good at her job. Thank God for it!

Violet reached for the brown prescription bottle in her bathroom. She popped a couple round, yellow pills. She knocked them back with a swig of the flat soda on her nightstand. Within minutes, she felt more relaxed. Oxy took the edge off. She felt ready to tackle the night.

This blissful ritual had become a newfound habit ever since she began a more grueling work schedule. In the beginning, Violet took Tylenol PM to ease her mild muscle aches. It helped her sleep better, so she took it diligently every night. Before long, the persistent aches returned. It was time to get the doctor involved; it was all too easy to get an OxyContin prescription. At first, the white 10 mg pill was prescribed, but recently the doctor increased the dose to the yellow 40 mg pill. Each time she took it, the pain subsided, and the euphoria kicked in. She had never needed its soothing ministrations more than tonight when her entire world had collapsed beneath her.

* * * * *

The growl of the bass reverberated through the establishment as Chanel took the stage for her pole routine. Meanwhile, Violet sat by a gentleman in a crisp button-down shirt who offered her a twenty-dollar bill for a half hour of her time. Her sleek hair was in a knot at the top of her head. Her apple-sized breasts were adorned in a leopard print balconette bra. It was a typical shift so far, and Violet was engaged with her surroundings, laser-focused on earning as much money as possible.

She smiled and blew a kiss to the patron before heading to the dressing room to count her money. Before her stage performance, she needed to refresh her makeup and add a few touches to her ensemble.

As she walked toward the row of vanity mirrors, a couple of the other dancers were primping before their acts. Violet extracted her makeup bag from under the desk and noticed the girl beside her wearing a ruched, ruffled pair of hot-pink panties with black trim. They accentuated her rounded asset—two voluptuous curves like a cherub's cheeks. Violet had chatted with her a couple of times before, finding out she was a dental school student at a prestigious institution in a nearby city, stripping to supplement her student loan.

"You've got cute bottoms," Violet said to her. "I'd love one like that."

The ambiguity of the comment caught the attention of another woman in the room, a chestnut-haired girl with thick black eyeliner swooped in the cat-eye style. Moreover, much like a lioness, the girl bared her teeth. "Excuse me? That's my girlfriend's ass you're talking about."

Violet froze. She'd seen this stripper taking lines of coke, ecstasy, any drugs she could get her hands on. Obviously, ecstasy wasn't the drug of choice tonight.

"No, not at all," she said, proceeding cautiously. "I meant the panties."

The dancer in the panties groaned. "Come on, babe. It's no big deal."

Nevertheless, the overprotective girlfriend was already in her face; Violet smelled alcohol. "You stay the fuck away."

They both exited the dressing room at the same time; the lioness's hand slapped the other dancer's butt as if to assert one more time that it belonged to her. Violet shook her head in disbelief and wondered what the hell she had just witnessed.

That woman is in the wrong business if her girlfriend will get bent out of shape when someone compliments her.

Something about the interaction was the cherry on top of her miserable day.

That night, Violet tackled her performance with unprecedented ferocity. Normally she was known for her mesmerizing, graceful style, a style no doubt developed from her years of ballet training. Nevertheless, tonight she exuded a dangerous, animalistic aura. The music started; she turned into a snake on the pole. Her body circled fluidly, all lean muscle and power. As soon as she heard the musical cue, she shed the leopard-print bra and pounced on the ground. Catching sight of a hollering man to the left of the stage, she slid over to him. She grabbed his bald head and jiggled her breasts in his face in an exaggerated motion. When she was done, she rolled her hips and shook her butt at the audience.

In the end, she glanced at the entry and spotted Edwin with wide eyes, his mouth hanging open.

Having earned a few hundred dollars early in the night, Violet felt drunk on power. A man brushed the back of her arm with a $100 bill and bent over to whisper in her ear. "Hey, sweetie, you do any private dances?"

Violet turned around and smiled. She had been apprehensive about the idea previously; tonight she decided to break her own rule. "I'd love to give you a private dance." She laced her fingers through his and led him to the private dance room upstairs. The "VIP room" was sparse, a small room with simple décor and a single red-velvet sofa. Violet guided the man to sit down. Standing opposite him, she began to gyrate her hips in a figure eight. She traced her body with her hands, teasing the man as she circled her breasts. She squatted and snapped her legs apart, rubbed her thighs, and closed her legs again.

The man's eyes widened with anticipation. She gazed into his eyes and stroked his chin.

Suddenly, she thought she saw Dylan in her peripheral vision, leaning against the wall in the corner, staring at her.

With a leg on either side of the man's lap, she continued to rub against him. With a sudden movement, she leaned back onto his lap, inverted herself, and wrapped her legs around his neck. She felt him harden beneath her, and for the first time that day Violet flashed a genuine, though bitter, smile. It felt good to be in control, to seek revenge. Revenge for what?

That's what you get for breaking my heart.

She glanced toward the corner. Dylan was no longer there.

It probably wasn't even him, she told herself.

It couldn't have been.

But really, what difference does it make either way?

PART FOUR

Chapter 24

Late November 2014, Los Angeles, CA

I'm doing well. I really am. I'm invulnerable.

Post-it notes scrawled with encouraging sentiments were scattered throughout the apartment. If Violet looked at the fridge, it reassured her that, "Nothing can affect me." Her toaster told her, "I'm happy by myself." By her bedside, her mint-green, ceramic lamp professed the words, "I'm immune to pain."

She moved through her morning routine while repeating each mantra that presented itself.

"Hello, Sunshine! It's going to be a beautiful day," the bathroom mirror declared.

Beside a well-used pot of Bobbi Brown metallic eyeshadow was the compliment, "You are beautiful," stuck to the dull yellow bathroom countertop. Absorbing positive energy from the notes, she inhaled and plastered a huge smile on her face. It was supposed to lift her mood. Her cheeks hurt within seconds. She glanced in the mirror to find dull, violet eyes glaring back at her.

"Hey, what do you think, little girl?" Violet asked, winking at Coco. The white fluff ball cocked her head before wagging her tail. She and Coco had become best buds since Chanel had become a virtual ghost.

Even at the club, Chanel was all business and didn't linger once the shift was over. Violet understood; she'd had those nights. Part of the reason why they always functioned so well as next-door neighbors and coworkers was that they respected each other's privacy. Violet had never divulged her past to Chanel; Chanel hadn't shared any of her own skeletons either. At that moment, Violet found herself wishing they could sit down for a nice long talk, really start opening up to one another.

Violet put on an ebony mesh open-cup shelf bra with a large satin bow. Gathering her thigh-highs, she gently pulled them up her leg and hooked her garter belt. Black stripper pumps completed the look, and she beheld herself in the mirror. Her thick lash extensions seemed to just weigh down her vacant eyes today. The darkness of her under-eye circles enhanced her dull look.

Out of nowhere came a deep voice in the back of her mind.

I am a woman with no soul.

Enormous emptiness and hopelessness enveloped her.

How did I get myself into this?

Violet suddenly found herself yanking open her bathroom drawer, ignoring the loud yellow Post-it that insisted, "You're all right!" She wrapped her fingers around the cylindrical bottle of happiness, twisted it open, and shook out the pills. She promptly swallowed the OxyContin with tap water.

She stared at every inch of herself in the mirror absentmindedly, as she waited for the comforting warmth to wash over her.

* * * * *

Business ebbed and flowed with the season. As Thanksgiving approached, the night was quiet. A couple of strippers called in sick, though Violet suspected they just didn't want to work for scant tips.

That night, Violet performed a Shakira-inspired routine. Once she'd stripped down, she embellished her dance with elements of belly dancing. Enthusiastic claps came from a far, dark corner—then came a holler that Violet recognized. Picking up a handful of dollar bills, she folded them and placed them in her G-string before hopping off the stage.

149

"How're you doing, Mr. Tomsen?" Violet approached and pulled out a chair beside a man whose features she could barely see in the dim light. She could make out the shape of his double chin as he nodded. Before either could speak, Chanel began her routine onstage. They watched her dance to a metal remix for several minutes.

Mr. Tomsen had been a regular for the past six months. He was a quiet, middle-aged man who only drank Miller Lite and never more than a couple of cans. He had requested a lap dance with Violet a couple of times after she started agreeing to them. While he was a man of few words, he was always courteous and tipped generously. Through the few words of conversation they had exchanged, Violet learned that he was a retired police officer who had lost his wife some time ago. Both of his children were grown and attended college out of state. Now he just did some private investigative work. No lack of work in the Hollywood area.

Chanel strutted onstage in her shimmering white blouse, her headband reflecting the light, giving it the appearance of a halo. She pivoted, popping her hips as she walked, and paused to glance at an audience member nearby. She licked her lips provocatively as she bent to display her breasts to the men in the front row.

In spite of the arousing spectacle before them, Violet noticed that Mr. Tomsen was looking at her instead of Chanel. Violet gave him a small smile.

Mr. Tomsen crushed his can of Miller Lite and pushed it toward the edge of the table, ignoring Chanel as she slowly unbuttoned her white blouse to reveal a lacy, cupless shelf bra. Aside from her pasties, only a garter belt and thong covered her.

Once Chanel's routine was over, Mr. Tomsen continued to sit silently—even more so than usual—so Violet decided to leave. She rose from her chair, leaned in, and kissed him on the right cheek.

"Goodnight, sir."

"Wait, stop." Mr. Tomsen reached into his pocket to extract his wallet. Violet accepted an easy $20 and walked past Edwin, who was on duty.

150

"Boss said we're gonna close early tonight," Edwin said just loud enough for her to hear. "Wanna do something?"

"Let's go grab a bite at Denny's," said a high pitched voice behind them. They turned around just in time to witness Chanel peeling off the two star-shaped pasties on her nipples.

Violet gave her a quizzical look. "Denny's? You hate diners. What's the occasion?"

Chanel pulled a burgundy sweater over her head and spoke in a chipper tone. "Just wanted to catch up." After a moment, she admitted, "Okay, fine. I have something to tell you both. Let's go. Denny's is just down the street."

Chanel turned to Edwin. "Come join us soon."

"Sure, I'll meet you guys there. I have to wrap up here."

"Sounds great."

Violet and Chanel exited the premises together. Violet's heart was galloping out of control.

What news would Chanel drop?

Can I take any more surprises?

* * * * *

The sounds of cheesy '90s love ballads filled the empty dinner at 2 a.m. Another couple ate quietly on the other side of the room. With an 18-wheeler parked in front of the Denny's and no other patrons, it was safe to assume they owned the big rig.

Violet ordered the bourbon chicken skillet while Chanel opted for pumpkin cream pancakes.

"Breakfast time?"

"Yeah. It'll be time for it in a few hours anyway."

After they ordered, the anxious bubble in Violet's chest rose and burst from her mouth. "So, don't keep me in suspense. What do you have to tell me? Just shoot!"

Chanel sighed. She looked down at her hands. "I'm leaving."

It felt like Chanel slapped Violet in the face with those words. "What? What are you talking about?"

"I'm going back to Iowa."

"But why? I thought you hated Iowa!"

"I did when I was there. Couldn't wait to get out," she said wryly.

"But what changed?"

An impish grin crossed Chanel's face. "A guy, *of course*!" She shrugged. "Actually, it's my high school boyfriend, Kevin. We reconnected on Facebook, and we've been getting hot and heavy ever since. He wants me to come back. Can you believe that? He's even brought up the m-word."

"Wow." Violet didn't know what to say. *Chanel married?*

"I know, right? Can you see me as a farmer's wife?"

"Honestly? No."

Unoffended, Chanel barked with laughter.

"But what about your musician boyfriend?"

Chanel scoffed. "That was never going anywhere. He thinks I'm fun, sexy, someone good to party with. Kevin's different. A really decent guy. He even knows about . . . the dancing. And he's still willing to—"

Before she could continue, their order arrived. Chanel grabbed the maple syrup bottle and drenched her pancakes. The brown liquid glistened and dribbled down the side.

"Hey, ladies. You didn't wait long." Edwin, dressed in a flannel shirt and jeans, slid in next to Violet.

Chanel extracted her finger from her mouth. "This is good stuff. Here, have a bite." She pushed her plate toward him.

"Girl, that looks nasty," Edwin said. "I'll take a club sandwich as usual." He looked back and forth between them. "So what did I miss?"

"Edwin, I want you to hear this from me, not someone else. I'm leaving the club."

Edwin promptly asked why, so Chanel explained again.

"Are you sure?" Edwin asked. "That's a big decision. It'll be a culture shock, for sure. I can't imagine ever going back to my hometown."

Chanel sighed. "Guys, to be honest, I'm tired of LA and this lifestyle. I'd like to be close to my family again. Maybe settle down and have my own."

A sharp pain seized Violet's heart.

"Well, we'll miss you," Edwin said with a good-natured shrug.

"Don't be a stranger," Violet added.

Chanel smiled. "Not a chance. I'll send you some canned fruit and homemade soap for Christmas."

Afterward, back in her apartment, Violet couldn't let go of Chanel's news. She was much more affected by it than she would have expected. Sure, Chanel was a friendly face, but they had never been exactly what she'd call close. So why did she care so much that Chanel was leaving?

Why did it feel so much like a . . . *betrayal*?

* * * * *

Over the next few days, Violet helped Chanel pack up her apartment. As they loaded her belongings into large cardboard boxes, Violet found her heart sinking as she recalled the memories associated with each item.

She helped Chanel load each of her beloved pairs of heels into a box and remembered how flabbergasted she was when she first saw the collection. She couldn't help but smile thinking about what a prude she used to be. In the kitchen, she packed up shot glasses and wine bottle openers and thought about their casual talks on the patio in the early morning hours as they decompressed from a long night at work at the beginning of their acquaintance.

However, probably the worst was packing up Coco's toys. Knowing that she wouldn't see Coco anymore was a hard pill to swallow. The little white bundle of love and energy had provided quite a bit of comfort to her. She was the perfect companion. No questions, no small talk, just pure affection.

One week later it was Chanel's moving day. Violet entered her neighbor's empty apartment to see Chanel standing in the middle of the room, her oversized metallic purse sitting on top of Coco's pet carrier. The day was chilly, so Chanel wore a powder-pink beanie and a North Face jacket.

"Look how dirty the floor is," Chanel said with a laugh, rubbing a patch of burnt carpet with her shoe. "I'm not going to get my deposit back."

Violet smiled. "Probably not."

"Well," Chanel said with a sigh, "I guess it's time to leave."

"I guess so." Violet's voice sounded hollow.

Chanel leaned in, and they embraced for a few moments. As she pulled away, she murmured, "Ya know, don't be afraid to put yourself out there. You're awesome, and people want to be there for you."

"Thanks, Chanel."

"Actually . . ." she said carefully, "it's Charity."

"Charity?" Violet asked, noticing that her friend was observing her

154

warily, as if she was afraid of being mocked.

Violet couldn't square that with the tough-girl image Chanel usually projected. "That's really . . . nice." She meant it.

Chanel—Charity—shrugged nonchalantly, but Violet could tell it mattered more than she let on. "Better than Chastity, right?"

Violet swallowed back her emotions as she hugged Charity one last time. "I hope it all works out for you," she said sincerely. "And don't forget me, Coco. I'm going to miss you too." Coco barked to her from inside the crate.

For a split second, Violet contemplated revealing her real name to Charity, but she suppressed the idea instantly.

She returned home feeling ten pounds heavier. Her first thought?

OXY!

She hurried to the bathroom, pulled the drawer open, shook one pill out of the bottle, and let it dissolve on her tongue. Closing her eyes, she awaited the imminent pleasure. Sure enough, the light sensation lifted her up. She floated away from reality.

Reality needed some augmentation.

Chapter 25

May 2015, Orange County, CA

Dylan sat in his study after dinner, as usual. His work at a local accounting firm usually drained him. However, that night belonged to a personal project. The light from the monitor reflected in Dylan's intense, thoughtful face. His thick eyebrows were knitted together. His fingers skipped across the keyboard as he typed about his time in the Peace Corps. He hoped these blog entries could eventually be compiled into a memoir about his experience. Tonight, he was in the zone. Many precious moments and memories were worth sharing. He wanted to recall them and put them into words before they faded away in the midst of the drudgery of his new, mundane life.

Suddenly, Tess's words cracked through the silence like thunder. "Dylan, help!"

Without thought, he sprang up at once and rushed to the bedroom. Tess lay in a heap on the floor. Foul odor assaulted Dylan's nostrils.

"I'm so sorry. I wanted to go to the bathroom, but I fell." She was trembling, overwhelmed with embarrassment. She'd had diarrhea for the last three days, and this was the second time she hadn't made it to the bathroom in time. Dylan turned his brain off and bent down to help her up. A foul yellow liquid dripped from her pajamas onto the beige carpet. Dylan would later discover it on his jeans.

"Let's go see the doctor in the morning." Dylan spoke calmly as he helped her change. Tess sat on the toilet while he returned to the bedroom to spray some Lysol and wipe the carpet.

"Maybe I should wear a diaper." Tess couldn't conceal her abject devastation. Dylan knew she had helped plenty of patients with incontinence and changed diapers hundreds and thousands of times. Now the tables had turned.

"Just get yourself to sleep. We can talk about it tomorrow. Call me if you need anything." Dylan helped her up from the toilet. She leaned against his arm as he guided her to bed and pulled the blanket up to her chin. While he didn't kiss her, he did give her a pat on the shoulder.

With Tess taken care of, he immediately walked into the bathroom. Cleaning himself was priority one.

He turned the shower dial almost all the way to the left. The scalding water began to steam, but Dylan jumped in anyway. It stung his skin, which quickly turned red and raw. However, the pain was oddly pleasant. He wanted to cleanse himself on a level that was more than skin-deep.

Am I a hypocrite? Is this the marriage I envisioned a few years ago? Would I be happier if I left her now—even in this situation?

Dylan had been taught to be dutiful and responsible by his stern father and admirable mother. While every fiber of his being cried out for him to leave, he knew his conscience would scream louder if he obeyed this temptation.

You don't dump a sick animal. How can you dump a person who took care of you and returned you to life when you were helpless? Keep giving back. It's the right thing to do.

He reached down to wash his flaccid penis. Once he touched it, Violet instantly appeared in his mind. He knew logically that he shouldn't heed this mental vision, but he couldn't stop. He stroked his penis slowly at first until it got firmer.

Oh Violet . . . .

He closed his eyes. His breathing quickened. His mouth gaped. The tingling sensation on his lips. He could feel those pink lips, her tongue. He pumped his dick harder and harder, his hand moving up and down faster and faster. A moan escaped his lips. His body convulsed as he found sweet release.

And just like that, the fantasy ended.

He opened his eyes and turned off the water, watching the last of it swirl down the drain before stepping from the shower. He was numb—inside and out.

I will leave this marriage as soon as Tess comes to terms with her condition and can manage without me. I don't know when, but I have to wait for her to be in a good place, able to survive on her own first. I'll do my duty, but I'm not giving up hope.

* * * * *

The marmoreal exterior of the medical building, with its mysterious dark-tinted windows, loomed ahead. Dylan pulled Tess against him to steady her gait. Even while exiting the car, she almost fell. As they approached the building, her knees wobbled; she could hardly maintain her balance. Each "MS attack," as they called them, weakened her further, with the length of remissions becoming shorter and shorter.

Dylan figured that Tess, as a healthcare provider, must know the severity of her condition. However, he hadn't asked—and she hadn't clued him in.

"I'm sure the doctor can find a cure. You'll be back to normal soon." He grabbed her elbow brusquely. Tess turned and shot him a wordless, stone-faced glare.

They were both quiet as they entered the building and headed for the elevator that would carry them to the fourth floor.

I hate hospitals! I hate the doctor's office! Dylan's childhood memories surged through his mind. There they lingered until the neurologist, Dr. Kao, entered the examination room.

Tess recounted the recent events to the doctor, a petite Asian woman with rimless glasses. Dylan glanced at the wall. Even though the doctor was soft-spoken, the array of honors and diplomas spoke loud and clear. This encouraged him—until he heard Dr. Kao's words.

"From the pattern of episodes and your history, you may have the progressive relapsing variety of MS." Dr. Kao searched for her words discreetly before she proceeded. "I'll be straight with you. It's very rare. It's often challenging for patients with this type to cope."

Each word burned into Dylan's consciousness. He maintained his silence, the words "progressive relapsing MS" tumbling through in his mind.

"Sir, you are her . . .?" Dr. Kao asked.

"Oh, this is my husband, Dylan," Tess asserted.

Dr. Kao failed to conceal her surprise, and Dylan figured he knew why. Tess's illness had aged her. Her state was even more apparent next to Dylan's relatively smooth, youthful appearance. Violet used to call it his "baby face." Now, sitting next to his haggard wife, he could be mistaken for her son.

Pushing the thought aside, he cleared his throat and asked the most pressing question: "Can this type of MS be cured?"

"The FDA has approved new drugs in recent years to manage it, but none are too promising. The majority of drugs have side effects. Of course, there are many options for managing MS . . ." Dr. Kao trailed off into a laundry list of options, but this long and complicated answer did not assuage Dylan.

"Can this type of MS be cured?" Dylan asked again.

Dr. Kao sensed his urgency and replied slowly and clearly. "As of this moment, no."

As if a cold lead block had fallen into Dylan's stomach, the panic and disappointment flew onward. Even worse, he could sense Tess's devastation radiating from her. How could he be so slighted when this was happening to her, not him?

But that's not even true. This is happening to me. Our fates are intertwined.

Dylan buried his head in his hands.

* * * * *

The night after the neurologist's visit, Dylan tossed and turned. After counting innumerable sheep, he abandoned the idea of sleep for the night. Sitting in his study, he pondered his life, his future, and his options . . . again!

The option of leaving Tess had been wrestled and ruled out. It was simply beyond his ethical comfort zone.

The second option: live like a trapped mouse feeling sorrow, anguish, and regret. *Life is too short to live as a captive in a miserable marriage. Do I really want to live this way for the rest of my life?*

He decided to go for the third option. *Time to make a change!* He didn't know exactly how to do it, but he was determined to give it a shot.

Tess had quit her nursing profession shortly after the diagnosis of MS and stayed home. Dylan had hired a caretaker to watch over her when he was at work. He decided to make a change. He sent an email requesting an appointment with his superior.

During the meeting, his boss granted his proposal and structured a work-from-home arrangement for most of his assignments. This way, he could spend more time with Tess.

Once he spent more time with Tess, he realized what a boring life she endured. With nothing else to do but watch TV and think about her condition, he was worried Tess would descend into depression, if she hadn't already.

He remembered all the card games and charades and sock puppet shows and improvised plays that Violet had instigated to keep her sister amused during those long, interminable days in the hospital while he had been entirely self-involved. If she could do that at nine years old, he could expect no less from himself. He took it on as his mission to support and encourage Tess in any way he could, to do for her everything he wished he had done for his mother.

One of the first things he tried was getting Tess into a support group. She resisted mightily. "What good will that do? Sitting around complaining will only make me feel worse," she said.

"Just try it," he coaxed. "You can't know if you don't try."

Finally, after weeks of badgering, she begrudgingly agreed to go. "Once," she warned. "That's it. And then you promise to get off my back, right?"

When she came back from the first meeting, he eagerly asked how it went.

"You said I only had to go once," she protested. "Well, I did it."

Dylan realized then that talk therapy wasn't going to work for someone whose go-to coping technique was avoidance.

Distraction it is.

Knowing that medical dramas were Tess's favorite, he ordered DVD sets of *ER, Gray's Anatomy, House, Nurse Jackie,* and *Chicago Med,* and he rationed them out so they'd last as long as possible. Tess got a kick out of telling him if they were realistic or not and stories about similar cases she'd seen. However briefly, it allowed her to feel like a nurse again, rather than a patient.

In his ongoing quest to bolster Tess's spirits, Dylan suggested they try meditation, which he learned from his host mother on the island during the Peace Corps, and praying, which his mother earnestly installed in him when she was alive.

He decided to make a practice of compassion and deliberately began employing loving-kindness whenever Tess was irritable or bad-tempered or said or did something that annoyed or exasperated him.

May you live with ease, may you be happy, may you be free from pain. His host mother used to mumble those words in her native tongue. He found himself doing that more and more these days.

To his surprise, he found that the more he practiced compassion, the less Tess rubbed him the wrong way. Was she less aggravating or

161

did it just bother him less? He couldn't tell. Did it matter?

May you live with ease, may you be happy, may you be free from pain.

May you live with ease, may you be happy, may you be free from pain.

* * * * *

August 2015, Orange County, CA

The dry heat of the Santa Ana winds swept over Southern California for a week. Air-conditioning couldn't defy such temperatures. Wildfires sprang up throughout the forests, ravaging 40,000 to 50,000 acres with ease. Hundreds, even thousands, of people were forced to evacuate. Even fire trucks were engulfed by flames.

The heat tortured Tess in her weakened state. Her muscles spasmed, and she fell more frequently. Before long, she submitted to using a walker, ultimately giving in to a wheelchair.

There was one bright spot in the middle of the heat wave: Dylan devoted more time to writing when it allowed. The series of stories about his experiences in the Peace Corps was coming along well. It was the only time of his life not overpowered by painful memories. The more he focused his thoughts on the lessons in simplicity and relationships that he had learned there, the more he was convinced it was a worthwhile project. He earnestly hoped the stories could eventually be compiled into a memoir about his experiences and be accepted by a publisher, or that he could have it published independently. The prospect delighted him.

Whenever he got a chance, he retreated to his office and let his fingers fly across the keyboard while his mind traveled back across time and space.

"Dylan!" Tess called from the next room.

Dylan sighed. He was in the zone. He briefly considered pretending he hadn't heard, but his conscience got the better of him. He pushed

162

away from the desk and walked out to the living room.

Tess didn't look up from her spot in the easy chair. "I don't know why I watch the news. Everything is depressing. What's going on in this world?" Her eyes remained glued to the screen.

"Maybe you should find something less gloomy. Do you want me to look for a movie?"

"No, I'm hungry."

"Okay, sure." Dylan went into the kitchen and looked in the freezer. "How about lasagna?"

"Whatever," she said.

He removed two frozen dinners and popped them into the microwave.

When they were done, he put them on trays and took them out to the couch. With her shaky hands, Tess struggled to feed herself. Dylan kept an eye on her, stepping in when needed. He tried to make his interventions as unobtrusive as possible to spare her pride. She hated being treated like a baby.

"I need to take a bath," she said as she finished her dinner. "The heat is killing me. I smell like a pig." It was his cue to draw her bath.

Getting the tub ready, he inserted the handheld thermometer to make sure the water was less than eighty-five degrees. He had learned that hot baths weren't good for people with MS. Once the tub was full, he helped Tess into the room, gently eased her out of the wheelchair, undressed her, and lowered her into the bathtub.

"Does that feel okay?" he asked.

"It's fine, thank you."

Tess bent her head and leaned slightly forward while Dylan gently washed her back with a sponge.

Then, Tess turned her head slowly and gazed at Dylan, her eyes brimming with feelings she was unable to verbalize, no matter how hard she tried. She finally gave up, shaking her head as she looked away from him. "You're rubbing me too hard!"

Dylan remained silent.

May you live with ease, may you be happy, may you be free from pain.

Chapter 26

Early December 2015, Los Angeles, CA

Another year went by. Violet's emotions were a fragile glass ball that she kept tucked away in safety, far from the reach of anyone who would seek to shatter them. She went through the motions of stripping, shaking her butt, rolling her head and body against the pole, against countless bodies in the club. Patrons cheered for her, but she felt nothing. She kept her distance from them, even during lap dances. She built an impenetrable wall around her. It was much better that way.

Each day, before the same old dog and pony show, she took a handful of Oxy. Her favorite ritual.

I'm not taking drugs. These are just painkillers. Plenty of people take these daily. Doctors prescribe them all the time. I'm okay.

OxyContin was easy to obtain through the online drugstore—not to mention cheaper. She carefully portioned out each day's dose. Over time, she upgraded to the stronger green pill. However, she occasionally took multiple doses to get an extra kick. She smashed the tablets into powder, mixed it in a glass of cheap wine, and gargled it. The warm pleasure came. She escaped the real world and entered her own realm.

Recently, she'd ordered a case of Flamin' Hot Mix Variety Packs of Hot Cheetos from Amazon. The Crunchy Flamin' Hot Lime had become her favorite.

Hot Cheetos and Oxy were the perfect combination!

There she remained, particularly on her days off. The world went by without a hitch.

* * * * *

It was 2:49 in the morning and Violet was up, unable to sleep, a not-unusual state of affairs.

She surfed the internet absentmindedly and soon found herself on Sarah and Blake's Bed, Bath & Beyond wedding registry page. Most of the items had already been bought. *It's nearly here.*

She knew Sarah had probably tried contacting her at the wrong number she gave her. *Did she think it was an accident, or did she realize it was intentional?*

Suddenly she felt an overwhelming desire to see the old crew again. Sarah, Blake, Tyler, Reese, Anita. How she missed them all!

Impulsively, she went to Sarah's Facebook page and typed a message:

"Hi, Sarah! I know your wedding is this Saturday, but I haven't gotten an invitation yet. I'd love to join you, assuming you still want me to come, that is!"

She hit Send and went to bed, sleeping more soundly than she had in months.

In the morning, she awoke to a new message:

"Hi Violet! I'm so glad you got in touch. I tried calling but must have had the wrong number. I am so thrilled you'll be at the wedding! I know it hasn't been an accident that you've kept your distance after all that happened and that you might feel weird about seeing Dylan…but I miss you, and everyone will be so glad to see you."

Violet's heart skipped a beat as her eyes floated over Dylan's name.

The truth came crashing down around her: Dylan was *married*. If she went to the wedding, she would very likely see his wife. The thought knocked the wind out of her, but she also couldn't blame Dylan. She was the one who pulled away all those years ago. It would be foolish to assume he would continue to wait for her.

She wouldn't go. Why torture herself?

Nonetheless, part of her was irresistibly drawn to the idea. Who was the woman who managed to steal his heart? Even while Violet still wore his?

* * * * *

On the day of the wedding, Violet put on a sexy, low-cut red dress. She examined herself in the mirror and clicked her tongue. *He'll see every single curve,* she thought. *Not so bad, if I may say so myself.* However, the dress was more like a second set of skin—far too slinky for a wedding ceremony.

She peeled it off and put on a black lace-overlay dress. The sheath style was classy, but the sleeves and cleavage area were sheer. *Maybe still a little too sexy.*

At last, she settled for a long-sleeved, plum maxi dress with a v-neck and cinched waist. Just the right amount of sexy and elegant. Just the right amount of attention to draw to herself.

She styled her hair in a sleek updo and set to work on her makeup. The expertly applied blue eyeshadow accented her eyes, which sparkled like two brilliant amethysts.

Even though the mirror assured her that she looked fantastic, fear still bubbled in her gut. All she could think about was coming face-to-face with Dylan and his wife. Could she handle seeing him? Right at that moment, she didn't think so.

Back to old faithful.

Violet extracted the Oxy bottle from her bathroom drawer, gulped down a few pills, and waited for the fear to melt away.

* * * * *

The wedding was at a country club overlooking a verdant golf course. It was dusk, and the sun and moon were about to switch

167

places. The clouds changed hues—from white, to deeper shades of blue, to violet. Lively piano music floated in the cool evening air. Violet stood on the balcony to absorb the view and soothe her nerves—nerves so strong that not even her trusted Oxy could relieve them. She made a mental note to grab a glass of champagne.

It will be okay it will be okay it will be okay. Just breathe.

Closing her eyes, she took several deep breaths before allowing the music to carry her inside the hall.

She barely noticed the polished antique furnishings and stunning oil paintings that adorned the hallway as she joined the crowd of people heading for the ceremony. Her heart pounded in her chest as she stepped through the doorway and back into Dylan's life.

And there he was. He stood not far from the doorway, deep in conversation with a group of others. Everything else washed away. Every sound was white noise. The universe became Dylan. Everyone in the room became invisible. Her eyes traced the curve of his cheek, watched the way his hazel eyes twinkled as he smiled at some faceless, nameless friend.

He turned. He saw her.

Their eyes locked. His mouth fell open before he closed it again. Violet was certain she could hear his heartbeat. He drifted toward her. She smelled his clean musk scent. His white shirt blinded her.

Dylan's right hand held a terribly wrapped gift. *He never was much good at it,* Violet fondly recalled. She watched his eyes travel down her body, stopping at her chest. Violet realized—she never removed her lovelock. She felt naked. *Is he wearing his?* Then again, why would he?

As Dylan reached out to her, his wedding band flashed like a brilliant neon light. It struck her like a blow to the head. The realization that he belonged to someone else overwhelmed her. The room seemed to spin as he took a few steps toward her, his eyes shimmering with passion. Then, a warm smile lit his face—a smile Violet remembered so well.

168

"Wow. How are you doing? I've missed you." Dylan's tender voice was like a dream. It tugged at Violet's heart.

Words flew away from her brain. She opened her mouth, but her throat was so dry that she could barely make a sound. "Oh, h-hi, Dylan. Wow, yeah, I'm doing great. Just great. Couldn't be better." She tried to speak with conviction but could only manage to ramble. "Nice seeing you. Really. I'll have to talk to you after the wedding."

Before Dylan could respond, Violet darted away, swallowing hard against the bile rising to her throat. She hurried down the hallway toward the women's restroom and barely made it into the stall before dropping to her knees and retching violently.

When she was done, she got to her feet and examined her dress. Thankfully, it was still clean. Exiting the stall, she observed herself in the mirror. Her eyes were red. Her makeup had smeared like a watercolor painting on canvas. She had no idea she had been crying. However, the feeling in her heart corroborated the sight at hand.

I'm such an idiot for thinking this would work, she thought as she dabbed at her face with a wet paper towel and rinsed her mouth.

Without a word to anyone, Violet slipped from the building through the back door. She stood at the curb and called for an Uber.

* * * * *

Violet returned home from the wedding and instantly downed some Oxy with a glass of cheap wine. She swallowed it all in a few gulps, crawled to her sofa bed.

There's nothing left for me.

The concept of death was no stranger to Violet. After all, death was the foundation of Dylan and Violet's connection.

Death was their companion back in elementary school during those interminable days in the hospital. While their friends invented games about imaginary villains, Dylan and Violet knew the worst foe of all. This was a game they could not escape once playtime was over.

"Do you think it'll be that bad?" Violet had asked one day on the school playground. She'd hoped that if she could wrap her mind around death it might help ease the pain of her sister's passing.

Dylan had drawn lines in the dirt with a stick. "I don't know. I wonder. Taking naps can be okay sometimes, especially when you're sick. So what if death is like a good nap?"

Violet had thought about it for a moment before pulling her purple windbreaker closer. "Do you believe in heaven?"

Dylan shrugged. "I dunno. I want it to be real, but that doesn't mean that it is."

Violet remembered Sister Grace and her extraordinary experience. What if heaven was real and as splendid and amazing as she said? Wouldn't it be fantastic to see Amber again? She was going to end up there anyway. Why not just go a little earlier and avoid all this suffering? Try as she might, she couldn't think of one good reason not to.

She dozed fitfully, coming in and out of consciousness throughout the night. Her body felt clammy and hot; her head hadn't stopped spinning since she saw Dylan. His face haunted her sleep, punctuating long bouts of darkness. Finally, a female voice reverberated through Violet's mind. A face appeared, similar to hers, framed by longer, light-chestnut hair and possessing a pointier nose.

Amber.

Her gaze, intense but sad, penetrated Violet to the core. She shook her head. "Stop it. Pull yourself out."

Stop it. Pull yourself out. Stop it. Pull yourself out. Violet chanted in her sleep, mumbling incoherently until the mantra woke her. The vision blurred, swirled away. Violet woke up with little recollection of anything except the cocktail that started it all.

Chapter 27

Two days after the wedding, Violet marched into the club without saying hi to Edwin or any of her colleagues. She made her way to the dressing room to prepare for another exhausting night. She glued her fake eyelashes on, swept the black tip of her eyeliner across her lid, and let a pill dissolve on her tongue before going out on the floor.

She was not surprised to see Mr. Tomsen sitting in his usual spot in the corner, sipping his beer. He nodded to her, indicating he'd like her to come over.

"Hi, Mr. Tomsen." Violet couldn't even fake a smile. As a stoic, impassive man himself, Mr. Tomsen didn't seem to mind. He inched closer to her so she could hear him above the loud beat of the music.

"You aren't happy," he said.

"That obvious? Yeah, I didn't have the best weekend." Violet wasn't sure why she was so honest. *It will probably come out of my tips.*

"Are you in some sort of trouble?" Mr. Tomsen asked.

"No, not really," Violet replied, a little perturbed by his shift to a fatherly, concerned tone. She rotated an empty beer bottle on the table to distract herself as she continued. "I was just curious . . . can you help me locate an old friend? I have a bit of information about him, but I've . . . uh, had some trouble tracking him down." She hoped she didn't sound suspicious. Truthfully, she felt silly asking him in the first place. She could have asked any of their college friends about Dylan's whereabouts, but she frankly couldn't bring herself to do that. She didn't want it getting back to him.

Besides, she was certain Sarah was pissed off at her for not staying for the ceremony. Violet didn't blame her.

Mr. Tomsen took a swig of beer before he replied. "I can certainly try. Depends, though. What info can you provide?"

Having anticipated this question, Violet told him she had it all on a piece of paper that was in her locker. "I'll give it to you when I can slip away for a little bit."

Later that night, as the lights dimmed and the bartenders announced "last call," Violet approached Mr. Tomsen. She apologized for taking so long, as it was a busy night. On the note card was Dylan's full name and date of birth.

Mr. Tomsen scanned the paper and looked up. "I'll help you, but you have to promise me you're not in any kind of trouble."

"Of course," Violet said. "Just trying to reconnect with an old, dear friend."

* * * * *

Two days later, Mr. Tomsen appeared at the strip club again in his usual corner spot. Once the hostess had given him his beer and he'd settled in, Violet darted over to him, her heart pounding.

"Any luck?" she ventured.

Mr. Tomsen nodded and patted his front pocket.

"How much do I owe you?"

"Nothing at all."

"I hate that you went to this trouble for free. I can give you a lap dance."

"No need. It wasn't any trouble. He came up right away."

Violet was overwhelmed at the unexpected kind gesture and wouldn't have been surprised if she appeared visibly moved. "Thank you. So kind of you."

Mr. Tomsen shifted in his seat before looking at her with his cool gaze. "You don't belong here, Bethany", he said, emphasizing her name. His words hung in the air a moment before they dissipated. He took a swig of his drink and let Violet process his words.

Violet frowned and wondered if she was imagining things. Did he know who she really was?

You don't belong here.

Should she be offended? For some reason the words cut into her, but not in a hurtful way. She felt exposed, as if she were naked on a crowded street corner.

Before she could think of a flippant response, her true feelings emerged. She simply said, "I know."

* * * * *

Violet sat in her car and desperately tried to catch her breath. The address, shakily scrawled on a piece of scratch paper, sat crinkled and folded in her lap. The ranch-style house across the street looked unassuming in the sleepy residential neighborhood. There was no car in Dylan's driveway, so she assumed he must be gone.

The small front yard was trimmed and modestly kept. Violet's mind swam with questions. Did Dylan enjoy working outside? Did his wife intend on planting flowers in the spring? Would there be children playing in the yard soon?

Still taking deep breaths, Violet surveyed his neighbors. Christmas lights lined the roofs of the houses beside them, but not Dylan's. The landscaping was more ornate than Dylan's, but then again, Dylan was only just starting out.

Why was she here? Was she a glutton for punishment? Some kind of masochist? She didn't know. All she knew was she was compelled to see the woman who Dylan has pledged his life to. What was she like? Did Dylan love her as much as he once did Violet? Were they happy together? She knew just seeing the other woman couldn't give her the answers she wanted, but still . . . .

Two hours passed; nothing happened. She checked the address Mr. Tomsen had given her and hoped it wasn't a cruel joke. It had been nerve-racking to ask him for help in the first place. She felt like a stalker. Actually, that's exactly what she was doing. She tried to figure out why she had to resort to using a retired investigator for this. Perhaps it was her deep sense of shame. Perhaps it was the fact that she felt vulnerable in showing interest in Dylan's whereabouts. She knew Mr. Tomsen wouldn't ask why.

The neighbors' Christmas lights flickered on one by one, and soon the neighborhood twinkled merrily. The daylight wore thin, but it wasn't dark yet.

Just as Violet began to wonder if she should leave, Dylan's garage door yawned open, revealing one car parked inside. The door from the house to the garage opened, and a silhouette appeared in the doorway. A woman in a wheelchair being pushed by a familiar figure.

Violet silently gushed!

Dylan!

Then it dawned on Violet. The woman was handicapped, sickly.

The woman had long, dark hair pulled back in a ponytail. She pointed to the mailbox and said something to Dylan. He glanced, nodded, and leaned down to tuck the folds of her blanket into the sides of the wheelchair. As he straightened up, he looked in the direction of Violet's car.

Oh my God!

Violet's heart almost leaped out of her throat.

Their eyes met and locked for several seconds. Violet fumbled to ignite the engine and drove away. From the side mirror, she saw Dylan gawking in her direction.

It was not until she was almost home that she noticed the death grip she had on the steering wheel, her knuckles bone-white. The gravity of the situation started to sink in.

Dylan's wife is handicapped.

He will never leave a woman like that.

Profound sorrow crushed her. She felt agony for the woman, for herself, but most of all for Dylan.

Chapter 28

December 23, 2015

Intoxicated and emotional, Violet had made up her mind.

Back in high school, she would read Virginia Woolf's works. The troubled author often fantasized about her death, eventually filling her overcoat pockets with stones, walking into a river, and drowning herself. Violet imagined the moment Woolf walked into the river. To an onlooker, she must have looked calm, resolute—slowly wading in, unsmiling, distant. Nevertheless, like the current of the river, her seemingly calm mind must have been turbulent under the surface. What coursed through her thoughts in those final moments?

I will find out soon enough.

Violet had bought a small exercising sandbag from a sporting goods store, along with a couple pairs of ankle and wrist weights for good measure. She also had half a bottle of cheap cooking whiskey. She packed them into an overnight bag with her beloved OxyContin and hot Cheetos.

* * * * *

Violet's hands gripped the steering wheel, but her eyes were dry. After all the crying she had done, she figured she must have finally used up all of her tears. She felt strangely calm, numb. Perhaps she'd come to the end of her feelings too.

She drove down Interstate 5 toward San Diego, speeding slightly but not enough to be pulled over. The roads were eerily empty. Violet had the peculiar feeling she was all alone. In a sense, she was. Everyone she'd ever cared about was gone. No one would miss her if she disappeared. Who would even notice?

Life is drama school? No. Life is a tragedy. Unfailingly, every life is a tragedy!

* * * * *

She pulled into the parking lot, the unmistakable three-tiered, red-pointed roof of Hotel del Coronado just ahead, gloriously illuminated like something out of a storybook. She shut off the engine and stepped out.

It's a one-man show. I am the actress, the director, the producer, stage designer . . . . Let the show unfold.

She headed straight toward the beach. It was dark and still, aside from the constant roar and retreat of the waves. There was a scattered group of people, a few solo joggers, and plenty of empty space.

She faced the black expanse of ocean. She slipped off her moccasins, rolled up the bottom of her blue jeans, and wiggled her toes into the wet sand.

She took in each sensation as if it was her last, with the foamy edge of the water sending a thrill through her spine. She waded further into the cold water, the winter wind blowing through her hair. Body and mind detached, she felt no fear. The sand underneath her shifted; she braced herself to regain balance. The waves rolled into her, and she could easily throw herself into the water beyond the drop-off and let it take her.

No, not here. She was here to have a ceremonial farewell to the origin of the lovelock, like a solemn ritual. If she threw herself in here, the chances of being discovered and rescued would be high.

She turned around and gazed at the hotel, it's twinkling lights defining the outline of the huge, historic structure.

In the distance, the merriment at the outdoor ice rink echoed in opposition to her mood.

Laughing and screeching, children glided around the rink, their glee filtered through the chilly air. Their innocent laughter reminded her of birthday parties she'd shared there with Amber. The familiar sharp ache thrust right into her chest. She remembered the smell of the old skates as they put them on, the thrill of acclimating to them, how she would pull Amber along behind her.

The laughter only enhanced her melancholy, and a voice prompted her . . .

Not yet. Not here. This is only the first act!

She pulled herself back to the shoreline and wandered toward the source of tantalizing warmth.

A sinking feeling in her chest drained her as she watched the flushed faces of joyful children beside their protective families. Some families cheered from the sidelines; others carefully skated alongside their energetic children. Then there were the newer families. Violet viewed a younger couple. The woman appeared to be in the earlier stages of pregnancy. The man weaved his fingers through her hair before drawing her close for a passionate kiss.

Violet turned away. *Will they still act that way five years from now? With a screaming child in tow?* Violet twisted her mouth and continued to walk to the tune of the Christmas music floating on the air. The festivities and dazzling lights surrounded her wherever she went. However, they couldn't break through her impassive exterior.

Why does everything feel surreal?

Yet, it was reality, even though it only seemed like yesterday that she and Dylan were here. That day Dylan gave her the lovelock.

When and how did it go so wrong?

She felt lonely, and the pervasive sense of isolation in her life was a plague she couldn't escape. Everyone she had cared about in her life inevitably left her. Chanel, Amber, her mother, Dylan . . . . Violet abruptly pivoted on her heels and returned to her car.

It's time for the next act.

She was soaking wet, but she didn't care. She sat in her car without a

178

towel to soak up the salty seawater. With a single-mindedness coming from God knows where, Violet drove through the quiet residential area toward the San Diego-Coronado Bay Bridge. The darkness enveloped the earth, as is typical for that time of year. The lights of the city and the stars twinkled in the remoteness of the great beyond. The stage was set for the next act.

She parked her car a little distance away, out of sight.

Solitude!

She put the ankle and wrist weights on and stuffed the small sandbags in the pockets of her sweat jacket.

Yes! Let the sandbag and weights pull me all the way down to the bottom of the ocean.

I'll vanish from the surface of the earth. No one will even notice.

She was ready.

Wait!

The whiskey. She twisted open the bottle and took several hot gulps. The burning sensation rushed down her esophagus into the pit of her stomach. She topped it off with a handful of Oxy. The floating sensation arrived . . . and she was ready.

Let the final act begin!

She tried to open the car door, but it felt jammed. Puzzled, she tried again. The door wouldn't budge. Violet dumped out the contents of her purse and fished around for her car key fob. Once she located it, she pushed the Unlock button. Pushed it again for good measure. Pushed on the handle. Nothing!

Violet's forehead crinkled. The car seemed sealed from the outside! Her frustration mounted, so she gulped the remaining whiskey. Hoping against reason that the booze gave her strength, she pushed her body against the door again. Sweat began to form in beads on her face. She slid over to the passenger side and pushed against the door with full force. Nevertheless, that door wouldn't budge either.

"What's going on?" she muttered. She glanced outside the door to see what barrier could be causing this but saw nothing. Nothing! There was nothing except her faint reflection in the window. She stared at it and then looked again. .

Violet couldn't believe her eyes. The face she was staring at—her face—moved, a hint of a sad smile appearing. Only she hadn't moved an inch . . . and she certainly wasn't smiling. She pressed her fingers into her eyes and inhaled deeply before taking another look. The face reflected back at her had hazel eyes with flecks of gold. It couldn't be!

"Amber? Is that you?" Violet gasped. The reflection was still. However, the pleading golden eyes mesmerized her.

Violet pushed even harder. She held the handle and applied her whole body to force the door open. It remained shut.

All of a sudden, a gush of cold air blasted in.

Chapter 29

Evening of December 23, 2015, Orange County, CA

After a simple dinner from Boston Market, Tess retreated to the bedroom. Her condition had continued to worsen with each episode. The recurrent urinary tract infections had weakened her further. Her primary physician stated that the infection was common for MS patients. Dylan worried about her.

"Here's the antibiotic. The doctor said you need to drink a lot of water with it." Dylan handed her a cup of warm water and the pill.

"Thanks."

"Do you want anything else, Tess?" Dylan asked gently.

"I'll be alright."

"Let me know if you need anything." He waited for a minute but got no response. Dylan closed the bedroom door quietly.

* * * * *

Dylan sat in his study in rare silence and attempted to summon a muse for his writing. However, he couldn't get his mind off Violet. Since their encounter at the wedding reception, her image lingered. She stood there in her dark purple gown champagne flute in hand, with wide, shocked eyes. She looked every bit as beautiful as he remembered, but she didn't seem quite right.

Then there was her totally unexpected visit to the house. He could barely believe it was her, but there she was in her Mini Cooper, the red one with the black top. He remembered choosing the car with her at the dealership right after their engagement. It was a gift from her parents, replacing the ten-year-old family car she had been using. He could even identify the dent in it from when Violet accidentally hit a pole outside a coffee shop.

Even though it would have undoubtedly been awkward, as it was seeing her at the wedding, he couldn't help but wonder why he didn't go over to talk to her. *What did she need?*

But he knew the reason.

In just a few years, he'd come to recognize that the more he took care of Tess, the more compassion he had toward her. He genuinely cared about her, and he hoped to compensate for what he should have done for his mother when she was ill years ago.

It's a form of love.

He had made peace with himself. Taking care of Tess was his mission, and he accepted the responsibility willingly and seriously. But his longing for Violet, keeping the memories of her alive, was an undeniable part of his existence. He cherished the memories of their love. In reality, his unrivaled passion for Violet provided him the strength to care for Tess. It sounded incomprehensible, but it was true. He forced himself to keep Violet and Tess isolated from each other in his mind, his feelings for them tucked discreetly into separate compartments in his heart. Somehow, they managed to coexist well. In the beginning of their marriage, to mollify Tess's jealousy and lessen the conflicts, Dylan had removed the chain he wore bearing the tiny lovelock key. However, he didn't have to wear it to feel its presence. The key and what it represented was all but embedded in his heart. No one could ever take it away from him.

As he sat in his study that night, concern for Violet dominated his every thought. It was inexplicable, but he couldn't shake off the feeling that she was in trouble. Raging worry overtook him like crashing waves. Not even his favorite opera could distract him. Dylan had to turn off Gounod's opera, *Faust,* an hour ago, as it was agitating him rather than soothing him. That's when he recalled the other gift his mother had bestowed upon him: prayer.

It was something Dylan didn't often do, but that night he was brought to his knees. He clasped his hands and bowed his head. "Dear God, please watch over Violet and keep her safe, no matter where she is, no matter what she's doing." He repeated those words over and over and over, like a frantic mantra.

Chapter 30

December 24, 2015, Coronado, CA

A blinding light shone on Violet's face, a light so intense that it penetrated her eyelids and prohibited her from opening her eyes.

Am I in heaven or in hell?

She felt heavy, lifeless. She tried to gain a sense of her surroundings. It was warm but not uncomfortably so. Sounds started to make their way to her eardrums—the distant sound of laughter and movement. With effort, she slowly opened her eyes and struggled to adjust to the light. She glanced down and saw that she was tucked under a tightly wrapped blanket in the back seat of her car. It was a blue blanket that she once purchased for a camping trip with Dylan back when they would go to Crystal Cove at Laguna Beach. It hadn't been touched for years . . . not since their engagement. She didn't even recall that it was in the back seat of her car.

Where did it come from?

Puzzled, she frowned and slowly sat up to assess the situation. The empty whiskey bottle and pill container were on the floor. Her scattered memories began to connect. She was startled when the image of Amber's pleading eyes floated to the surface.

Those two golden eyes, so familiar, as welcoming as the front porch light of her childhood home. Nevertheless, they appeared so . . . so sad.

It's not your time.

Was that a real voice or only in her mind? Could the drugs and alcohol have befouled her brain?

Violet sighed and rested her forehead against the smooth glass of the window. The distant caw of seagulls could be heard outside. It was a sunny day with only a few patches of clouds, so she decided to get out and stretch her legs. After taking only a few steps, the sprawling bay view and all its mighty skyscrapers came into sight. A replica Friendship sloop filled to the brim with joyful tourists sailed on the glassy, dark-blue water toward the bridge.

The profound loneliness enveloped her once again. A familiar sharp stab of ache overtook her.

Violet returned to her car. She began sobbing uncontrollably. She was done. Spent. She couldn't move forward; she couldn't go back.

Just then, her cell phone rang.

Startled, she looked down and recognized the name on the screen. She wiped the tears from her face, struggling to get her emotions in check, and took a deep breath before answering it.

"Merry Christmas!" a familiar voice boomed before she could speak.

The ebullient warmth was enough to start the tears flowing again.

"Hi, Edwin," Violet hiccupped.

"Bethany, what's wrong?" he said, obviously alarmed.

She couldn't answer. She didn't want to lie, but a lifetime of pretending to be all right was hard to break.

"Listen, are you okay? Where are you? I thought of you last night. You didn't look too happy when you left the other night."

All Violet could muster up in reply was her location.

"What the hell are you doing there? Don't do anything stupid." Edwin sighed and decided against waiting for her reply. "Drive downtown, find a place to eat. Stay there. It's Christmas Eve, but I bet you can find a Chinese restaurant that's open. Once you get there, text me the location. Peter and I will come get you." He spoke earnestly, and it warmed Violet's soul to hear his concern for her in his voice. It nearly left her speechless.

"Bethany, listen to me. Promise me that you'll do what I just said."

She blinked back hot tears before emitting a squeak of a reply. "Okay. I promise."

* * * * *

Violet grew up in San Diego and knew her old hometown well. An old Chinese restaurant she used to frequent, The Golden Dragon, was open as usual. It observed the holiday with a seven-foot-high Christmas tree beside the big fish tank, next to a five-foot smiling golden Buddha. Violet was seated quickly. Once she slid into the booth, she retrieved her phone from her purse to text Edwin. She ordered just an appetizer-sized portion of wonton soup as she waited. The steamy broth was comforting; she let herself zone out as she swirled the soup with her spoon.

Edwin and his new partner, Peter, rushed into the restaurant sooner than Violet expected. She rose to give Edwin a hug. When she pulled away, she saw a bead of sweat on his brow. He breathed heavily, as if he had dashed there on foot.

"Bethany, are you alright?" he asked, searching her face, looking for clues to her mindset.

She managed a small smile. "Thanks for driving so far on Christmas Eve, Edwin. And you too, Peter." She turned to give Peter, a rail of a man wearing an argyle sweater, a slight hug. She couldn't help but think about what an odd couple they made—total opposites physically. "Merry Christmas to you both."

"Not a problem," Peter replied, waving his hand in the air nonchalantly. He removed his scarf and added, "The more people to spend Christmas with, the more fun it is."

The thought of the trouble Edwin and Peter went to in order to join her for mediocre sweet and sour pork in San Diego burdened Violet. She started to thaw a little as Edwin cheerfully engaged her during the meal.

"That Mr. Tomsen guy is your number one fan. Doesn't he creep you out at all?" he asked.

Violet chuckled, even with a mouthful of fried rice. "He's nice, but he's an odd duck, all right."

"I'm concerned he's trying to earn your trust by acting like a gentleman. But then, when you least expect it, he's gonna capture you and make you live in his basement."

"You've read too many suspense-thriller-murder books." Peter gently elbowed Edwin and laughed.

"You know, I could kind of see that. He really puts on this noble guy persona. And I'm like, dude, you're in a strip club." They all shared a hearty laugh.

After they finished eating, Edwin dabbed his mouth with his napkin. "Alright," he said to Violet, "I'm going to get the check, and then you're coming back to our apartment with us."

"Oh, no, I couldn't possibly—"

"That ain't us asking for permission. You're coming," Peter said in his deadpan way.

"Are you sure? I don't want to impose." She felt guilty putting them out, but at the same time, going back to her lonely apartment was more than she could bear to contemplate.

"No argument. It's settled. We're going home, having some drinks, playing some music . . . ."

"Fine, as long as there's no midnight Mass," Violet joked.

"Nah, we already went this morning," Edwin replied.

Surprised, Violet looked up to see if he was teasing. He wasn't. "What, you mean you still go to Mass? After everything . . .?"

"I know, right?" said Peter triumphantly. "That's what *I* say!"

"The church isn't perfect," Edwin admitted. "They make mistakes.

187

But it's like people. If you love them, you don't just leave when they screw up."

Peter rolled his eyes, but his bedrock affection was evident. Violet, however, was blown away by Edwin's words. They cut her to the core.

"I'll even ride back with you. Peter can drive my car back."

Peter looked at Edwin over his glasses as if he wanted to tease him but reconsidered due to the circumstances. Violet clutched at the plastic bag containing her Chinese to-go box as she nodded at them.

"Good, now give me your key." Edwin held out his hand.

Violet cocked her head and glared at him. "You know I can drive, right?"

"Yeah, but why don't you just nap on the way home? I got this."

Before Violet could answer, Edwin gently removed the key from her hand and patted her on the shoulder.

Violet kicked the whiskey bottle, empty hot Cheetos bags, and other mess under her seat as Edwin slid behind the wheel. Once the motor had started, it hummed Violet into a peaceful, dreamless sleep.

* * * * *

She awoke to Edwin gently nudging her shoulder. She rubbed her eyes and glanced out the window to see their apartment. It was a gray, four-story building in Culver City, slightly trendy-looking with its industrial appearance. Edwin grabbed her duffel bag from the back seat and guided her upstairs.

When she entered, she was rather impressed. The living room had quite the entertainment system and a sleek, black leather sofa. A piece of modern abstract art sat above the couch, a 3D piece that had recycled materials attached for added texture. Violet glanced into one of the two bedrooms and saw that it had been converted to a home gym, judging from all the dumbbells on the ground.

188

"Nice place," Violet said. She wasn't sure how much a club bouncer made, but she knew Peter had a good job in advertising.

"Thank you. Please go sit down, and we'll get you a drink," Peter said.

The men went to the kitchen to put away the leftovers, so Violet did as she was told. She flipped on the television and saw that the *Twilight Zone* was on. The scene depicted a woman lying on a hospital bed with thick bandages around her head. A muffled female voice could be heard underneath, pleading with them to remove the bandages. "Do I look like everyone else now?" the patient asked earnestly.

Violet had already seen this episode and knew the twist: the girl was beautiful, and to be "normal" in the *Twilight Zone* she must become what the audience would deem ugly. The acting, directing, lighting, and camera angles throughout the entire show still drew her in every time. She smiled wanly.

Here I am being a drama nerd again.

She missed acting—real acting. How her life ended up this way still seemed unreal—like she was in a Twilight Zone of her own.

Moreover, if she wasn't already in it, then she certainly had fallen into the Twilight Zone the night before.

Amber was with me last night. I just know it. I felt her.

Edwin jerked Violet from her reverie. "Peter is making pecan-apple pie and cinnamon roasted almonds for us. Would you like something to drink?" Edwin maintained his gentle, upbeat spirit. Violet couldn't help but reflect on how grateful she was that he had avoided asking her any personal questions, though the concern was still visible in the lines of his forehead.

"I know just the thing to make for you, Bethany. I know you'll love it."

Violet continued watching "The Eye of the Beholder" as it slowly unfolded on the large LED flat-screen TV. Just like the first time she saw it, the anticipation of the ending never got old. The doctor and nurse, whose faces were shrouded in darkness, slowly unwrapped the bandage for the disfigured woman. Edwin handed her a cocktail, something a milky yellow. Violet sniffed it; a pleasant, sweet vanilla and cinnamon scent filled her nostrils. She took a sip and discovered that it was warm eggnog with a touch of rum.

Another *Twilight Zone* played. That particular episode featured a young William Shatner staring at the wing of his airplane, which was on the verge of breaking down. It was another one of Violet's favorites. Momentarily, she felt transported to a simpler time as she savored the nostalgic flavor of the eggnog and retreated into one of her favorite old television shows. Soon the warmth of the rum started to soothe her but not to the point of inebriation; it was just enough to help her relax in her new surroundings.

As she heard clangs and scrapes in the kitchen, she recalled her mother making the same painstaking efforts for their family Christmas dinners—prior to Amber's illness, anyway.

"Does he need any help in there?" she asked as more loud banging issued from the kitchen.

"Nah. That's all for show," Edwin scoffed. "He just wants us to know how hard he's working. If we tried to help, he'd run us out. The kitchen is his kingdom; everything has to be *just so*. You put a fork in the dishwasher upside down and he has a coronary. But I can't complain. He is the most tremendous cook." He rubbed his stomach with satisfaction. "I've gained fifteen pounds since we got together."

Soon the toasty apartment was redolent with the smell of vanilla, cinnamon, and apples. Peter emerged from the kitchen bearing a beautiful, golden-brown pie.

"See, what did I tell you?" Edwin said proudly. "Have you ever seen such a perfect pie? It belongs on the Food Network!" Peter couldn't help but smile.

Edwin grabbed a dishrag and popped open a bottle of champagne, filling three flutes with the energetically bubbling liquid.

They gathered around the table, where Edwin passed out the drinks. He held one up and looked at Violet fondly before saying, "To being with some of my favorite people this Christmas. I know once the holidays are over, the next year is going to look up for all of us. Cheers." They merrily clinked their glasses and sipped the drink.

Violet looked at a smiling Edwin and her heart soared with gratitude. For some reason, the warmth of the evening penetrated Violet's injured soul. She felt vulnerable yet unafraid. These two men dropped everything to tend to her and welcomed her into their home. The kindness and a true sense of family touched Violet.

It's been so long.

As they enjoyed generous helpings of warm, gooey pie, Violet suddenly felt compelled to unload the weight that threatened to drown her. With her guard down, she wanted to cast off her emotional burdens. She wanted to tell her story.

Therefore, after two more bites of pie, Violet pushed it aside and looked Edwin in the eye. "Edwin, it's time I told you something . . . about how I ended up at the club."

Edwin gaped at her, wide-eyed, no doubt ravenous to have his curiosity about his isolated friend finally quenched. "Yes, whatever you're comfortable telling."

Violet looked down at her plate of half-eaten pie. "It's kind of a long story. I don't know exactly where to start."

"Well, why not start at the beginning? We've got all night."

Violet took a deep breath, preparing herself to revisit the memories she spent so much of her energy trying to suppress. Apprehensively, she cast her mind back . . .

PART FIVE

Chapter 31

January 2010, The Swanson's Residence

Violet fretted as she peered into the oven to check on the lasagna.

Please, please let everything go alright tonight.

Dylan and his father were due any minute for dinner. Even though she and Dylan had been dating ever since freshman year, this would be the first time Dylan and his father were invited to Violet's family's house. Violet told herself that she was protecting her mother by sparing her the reminder of that bleak time. In truth, she didn't want Dylan to see for himself how dark and dysfunctional her family really was.

Little did her parents know that they wouldn't just be having dinner with her boyfriend's father, but her soon-to-be father-in-law! They planned to announce their engagement tonight, assuming everything went well.

Violet had shouldered all the preparations, cleaning the house and cooking the meal herself. All her mother had to do was dress and show up.

That's not too much to ask.

"It smells great," her father said. "Anything I can do to help?"

"Can you put the salad on the table?"

The doorbell rang. Violet was startled. Her mother still hadn't come down. Was something the matter? She hurried to the door and opened it to see Dylan and his father standing on the step. Just seeing Dylan soothed Violet's nerves. No matter what happened, they were in this together.

"Violet!" Gordon said warmly. "So nice to see you. And you too, Wanda."

Violet whipped around and saw her mother descending the staircase. The red sheath was loose on her thin frame, but she looked stunning. Her hair was washed and pulled back into a low chignon, and her makeup was perfect. Violet's heart swelled. She'd indeed made an effort!

"And you, Gordon," Wanda said in a casual way, as if she did this every day.

"Wanda!" Aidan said from the dining room doorway, awestruck by his wife's transformation. "You look . . . amazing, darling." Wanda flashed him a smile.

With difficulty, Aidan tore his eyes away from his wife and stretched out his hand to the other man. "Gordon," he said, pumping his hand in earnest.

"Hello there, Mr. Mayor," Gordon said. "Congratulations."

"It's been a learning curve," Aidan said.

"Careful, he may try to recruit you," Wanda warned, arriving at the foot of the stairs. They all moved toward the dining room.

Aidan chuckled. "There's an opening on city council that needs filling. And I hear you've just retired?"

"That's right. I've still got the business, but I've stepped away from the day-to-day management."

"Well, if you're looking for something to do with yourself, we could always use people with good business sense." He was joking, but not entirely.

They reached the dining room, and everyone remarked on how beautifully the table was set, with the planter box centerpiece filled with succulents and candles. "I can't take any credit," Wanda said.

"It's all Violet's doing." Violet blushed.

"She's got her mother's eye for detail," Aidan said. "Wanda's a fantastic decorator." His wife shook her head with a modest smile.

After they were seated, Wanda got serious all of a sudden. "Gordon, before we go any further, I want to apologize to you."

Violet and Dylan exchanged a look of alarm. Gordon frowned. "For what?"

"For not coming to the funeral. It was awful of me. But it was so close to Amber's . . ." She paused to compose herself. "I wasn't doing well. But still, I should have been there for you. I feel just terrible."

"Don't give it another thought," Gordon said. "I know what you were going through. I was in a fog for months afterward."

"And how are you doing now? Really?" Wanda asked. It was a real question, not just being polite.

"To be honest, I still haven't really gotten over it. I can't bring myself to get rid of her things. I still sleep on my side of the bed," he confided with a wry smile.

"That's no good," said Aidan. "You've got to move on, mate."

"That's what Dylan keeps telling me," Gordon said, chuckling. "He keeps trying to get me to try online dating. But the dating scene just doesn't interest me. I've gone out with a couple of women, but no one comes even close to . . . ."

"Well, no one *likes* dating," said Aidan, "but it's a necessary evil. You're still young. Successful. You'd be quite a catch. You've got to get out there!"

"Now, Aidan!" Wanda lightly reprimanded him. "Leave him be. Everyone grieves in their own way, in their own time."

"Sorry," said Aidan sheepishly.

194

"If you ever do decide it's time to go through her things, I'd be happy to help," Wanda said. "I know it can seem overwhelming."

Gordon shot her a grateful look. "I just might take you up on that. Dylan's right; it has been too long."

Aidan looked around the table. "So, can you believe our kids? All grown up and dating each other? Who would have thought?"

Violet felt her heart jump into her throat. *This is it!*

"Actually," said Dylan, "there is a reason we wanted to get you together. There's something we wanted to tell you." He glanced at Violet. "You see, I've asked Violet to marry me. And she's said yes."

The three adults stared at him in silence, and then at her. Violet could feel the force of their collective disapproval hit her like a wave.

"I know it must seem sudden to you," she rushed to explain before they could voice their objections. "You've barely even seen Dylan. This is my fault. But we've been going out three years now. We spend practically all our time together at school. We're not rushing into anything."

"But you're too young!" her father thundered.

"They're just a year younger than we were, honey," her mother reminded him. Violet was shocked. Support from an unexpected quarter!

"I know we're young," Dylan said, "but the very first time I saw Violet at school, I knew I wanted to spend the rest of my life with her."

Violet swung around to him, her eyes wide. "You did? You never told me that!"

"It was like I found my missing piece," he continued. "Everything makes sense when we're together. I can't explain it. We just *fit*."

Everyone was quiet.

"That's exactly how I felt about Kendra," Gordon said, reminiscing. "I just knew."

Aidan's eyes flew to Wanda. "Me too," he said. "I remember the first time I saw her. In that yellow dress with the big skirt." His face glowed, his love undimmed by the years.

Violet shot Dylan a hopeful smile. Maybe all her worrying was for nothing.

Chapter 32

Spring Break, 2010, The Swanson's Residence

"You're home for the weekend?" Wanda asked with a brilliant smile. She stood at the granite countertop in the kitchen, huddled over a vase of fragrant red, pink, and yellow roses.

Perhaps more remarkable was the fact her hair was highlighted and cut in a new layered style. She was wearing a lovely red blouse and a pair of dark-wash jeans instead of the usual sweats. She'd even gained some weight. Her father had said that Wanda had been feeling better since the engagement dinner, but Violet had never imagined she was this much improved.

"No, just stopping by. Had to pick up a few things for our trip."

"Trip?" Wanda asked. "Oh, New Orleans with Dylan?"

Violet was surprised her mother remembered. "Yep, it's our last spring break. Gotta make it count. Are those from the garden?" Violet asked. She figured she would stay and make conversation while she caught her mother in rare form.

"Oh yes. They've done well this season. These roses are just gorgeous. Just have to watch those thorns. I always forget about that part!" Wanda carefully picked one up and swirled it under her nose as if she were appreciating a fine wine. "Love the smell. This yellow one with the red tips is my favorite. You know, I was thinking . . . if you wanted, I could do the flowers for your wedding."

Violet felt a warm, contented feeling in her chest. She couldn't remember the last time she and her mother conversed like this.

"I would love that, Mom. You've always had such a good eye."

"How about purple calla lilies and white roses? With some green and white sprigs?"

"Sounds perfect."

Wanda smiled broadly. "I just assume you'll have violet as one of your colors, won't you?"

Violet shrugged. "I hadn't really thought about it yet, but yeah, sure."

"You *must*! It's *your* color." She took Violet's chin and tilted her head, so they were looking eye to eye. "My beautiful, beautiful girl," Wanda said before pulling Violet into a tight embrace.

Stunned, Violet was too overcome with emotion to do anything but submit.

When her mother released her, Violet excused herself in haste before her mother saw the tears in her eyes. She stumbled to her room with a faraway smile. Perhaps having to pull herself together for the engagement dinner had somehow thrust her mother onto a different track. Maybe they'd finally found the right meds, or maybe it was just the simple passage of time. No matter what the reason was, Violet was thrilled to see her mother in such high spirits. *I just hope it lasts.*

As she grabbed her weekend bag and began stuffing it with clothes, she imagined herself and her mother crafting table centerpieces for the reception, shopping for a wedding gown together, planning a bridal shower, and doing all the other traditional mother-daughter activities that surround a wedding. It would be the best gift she could ever hope for.

When she returned to the kitchen, her mother was half-humming, half-singing "Somewhere Over the Rainbow."

"Oh, honey, I wasn't going to tell you yet, but . . ." Wanda said, giggling like a little girl with a secret, "we're booking you the Crown Room at The Del for your reception!"

Violet gasped. "The Del Coronado?"

Wanda grinned. "Now, I know it's expensive, but Gordon has a contact there *and* he wants to split the cost."

Seeing Violet's confused expression, Wanda explained. "We've been having Gordon over for dinner practically every week since you first got engaged. He seems to really appreciate it. He's got all that time on his hands now that he's stepped away from the business, and with Dylan at school, he's all alone with nothing to do. I think he's lonely," she said.

Violet hadn't realized their parents had renewed their friendship.

How awesome that their in-laws got along! She flashed forward to Christmas mornings, beach vacations, and Saturday afternoon barbeques with both Dylan's father and her parents, surrounded by their many towheaded grandchildren.

Maybe her marriage wouldn't just mend her heart. Maybe it would heal them all.

Chapter 33

July 2010, San Diego

Violet's wedding dress hung by the window, the small crystal beads catching the sunlight and illuminating the dress in an angelic glow. The wedding was only two days away, and Violet was busy with all the last-minute details, emailing and phoning each vendor to ensure everything was on track.

She couldn't believe how much work went into just a one-day event. No wonder it took most brides a year! If her mom and Dylan's dad hadn't helped out so much with the planning, she never would have gotten it all done on such an abbreviated timeline.

She finished up with all the vendors—all except the hotel, for which her mother had been the point person. Violet checked her mother's bedroom, which was empty, and then headed downstairs. She found Aidan in the kitchen, fixing a sandwich.

"Hey, Dad, where's Mom?"

"Eleventh-hour shopping. Looking for shoes for the big day."

"But I thought she was wearing her silver heels?"

Her father shrugged. "You know your mom. She just wants everything *perfect*." They shared a knowing smile. "Why? What did you need her for? Anything I can help with? I feel like I've gotten off easy."

"Yeah, you and Dylan both," she teased. "I just wanted to know if the woman from the hotel ever emailed us back about whether they had an extra room available now that the McMichaels are coming. If not, we'll need to find them another place."

"I don't know. I can check her email and see," he said.

Violet grabbed a banana and went back upstairs to tackle the next item on her to-do list: making sure her suitcase for the honeymoon was packed and ready. As much as she was looking forward to the wedding, she had to admit she was even more excited about the honeymoon. The wedding was going to be a bit of a spectacle, with as many of their fathers' business associates and clients on the guest list as their own friends. The honeymoon would be just them. Man and wife!

As she went through everything she had already packed, she hoped she had the right clothes for the weather and whatever activities they ended up doing. Although they'd done lots of research, you couldn't know what another place was really like until you were there. What would Japan be like? Their plan was to tour Tokyo and then take the bullet train to Kyoto to tour the Buddhist shrines and temples. She couldn't wait to take in the sights and sounds of a very different way of life.

She folded her brand-new, itsy-bitsy-teeny-weeny aquamarine bikini and tucked it in next to her cosmetics bag. She envisioned wearing it as she strolled hand in hand with Dylan on an exotic beach in Thailand, where they would be island-hopping after Japan. She grinned, anticipating Dylan's reaction to the sexy suit that left nothing to the imagination.

Shutting the suitcase, she shot Dylan a quick text. "Everything is ready. I can't believe we're about to do this."

Within seconds Dylan replied, "Is it too late to back out?"

Violet smiled. Before she could decide on a suitable reply, she heard the front door slam. Then there was a squealing of tires, followed by a loud crash.

Violet's heart leaped to her throat. She bolted out of her room and down the stairs and threw open the front door.

Her father's Mercedes was embedded in the large oak at the end of the driveway. Apparently, he'd been trying to maneuver around her car and had hit the tree instead—at an unusually high speed from the looks of it.

Instead of getting out and assessing the damage, Aidan drove forward a few feet, slammed the car into reverse again—bypassing the tree this time—and then veered out onto the road, his rear taillight completely smashed.

Violet felt ill. Something was wrong. It was just a gut feeling, but somehow she knew she had to follow him. She grabbed her keys from the foyer table and ran to her car. It was rush hour, so he couldn't have gotten too far.

She sped over to the closest main road and craned her neck to see around the two cars in front of her. *There he is!* His normal careful driving went out the window, as he got right on the other driver's bumper and leaned on the horn. After a few blocks, Violet realized that her father was driving toward Dylan's house. He ignored the stop sign and accelerated.

What could've happened? What if it had to do with Dylan? Was Dylan okay? The blood drained from her face, and she fought the urge to vomit.

Nevertheless, she sped to Dylan's without slowing. There, she saw her father's car parked next to her mother's in the driveway. What was her mother doing there?

Violet flew from the car and rushed to the front door, which was not only unlocked but ajar. She heard screams from the master bedroom. She ran toward the commotion and walked in on a scene she would never forget. Her father stood over her mother, who was on the floor beside the bed. She clutched a sheet to her chest; her face was purple and tearstained.

Standing beside her was Gordon, naked from head to toe. Violet didn't even have time to react. She couldn't utter a sound.

Gordon tried to speak calmly but was visibly shaking. "Calm down, Aidan! Aidan, let's talk this through. Away from Wanda."

That's when Violet saw the .45-caliber handgun in her father's hand. She let out a scream as Aidan lifted it coolly and shot Gordon twice in the shoulder. Another bullet shattered the picture above the bed.

Violet screamed at the explosion of blood soaking the bed behind him. Gordon crumpled to the floor. Wanda screamed. Aidan walked over to Gordon, still pointing the gun at him.

"Dad, no!"

Aidan either didn't hear her in his murderous rage or didn't care. He kicked Gordon's body over and shot twice more between his eyes. Gordon's face shattered.

"Dad!" Violet shrieked. Only he wasn't her dad; he was a man possessed. He snapped.

Aidan turned to her, his eyes bloodshot. Her knees buckled beneath her; she didn't have the strength to watch this madman another second. He abruptly pushed Violet aside without a word. As she fell, her head slammed hard into a dresser.

All was dark.

Chapter 34

Violet awoke in the hospital, her head pounding. She was groggy, confused. Dylan was by her side, holding her hand.

His face was haggard, his eyes sunken. He looked years older. When he saw Violet looking at him, his face brightened for a split second. However, an infinite sadness immediately snapped back into place.

The memory of what had happened came rushing back. Violet sensed the bile rise in her throat. *Oh my God, oh my God, oh my God. This can't be happening.*

Dylan held her hand tight, seeing the agony flash across her face.

"Are you alright?"

"No. No, I'm not," was all Violet could say. She wished it were the most horrific of nightmares. Though she knew deep down in her gut it wasn't. It was a reality, a revolting new reality that she would never escape.

Dylan hugged her. He buried his head on her shoulder and cried, shuddering with each sob.

"I'm so sorry," he said after he drew back.

Sorry? she wondered. For what? It was *her* father who had committed this vile, unspeakable act. She felt not only revulsion but deep, deep shame as well.

They sat in silence until a nurse came in and, after some tests, told Violet that she had a mild concussion but hadn't suffered any permanent damage.

Violet nearly laughed. No permanent damage? Was she kidding?

When the nurse left, two cops came in to question her. She recounted what she had seen in a dull, detached voice, displaying no more emotion than a computer. She couldn't think, couldn't feel.

Dylan escorted her to the parking lot and helped her into his car. It wasn't until Violet asked, "Where are we going?" that Dylan spoke.

"I'm taking you home. To be with your mother."

Violet's stomach churned with emotion. Rage cut through the grief and numbness. How could her mother have done this? Her sense of betrayal was overwhelming. After all her father had done for her all these years, after all he had put up with, to do *this* to him? No wonder he snapped!

"I can't look at her right now!"

"She needs to see you," Dylan said. "They had to sedate her. That's why she wasn't at the hospital. I know it's hard, but I think we all need to work through this together."

Violet didn't want to work through anything. She didn't want to see or talk to anyone, not even Dylan. She just wanted to be alone. She was bone tired, more exhausted than she ever remembered feeling before in her entire life. All she wanted to do was sleep and never wake up.

She was not surprised to see a cop car in the driveway. No doubt Wanda was being questioned as well.

Violet reluctantly walked into the house, not knowing how to face her mother. What would she do? Violet wondered. Scream at her? Shake her? Just weep?

As they entered the foyer, they heard a commotion in her mother's bedroom.

They looked at each other without a word. Violet took the stairs two at a time, Dylan right behind her. She heard frantic voices behind the door and pushed it open.

A heavyset cop jumped up and stood in front of her, attempting to block her view.

Eichin Chang-Lim

"Ma'am, please step back—"

But it was too late.

Violet saw it.

Her mother.

Hanging from the bedpost. Her lifeless body in the red dress from her engagement party.

Face blue, swollen. Tongue purple, protruded.

Violet shrieked and fell to her knees. Only this time there was no blessing of unconsciousness.

* * * * *

Instead of celebrating her wedding, Violet found herself in the unbelievable position of planning her mother's memorial service. It was so surreal. Violet was repeatedly struck by how similar the two occasions were. Flowers, music, readings, limo services . . . . Sometimes she used the same vendors and was even able to exchange services from one to the other.

Luckily, she could do nearly everything by phone. Violet was practically a prisoner in her own home. Whenever she attempted to leave, she was accosted by paparazzi clamoring for quotes and photos. The lurid story became an instant sensation. No matter how much she tried to avoid the media, she couldn't entirely escape the screaming headlines:

"The mayor, a respected defense lawyer, shoots his wife's lover in cold blood!"

"Prominent businessman killed. His mistress, the mayor's wife, hangs herself soon afterward."

"A young couple's wedding triggers shocking murder-suicide."

Meanwhile, Dylan was staying across town in a condo that his aunt—his father's sister—had rented for them. Gordon's next of kin

206

and Dylan's godmother, she had come down from Seattle to help with the funeral arrangements.

Trapped in their respective residences, they tried to keep in touch by phone, but the enormity of what had happened was too big for words. Their conversations were full of long, painful silences and often it was easier not to call at all.

Violet hadn't seen her father since the shooting—and didn't plan to. As far as she was concerned, he was dead to her. She vowed she would have nothing to do with him. Not now, not ever! Neither of her parents had siblings or living parents. After her many years of depression, her mother didn't even have any close friends that Violet could lean on for support. She was entirely on her own.

In some ways, as difficult as it was, planning the funeral was a blessing. It gave her something to concentrate on. Trying to get everything arranged in just two days was a Herculean task. She was busy every waking moment.

The day of Wanda's memorial came quickly. The service was a blur. Dylan was at her side the entire time. A string of familiar figures, many of whom were supposed to be their wedding guests, murmured condolences. A few held Violet close; a couple of distant family members who Violet barely recognized tried their utmost to utter some sort of consolation. However, such words were impossible to come by.

Afterward, physically and emotionally exhausted, Violet fell into bed knowing that the next day she would have to do it all again. Only this time, she would be by Dylan's side.

In the morning, braving the rabid press, Violet ran to her car and hurried to the Methodist church where Gordon's service was to be held. She was early, wanting to have some time with Dylan before the guests began to arrive.

At the door, she was met by a kind-looking man in an ill-fitting suit, holding a clipboard. "May I have your name? Because of the publicity around the deceased's passing, this is a private ceremony. Only authorized guests will be admitted."

"Of course," she replied. "Violet Swanson." She hated even saying it. No doubt he'd heard the story. Now people would look at her as *that* girl—the daughter of the adulterer and the murderer.

If he recognized her name, he didn't show it. He scanned his list. "I'm sorry, you don't seem to be on here."

"I'm sure that's just an oversight," she said. "I'm Dylan's fiancée. He probably didn't even think to put me on the list."

"I'm sure it is," he said calmly. "Let me just go in and check. I'll be back in a minute." He closed the door behind him, leaving Violet uncomfortable on the step.

She looked around nervously, hoping he came back quickly. Reporters could show up at any moment. If they did, she'd be trapped with no way out.

A moment later, the door opened. Instead of the man, a woman appeared.

"How *dare* you come here?" she hissed, giving Violet a withering glare. "Anyone with any common decency would know to stay away! But common decency probably wasn't something they taught in *your* family!"

Violet was dumbfounded. After so many losses, so many demands, she didn't have anything left to deal with yet another onslaught.

"Please," she whispered. "Just let me see Dylan for a min—"

"Absolutely not!" the woman snapped. "Leave him alone! He's better off without you. You don't think you can still get married, do you? When your father *murdered* my brother?" She laughed as if the very idea was preposterous. "You could try, but it would never last. Better just to let it go now. We'll take care of Dylan. He doesn't need you."

With that, she slammed the door.

In a daze, Violet stumbled back to her car.

Chapter 35

Was it days or hours that passed before Violet found herself admitted? She wept. She frequently spoke about the pointlessness of living. Everything was stolen from her: Amber, her mother, her father, now Dylan. His aunt was right. How could he continue to love her after what happened? After her own flesh and blood murdered his? He could try to see beyond it, tell himself it didn't matter. Nevertheless, it would always be there, standing between them.

Violet found herself in a regular hospital room first, but she couldn't stop babbling nonsense and crying. She tried to use the plastic dinner fork to stab her wrist, the frantic rage surging when the fork broke. She heard a doctor mutter the word "suicidal."

Was it hours? Or days? Reality and fiction became one and the same. Sedation provided little relief.

Before long, she became aware of where she was heading: the psychiatric ward. It seemed unfair. She couldn't live anymore. Why would anyone hijack the right to die from her? It was the only escape from hell.

Dylan visited her. He bit his lip and searched for the right words. His eyes were red, the bags beneath them pronounced. He didn't touch her. Was he afraid of her? Did he think she was crazy? Depressed and suicidal, just like her mother?

"Why are you here?" Violet finally asked dully.

Dylan groaned. "Violet, why wouldn't I be here? I love you. You're my everything."

Violet shook her head. She was too weary to cry. "We can't be together. Not after everything that has happened."

Dylan shook his head, tentatively reached for her hands. Violet pushed them back. "No," she hissed. "Don't touch me!"

"Violet," Dylan said, his voice breaking. "I'm not leaving you. I'll never leave you. Least of all right now."

Violet felt despair like a black hole erupting in her chest. He was the crazy one. Crazy for thinking this was something they could overcome. He would come to hate her for what her father did. He just didn't know it yet.

Their loved ones were dead. So was their relationship.

"I want you to leave, Dylan. Never come back," Violet whispered. "I can't be with you. We can't be with each other."

Dylan shook his head vigorously. "Absolutely not. I'm not leaving you."

"Leave!" she screamed at the top of her lungs. She jumped up, whipping her arm toward the door. "Leave! Don't come back!"

Dylan broke down, crying as she went into a fit. Security came and pulled Violet away. Dylan was ushered out.

He tried coming back a few more times, but Violet turned him away each time. Finally, three weeks later, she agreed to one last visit. She was done; he had to know it. They needed to talk calmly.

Dylan was waiting in a chair, arms folded, lower lip protruding as he sat in deep thought. When he turned to Violet, she noticed the changes in him. He looked like hell. His face was unshaven. The bags under his eyes were darker. His plaid shirt hung from his gaunt frame and looked at least two sizes too big.

"What are you doing back here?" Violet said in a robotic voice, staring down at her fingers. "I told you I didn't want to see you."

Dylan held up his hand and said, "Look. This is different. I love you, Violet. I still want to marry you. But if you don't want me around, if you need time . . . I can't deny you that." His voice shook, but he remained composed. "I get it. We could both use a little space, some

210

time to get back on our feet. So I've joined the Peace Corps."

Violet stared at him dubiously. "Peace Corps," she repeated. "What?"

"My godfather is one of the program managers, and he was able to pull some strings to get me in as a replacement for someone who dropped out at the last minute. He thinks it will be a good opportunity for me to get away from everything for a while. It's a two-year contract. It will give us both time to heal."

Violet gulped. Wasn't that what she had asked for, to be left alone?

"So you're leaving soon," she mumbled.

"I am. I'll leave you be. Just like you asked me to. But in two years, I'm coming back for you. I promise. I hope this will help you get to a better place emotionally."

He looked at her, fighting back the hot tears that threatened to spill down his cheeks. Finally, he reached over and gently embraced her. She didn't reciprocate. When he pulled away, she cast him a hollow stare.

With that, Dylan got to his feet and left without a word. He didn't even turn around to face her.

* * * * *

He was gone. She knew he'd leave her at some point, and he did.

Violet spent weeks obsessing over Dylan's decision. She hated herself for it.

She howled uncontrollably. Nurses came in to force pills down her throat or gave her shots to sedate her. Eventually, no more feelings remained. She was a walking dead.

One day, a middle-aged man in a white coat appeared in Violet's sterile room.

"How are you doing today, Violet? I'm Dr. Johnson, your

psychiatrist. You remember me, right?" Violet stared at him, blank and empty.

"After discussing your case with other staff doctors in this unit, we think you're a good candidate for an experimental drug combined with other treatments." He paused, waiting for her reaction. Nothing.

"Violet, you are not only suffering from a condition called post-traumatic stress disorder, but you are also dealing with underlying long-term depression and unresolved anger." The doctor maintained his pleasant voice and attempted to communicate with her as if she understood his words. Violet saw his mouth moving but registered only bits and pieces.

Not long after that, she was transferred to a mental health center in Arizona that looked more like a ranch than a hospital. Besides taking the so-called "experimental drugs," she went through an intense regimen of talk therapy, desensitization, and reprocessing therapy. Her treatment also included scheduled yoga and horseback riding—two things that provided relief, however temporary.

Later on, she learned that one of her father's distant cousins who bore the same family name cosigned the consent form for her to be in this clinical trial program.

As she gradually recovered, her memories of Dylan's love returned. She craved his touch, his comfort. He didn't want to give up on her. Would he really come back? Did he really want to return to her and face their demons together?

Violet stared into the Arizona desert. The arid, inhospitable landscape, dotted with cacti, somehow aroused both comfort and provocation. As the sun fell below the horizon and the sky became liquid gold and indigo, she thought about the future.

Maybe Dylan will keep his promise. Maybe he loves me in spite of everything. We're both victims, after all.

But if he doesn't choose me again, I understand. I couldn't blame him.

Violet did her best to prepare herself for the worse-case scenario.

* * * * *

Violet had resolved to have no contact with the outside world during the fifteen months she was an in-patient at the mental health center in Arizona. *Better that way.* She had no intention of communicating with any of her friends or anyone who had known her.

Finally, the day arrived. "You are ready to be released from this program, Violet," the program director, Dr. Turner, said with a warm voice and a pleasant smile. "You have recovered remarkably. We, as a team, are pleased with your progress." She paused.

"Thank you for all the care," Violet said.

"However, you need to return to the center for follow-ups every two months for the next year to ensure you don't regress. You may relapse. Your symptoms may return if triggered. Remember to take deep breaths and apply the techniques we've taught you to use when you feel uptight." She gently patted Violet's hand and squeezed it.

Violet nodded but had other thoughts.

Never mind the follow-ups.

She signed some forms, said her goodbyes—complete with hugs and even a tear or two—and left the center without a backward glance.

Next stop: Los Angeles.

She continuously shunned communication with her old friends, hid her real identity, and invented a new name, Bethany Curtis.

She was Bethany Curtis from that point on.

PART SIX

Chapter 36

Christmas Eve, 2015, Edwin's Apartment

Violet found Edwin and Peter staring at her, mouths agape. Their faces revealed their mixed emotions—at once sympathetic, fascinated, and repulsed. Edwin reached over for Violet's hand and held it in his. "Wow," he said softly. "I heard about the murder-suicide years ago. I just can't believe that was you."

Violet sighed and stared at the table. "Yeah . . . it's insane."

Edwin and Peter were quiet for a moment before Peter asked, "So what about Dylan? Did you hear from him when he got back from the Peace Corps?"

"No," she answered slowly. "But I didn't exactly make it easy for him to find me."

"But why?" Peter asked, his forehead furrowed in confusion. "It sounds like he loved you a lot. You *really* didn't think he could get over what happened?"

Violet shrugged. "That's what I thought at the time."

Edwin peered at her thoughtfully. Then he shook his head. "Nah, I don't think that's it."

"What?" Violet snapped.

"I don't think you pushed him away because you were afraid he couldn't get over it. I think you were afraid he could."

She frowned at him. "What do you mean by that?"

"If he came back and still wanted to marry you, you'd have to admit he *really* loved you."

Violet snorted and shook her head. "So what? Why would that be a problem?"

Edwin looked her right in the eye. "I don't know. Why would it?"

Violet's head began to throb. Her chest was tight, and her back ached. She needed some Oxy.

"Do you have any painkillers?" she asked. "I've got a killer headache."

"I've got some Tylenol PM," he said.

"Don't you have something a little, uh, stronger?"

"No, sorry."

Violet caught him exchanging a knowing glance with Peter. Her temper escalated.

"I know what you're thinking, but you don't get it! This pain is unbearable."

Edwin calmly walked to the kitchen to warm up a cup of milk and get the bottle of Tylenol PM. He handed them to her and said, "I hope this does the trick. It's all I got."

Violet mumbled and tossed the Tylenol PM back, after which Edwin coaxed her to the spare bedroom.

"Go to sleep and you won't even have to think about it anymore."

Violet tried to swallow back her tears. Between what had happened—or nearly happened—at the beach and the emotional toll of telling her story, she was completely drained. Nevertheless, the peace of sleep eluded her. She tossed and turned for hours before falling into a troubled slumber near dawn.

* * * * *

"Rise and shine, sunshine! Merry Christmas!"

Violet blinked groggily. "W-what time is it?"

"Time to get up!" Edwin bellowed. Violet wasn't sure if he was yelling or if it was just her head. It felt like a truck had run over her in her sleep.

She groaned and pulled the pillow over her face. "Why? I thought you said they slept all day on Christmas in Argentina."

"They do," said Edwin. "But this ain't Argentina, baby. We've got our own traditions here. We're going to the Mission."

Violet peeked out from under the pillow. "The Mission?"

"Yep, we're going to help serve Christmas dinner. I do it every year."

She sat up, her curiosity piqued. "Why?"

"I went there my first Christmas in this country. I didn't have any money, didn't know anyone. They treated me like a real person, not like a charity case. Ever since then, I've gone every year. Not for them—for me. Helps me get through Christmas. There's no better cure for self-pity than doing something for someone else."

Peter, in a tartan robe and carrying a tray of food, appeared behind Edwin. He gave her a sly smile and said in a singsong voice, "Hello there, sleepyhead. You ready for some breakfast?"

"Yes, thank you," Violet said. She glanced at the plate of picture-perfect waffles. "Nice presentation. You really missed your calling. You should be a chef."

"I thought about it. But the hours are shit. Besides, you should never mix business and pleasure, right?"

"Well, if anything is going to revive me after a tough night, it's definitely this." Even as she said it, Violet knew what would *really*

216

revive her was some Oxy. Instead, she ate her waffles, took a long shower, and trundled into the back seat of Edwin's car.

At the Mission, after they were checked in and assigned their stations, Violet nudged Edwin. "Doors don't open for another twenty minutes," she said. "I'm going to run out for coffee. You want anything?"

"There's free coffee right over there," he said, pointing to a percolator in the corner.

Violet wrinkled her nose. "Ugh! I need some *decent* coffee."

"Snob," he said, reaching for his wallet. "I suppose you'll be needing some money?"

"Thanks," she said. "I'll be back in a jiff."

She darted out. As she suspected, there was a crowd of skid row residents milling around waiting, for the doors to open. *I can definitely score an Oxy from one of these guys*. After the night she'd had, she deserved it. *It'll just take the edge off,* she told herself.

After scanning the available prospects, she approached the most promising candidate, a rail-thin young man with stringy hair and tattered jeans. He didn't have what she was looking for, but he pointed her in the direction of a large Latino man who could help her out.

Five minutes later, Violet was back in the Mission, feeling much more relaxed and ready to tackle the day.

She put on a hair net and gloves and started serving mashed potatoes to the long line of castoffs and throwaways. The junkies and the mentally ill, the immigrants who didn't speak English, and the poor single moms with young children in tow . . .Violet tried to give them each a big smile as they came down the line. She wondered if that was an uncommon event for many of them.

When her shift was over, Sister Mary, the nun supervising the volunteers, told Violet to grab herself a plate and mingle. Violet

217

scanned the room and took a seat next to a woman who looked to be in her late thirties. Her clothes weren't stylish, but they were clean, and she was well-groomed. Violet wondered if she might be another volunteer.

"Hello," she said, "I'm Bethany."

"I'm Irene," the woman said. Without being asked, Irene immediately launched into a colorful and unvarnished account of her tumultuous life story. Unabashed, she told Violet that she had been sexually abused by her own father and thrown out of the house by her mother when Irene tried to tell her about the abuse. She was just sixteen. From there, she had been involved in several abusive relationships, developed a serious drug habit, and eventually began supporting her habit through prostitution. Now she was in rehab, two months clean.

Having barely gotten in two words edgewise for the entire meal, Violet congratulated Irene on her sobriety and wished her a Merry Christmas and the best of luck with her continued recovery.

On the way home, Violet was quiet as she contemplated everything she'd seen in the Mission. She was so used to feeling like a pariah, a victim of experiences far outside the norm. It was a shock to her system to realize that there were many tales of tragedy out there that rivaled her own. Abused by her own father? Violet couldn't even imagine it. Some of her anger over the unfairness of everything that had happened to her began to dissipate a little.

When they got back to the apartment, Violet sat down in the living room with Edwin and Peter.

"Thank you for taking me there," she said. "It gave me a lot to think about. And . . . what you said last night? About Dylan?"

Edwin merely raised his eyebrows, encouraging her to continue.

"I thought about it all night, and you may be right." She sighed. "After my mom died, I was in so much pain. I just wanted to be alone. I didn't want to think, didn't want to feel. I *especially* didn't want to be close to anyone. Being close to someone just meant pain.

I loved Dylan *so* much. I couldn't stand to lose him. I seriously thought it would kill me. So I pushed him away." She laughed bitterly. "I was so scared of losing him that I made him leave. How stupid is that?"

Edwin stroked his chin. "It makes a lot of sense, actually."

Violet cocked her head at him. Emboldened by his nonjudgmental attitude, she continued. "I think that may be why I started stripping, too. It's a surefire way of keeping people away."

"It is that."

They sat in silence for a long moment. Then Violet finally said, "Ya know, I think I'm ready to quit."

"Really?" Edwin said.

"Maybe you can even find Dylan," Peter piped up in excitement.

"He's married," she said softly. "Not long after he got back to the States."

"Bummer," Peter said, genuinely disappointed.

Violet brushed off his sympathy. She was still too raw to go there. "It's too late for us," she said in a beat, "but I need to move on. For me."

"I'm so glad to hear you say that," Edwin said. Then he glanced at Peter, who gave him a slight nod. "There's something else I wanted to talk to you about."

Violet frowned. It didn't sound like it was going to be good.

"Bethany, look, sweetie, I want to give you some tough love. It's these pills you're taking. You seem to have a dependence on them. I love you, and I care about you, and that's why I'm bringing it up."

Violet's defenses shot up. "You're wrong. I need them for the pain. Have you lived with chronic pain? It sucks."

"Yeah, actually I have," Edwin said. "I hurt my shoulder back in high school, and painkillers are a slippery slope." He softened and rubbed his temples. "Sorry, Bethany. I don't mean to accuse you. I know you've been dealt a shitty hand in life, and you're trying to deal with it as best you can. But don't you think the pills might just be another way of numbing yourself from the pain? I think they are hurting you more than helping."

Violet started to cry. She couldn't contain the sobs that erupted from her. Oxy was the only thing she had that helped her deal; she couldn't imagine trying to go without it.

She buried her face in her hands and soon felt Edwin's strong hand rubbing her shoulder. He gave her a squeeze as her shoulders shook with sobs. She finally turned around, her face undoubtedly blotchy and haggard, "What do I even do next? I'm lost."

He smiled. "I'm glad you asked. You know Sister Mary that you met at the Mission? She also runs St. Jeanne's Women's Rehab and New Life Treatment Center. It's a really great place. I know you can do this. Will you try? We can drive you to the rehab in the morning. We'll be right there with you, helping we can."

Violet found herself feeling weak, so weak. She nodded feebly, unable to resist anymore. It was a relief having someone tell her what to do.

"Okay," she whispered. "Okay. Let's do this. And by the way, my real name is Violet Swanson. Please call me Violet from now on."

Chapter 37

Spring 2016, High Desert, Outside of Los Angeles

Pain. There's so much pain.

Muscle aches. Chills. Sweating. Violet became obsessed with her physical state. Even though the St. Jeanne's Women's Rehab and New Life Treatment Center was situated in a picturesque high desert, far removed from any sign of the outside world, Violet could not relish the beauty and the remoteness as she normally would. She turned inward, collapsing into herself.

She knew she couldn't continue her addiction. She also knew she could never, never feel this way again. With that, the only way forward was to dig her heels in and fight.

Violet cut the cord from her old way of life. She had quit the strip club, abandoned her fake name, and reverted back to her real name. With Edwin's help, she settled in at St. Jeanne's with no impediment. The director, Sister Mary, appeared cold at first glance. Violet mentally referred to her as "the stone woman." Stern lines framed her mouth, as did wrinkles—from years of chain-smoking, Violet would soon learn. Nevertheless, this hardened appearance was misleading. Sister Mary was a tireless, compassionate woman and her voice was gentle. The rough exterior was nothing more than a testament to her turbulent youth—a troublesome era that God plucked her from, gifting her with a greater purpose and infinitely more fulfillment than she ever would've thought possible.

Sister Mary knew Violet's struggle. She was empathetic but gave her the tough love she often needed. It was the first step . . . arguably the hardest, to be sure.

"I know you're having a hard time," Sister Mary said. "I have a Seroxat prescription from Dr. Stanley for you. It can help with the withdrawals."

Violet stared down at her fingers, gnawed raw. She understood meds were an option; nevertheless, she couldn't understand why she felt so resistant to the idea. In her entire adult life, she had stuck a Band-Aid on her emotions. It occurred with her meds after her psychotic episode; it happened again with her painkillers. She slowly lifted her head and said, "I can't. I want to feel this. All of it."

Sister Mary looked at her over her glasses, which had fallen to the bridge of her pointed nose. "It seems counterintuitive, doesn't it, that we'd dig into our negative emotions? Is feeling this way a negative thing in the first place? One could argue it's a necessary part of the human experience." The nun paused for a second. "Very good. That's one of the biggest things we'll be working on—experiencing your negative emotions. Being able to tolerate them without numbing them out. One thing I've found that helps is to find something I love. Something I loved that wasn't cocaine, anyway." She cracked a smile and chuckled. "I've always needed to devote myself to something. I just had to find something that nurture me instead of destroy me."

Violet tried to think about what she loved. All she came up with was acting. Their conversation lingered in her head for a long time afterward.

She sat deep in thought at a reading nook by a window, glancing down at the cluster of cacti and succulents below. Such beautiful magenta flowers bloomed from the cacti. Somehow, in spite of the lack of water and the harsh conditions, the flower bloomed from the thorned plant. Violet wanted to flower in spite of her circumstances—maybe because of them. Hell, she felt she almost had. Acting had been her refuge after Amber died. It had been therapeutic. And now . . . now she knew it was what had kept her alive and would continue to keep her alive. Her aim was no longer to be a movie star or celebrity, but something else. She had an idea and dream. Even if she failed, it didn't matter. It was her passion.

With that realization came Violet's determination. She asked Sister Mary if there was a drama club in the rehab center. The director's eyes widened. "No, Violet. No there isn't."

"Well, that's about to change, I hope," Violet said. "With your blessing, I'd like to start one."

Sister Mary grinned. After a few provisions and stipulations, she gave her the green light.

* * * * *

Violet took a few sheets of computer paper and headed to the arts and crafts room. She designed five fliers, each one elaborately decorated. On some, she used watercolors, and others were boldly decorated using multicolored Sharpies. She hoped the eye-catching design would reel more people in.

Friday at 3 p.m. rolled around, and a dozen women showed up. Violet felt less nervous than she'd expected; this was a good-sized group. She began by introducing herself and asking how many people had acted before. Five people raised their hands. Others had been interested for some time but didn't have the courage to give it a go. Others just wanted a much-needed distraction from their pain.

"Thank you for sharing," Violet said. "Those are all perfectly fine motivations. I've always loved acting, ever since I was a kid. It's been something very rewarding in my life, and I'd love to share what I know with others. Plus, it's just plain fun. I really do want this to be something we can all get something from. Whether it's improvisation, one-act plays, or even Shakespeare, let me know what you'd like to do, and we can change it up."

After engaging the group, they decided to switch up the focus each session. While it was fun to do so, Violet soon felt like a grand project would genuinely motivate them and bring them together. That's when she remembered a play she had been a part of in college.

"It's called *Quilters*," Violet said, dropping the script on the table for the ladies. "We're all girls here, and this play is about several pioneer women talking about the tough life of the frontier and . . . general women's issues, really."

"Women issues? Does it talk about periods?" someone asked with a snicker.

"Oh yeah, there's a whole song on that," Violet joked back. "I know it's a musical, but wouldn't it be fun to lip-sync? It would be like fake karaoke or something. That way we can simply focus on stage presence and really have fun with it. It'd be a good first production."

The girls agreed that it sounded like a great idea. They began the process of not only practicing their parts but also preparing the stage itself. One curly haired, middle-aged woman, Peggy, mentioned that she was an avid quilter. "Back before I was hitting the bottle every day, I actually owned a craft shop," she confided to Violet. "I'd love to put the show's quilt together."

Violet was thrilled to hear they could use a real quilt for the show. "Sure, I would love your help," she said, but added after a pause, "You get total control over this under one condition: You teach me how to quilt."

Peggy smiled. "It's a deal."

Violet met with Sister Mary and told her about their progress. Sister Mary was impressed to hear about the scope of the production and complimented Violet. "The women who are part of your group only have the best things to say about it. I can see some confidence shining through. Great job, Violet. Now, the question is, will this be open to the public?"

Violet could swear that her heart stopped at the mention of it being public. Her instant thought: *this rinky-dink production?* Then she considered the women and how much work they'd put in and how excited they were. Who was she to belittle their efforts? Why couldn't they put on a show worth being paid for?

Violet contemplated for a minute. "That's not a bad idea," she said. "Maybe we can charge five dollars or so, put it toward a fundraiser. Maybe help with some of the bills." It wasn't cheap to run a nonprofit organization. The proceeds would be a much-needed donation.

"That's a very considerate thought," Sister Mary said, a twinkle in her eye.

* * * * *

It was opening night. Violet was a bundle of nerves. She didn't even remember feeling so nervous when she was in her first production. This one was different somehow. She had poured her heart and soul into this; its success fell entirely on her shoulders. She knew word had leaked to the media about the performance. One of the performer's cousins was a reporter and had done a nice feature about the new drama program at St. Jeanne's.

The result of that coverage? A full house!

"If nothing else, it's only five dollars, and it's going toward a noble cause," Violet murmured to herself. "And hell, we're all having fun."

However, the worries were completely unnecessary. The women came alive on stage. *Quilters* was electric, the actors' joy and enthusiasm contagious. The crowd erupted into applause at the end, and the cast proudly took their bows to a standing ovation.

The women smothered Violet with hugs after the curtain came down. She was laughing and crying all at once. "You guys did it, not me! You!" She could not hold back her tears, tears of delight.

It took the title of Violet's new favorite memory in life with no reservation. A memory she could recall without pain.

* * * * *

Sister Mary appointed Violet as the volunteer director of fundraising for the rehab center. After the play, Violet felt even more inspired to carry out new projects. She organized the women in the center to practice quilting and other crafts as informal art therapy. Soon they set up an online business to sell products made by the women at the center. With the extra funding, the center encouraged the women to sign up for online classes to learn real-life skills so that they could become independent and contributing members of society.

From a seed grows a tree, Violet thought. All she'd wanted was to share her passion with a few women who might benefit. She could never have imagined this transformation in herself.

"I owe it to you," she told Sister Mary. "You believed in me, entrusted me with extra responsibility. You understood what I needed before I did. I don't know how to repay you."

Sister Mary's stern face cracked into a grin. "Don't be silly, child. This was you. I'm just emotional support."

Violet wanted to hug her, but all she could manage was, "I truly admire you."

"The feeling is mutual."

They sat in comfortable silence for a few moments before Violet shyly asked, "Do you mind if I ask how you decided to become a nun? I . . . I've been thinking about it, to be honest. I grew up Catholic, you know."

Sister Mary appeared surprised but not unpleasantly so. "Oh? What led you to that?"

Violet sighed and wondered how to put her jumbled thoughts into words. Over the past few weeks, she couldn't stop thinking about Amber visiting her Christmas Eve in the car by the bridge and how divine intervention kept her alive. God must have had some reason for saving her, some plan for her life. All these things she'd gone through—losing her family, her breakdown, the drug addiction, stripping—why not use them to help others?

"You're selfless, so loving . . . and happy, just like another nun I used to know. In spite of your own demons, you created something great here. I want to continue to help these women I love, and I realized the first step to do that is to stop thinking about myself. It's about looking outward and making a difference where you can."

Sister Mary looked touched. "I appreciate your kind words, Violet. Really. I would never try to convince you to live your life one way or another—aside from being clean, of course, and treating yourself with respect. It's a big decision. All I can advise you to do is pray about it. Listen for God. Heed what He wants for you. Serving Him has given me greater purpose and infinitely more fulfillment than I ever would've thought possible, but sometimes the church can be an escape too. You have to be sure you're doing it for the right reasons."

Violet nodded solemnly.

* * * * *

The next day, Violet sought out quiet time for reflection. She visited the small chapel on the premises. In the room, two statues flanked a painting of Jesus on the cross. Entering the second row, she pushed down the cushion for her knees and bowed her head. Slowly closing her eyes, she inhaled deeply and thought about her guilt. All these years she had been crushed by the weight of it. Guilt for living while Amber was dead. Guilt for hating her mother, who consistently rejected her only living daughter. Guilt for being the daughter of a murderer. Guilt for pushing Dylan away. Guilt for being a stripper and a drug addict.

Violet opened her eyes. The first thing she saw was the painting, which looked so incredibly real. Jesus was taking his last, ragged breath. She could feel his agony. Violet knew her emotional burdens couldn't compare with carrying the weight of all the sins of the world on his shoulders. Somehow, she identified with the sense of being alone, the torture. Dying on the cross was a battle Jesus had had to endure alone, but it was the ultimate price to pay to make way for the world's greatest gift.

All of a sudden, Violet felt goose bumps rising, prickling at her skin. The room was cold. And yet . . . an undeniable sense of warmth enveloped her. She felt like someone was embracing her, providing the utmost relief and comfort. The intense eyes of the angels seemed to beckon her forth, to join them in serving God.

Only in God could she find relief now. She was tired of bearing her burdens alone. She couldn't—and wouldn't.

"If this is what you want for me," Violet whispered, "I will serve

227

you all my days. Just give me a sign."

* * * * *

Six months later, Violet was well on her way to becoming a nun.

After several conversations with Sister Mary and other young women preparing to take the vow, she had gotten a clearer idea of what lay in store. First, she would be a novice, where she would gradually begin to let go of her worldly attitude, activities, and identity. She would even get a new religious name. Then, after her period of novitiate was over, she would take her vows and fully enter the monastic life. She would be consecrated to God until death.

When she told Edwin and Peter her new plan, they were stunned.

"Why would you want to do that?" Peter asked, appalled. "The Catholic Church is nothing but a hypocritical, sexist, homophobic, pedophile-protecting cult."

Edwin shot him a silencing look. "Now, I wouldn't say that, but a *nun*? Are you sure? That's a major decision. You know, in AA they say not to make any major life changes in the first year of recovery. Being a nun, that's a lifelong commitment!"

"I'm not rushing into anything," she said. "That's what being a novice is all about. Easing into the life to make sure it is the right decision."

"Alright," Edwin said in an attempt to conceal his apprehension. "As long as you're sure."

* * * * *

At the center, Sister Mary began to give her more responsibilities. In addition to the drama program, Sister Mary charged Violet with helping to welcome new patients into the program, making them feel comfortable and answering their questions about what to expect.

As she tried to find ways to connect with the women, Violet began to open up more and more about her own story, the things that had led to her addiction and recovery journey. She found that the healing power of telling her story was beyond her imagination, even more than the therapy she'd had with the center's counselors. Something deep inside her began to unspool.

The new women looked up to Violet as a role model, despite the fact that she was younger than many of them. Each day that she spent ministering to others, seeing the good she was able to do, made her more confident in her decision, relieved to finally have a path she could be proud of.

Nevertheless, at night, her dreams suggested otherwise. Dylan's face appeared to her in her dreams. She remembered the incomparable feeling of being loved by him. She could still feel the pleasant tickle of his unshaven chin on her shoulder as he kissed her neck. Many nights she dreamed of being intimate with him, holding his broad torso against her body as he plunged into her. It was a feeling of warmth and happiness so powerful that she woke up with tears in her eyes. The unshakable passion of Dylan overtook her.

If she could only get past those dreams, life would be so much easier. Staring into the mirror after awakening from another dream so vivid and lifelike it took her breath away, Violet prayed for clarity. Perhaps she needed to mourn that long-past period of her life. Undoubtedly, that was all it was. She just needed more time.

Her hand went to her neck and the lovelock. She could easily imagine giving up everything in her life: her friends, her freedom, any future family, even her name. The one thing she couldn't yet let go of was the lovelock. She knew that she would have to take it off when she took her vows.

Not yet. Someday. But not yet.

Chapter 38

Early Fall 2017, Orange County, CA

"Are you okay?" Dylan asked Tess with concern. Her weakness was nothing unusual, but what was worrisome was her new cough. She watched TV on the couch, weak and quiet except for the sporadic fits. "I'm nervous about leaving, not gonna lie."

"It's just three days. I'll be fine," Tess replied in a whisper, reaching for the water bottle on the side table.

Dylan was about to leave for Florida for a CPE conference, a valuable opportunity to knock out most of his annual continuing education (CPE) requirements to maintain his accounting license. With Tess's condition, he hadn't been as diligent about earning them as he liked to be. Tess's illness had been like an emotional and physical beating for both of them. In a few months, she had declined rapidly. He was grateful the caretaker, Julia, had been around to help out. Julia was a strong, rather rotund woman—gentle but tough, able to lift Tess single-handedly if need be. He trusted Julia to care for Tess; however, he felt increasingly guilty about leaving.

Tess was mostly quiet, buried in one Netflix show or another. She particularly loved *Breaking Bad* and had watched it several times—a show about a high school chemistry teacher who discovers he has terminal cancer and goes into the drug business to help pay his medical bills and prevent his family from falling into debt. It was no wonder why she enjoyed it; Dylan knew she hated being dependent on anyone. She'd love to take the power back if she could. Exerting a sense of control in her life was a luxury she no longer had.

She was just as still when Dylan packed to leave in the wee hours of the morning. He gave her a tight hug and kissed her on her worn cheek as she sat on the couch watching her show with languid eyes. Her black hair was in messy braids that Julia plaited for her a couple of days before.

"I'll be back soon. Call me if you need anything," he said quietly.

She stirred and yawned before replying, "I will."

A wave of guilt washed over him. He tried to swallow it back.

* * * * *

Dylan flew into Orlando for his conference. It was ninety degrees but felt hotter than Hades, thanks to the Florida humidity. He wiped the back of his hand across his brow as he carried his suitcase to the Gaylord hotel where the conference was taking place. There were hundreds of other CPAs in attendance. The air vibrated with excitement. In the midst of interacting with other professional colleagues, Julia kept him updated about Tess's condition.

"She feels under the weather, very tired. But OK. Just want to assure you," she texted him the next day.

This allowed Dylan to feel he could dive into his continuing education sessions and mingle a little with other attendees. He was torn in two, enjoying the ability to focus on himself for a couple days, yet unable to shake off the feeling that something was amiss at home. It left him tossing and turning the first two nights away.

You're never gone. Of course, you'd worry.

On day three, the final day of the conference, he visited the coffee stand to pour himself a tumbler of coffee. He stirred a teaspoon of sugar into his indispensable caffeine when he felt his pocket buzzing.

It was Julia. "Are you free? Call me now. Urgent."

Dylan's stomach dropped. He absentmindedly placed his coffee on the table and stepped into a hallway, away from the crowd.

"What is it?" he asked.

"It's Tess. She had a seizure. We're at the ER, and she has a very high fever. I just knew I had to let you know immediately."

"Christ," Dylan said quietly, raking his fingers through his messy brown hair. "Okay. Okay, yeah, I'll get to the airport soon. I'll be there as soon as I can."

Dylan caught the first plane he could. The flight was torturous.

After a frenzied cab ride, he arrived at the hospital room only to find a nurse consoling Julia, who was attempting to wipe her tears away with the sleeve of her shirt. "What happened?" Dylan asked hoarsely. He knew the answer before he was told: Tess had passed away.

"She wanted me to give you this," Julia said, handing him an envelope.

* * * * *

Dylan plunged into the most confusing period of his life. The doctors said it was pneumonia and sepsis that killed Tess. While she did suffer a cough and some chest pains in her final days, and while MS could reduce the immune system and increase the risk of an earlier death, Dylan was certain she died because she utterly lost the will to live.

He poured himself into planning her memorial service to ensure it was as respectful as she deserved.

Once all had been done and settled, he sat in his study. He reread the letter Tess left him over and over:

My dear Dylan,

Thank you for being here for me through my illness. I know you did not sign up for this, yet you stood by my side till the end. I hope it's not too late to let you know how grateful I am.

There's something that I have meant to tell you; however, time after time, my attempt failed me. I am sorry that I lied to you: the girl you searched and waited for had never come to the hospital. I saw her picture in your wallet, the two of you, and you looked so happy, so in love, wearing the matching lovelock. When you told me how she pushed you away, didn't want to see you anymore, I thought she didn't deserve you. That it would be better for you to make a clean break. My intention was to help you move on. Please forgive me for not telling you the truth sooner. I was afraid of losing you. Dylan, I loved you from the moment I met you. Having you around was the best thing in my life.

Again and again, thank you for all you have done for me.

Love,

Tess

On the card, she wrote:

I hope for you all the love and happiness you have given me.

* * * * *

He grabbed the knob of the study's desk drawer. Inside, scattered among pens, Post-its and highlighters, was the lovelock. He picked up the key, letting the chain pool in his hand, and lifted it to his cheek.

Chapter 39

Today is the day. Finally. I can't believe it's really happening.

Dylan stood in front of the mirror, scrutinizing his reflection. His brown hair had a few noticeable strands of gray. His face appeared more lined, particularly around the eyes, than the last time they saw each other.

Will she notice? Has she changed too?

After throwing a brown leather jacket over his black V-neck, he headed out to his car and plugged the address into the GPS. It showed an arrival time of fifty-seven minutes. All this time she'd been less than an hour away!

His thoughts were all over the place as he sped down the road. Would she still be there? Was he too late? Would she agree to see him? What would he say? Was she the same girl he remembered, or was she someone entirely different now? Had he been in love with a fantasy all this time? Was this the day his dreams came true or were crushed forever? His hands were slick with sweat on the steering wheel.

After what was surely the longest hour of his life, he pulled into the parking lot of St. Jeanne's Women's Rehab and New Life Treatment Center. For a second, he worried that he wouldn't be let in. Didn't places like this restrict visitors and keep their clients confidential? Even if she was there, they might not be able to tell him. At the very least he could leave her a note and hope she responded.

Heart pounding, he opened the front door and went inside. Instead of a sterile medical setting, he found a welcoming, homey room with several clusters of comfy chairs and potted plants. A couple of women were seated together. A thin Latina woman was facing in his direction. Across from her, her back to him, was a woman with long, honey-colored hair.

His heart stopped. *It can't be!*

"Cheetos?"

The woman froze and then slowly turned. He found himself staring into enormous lavender eyes.

"Dylan?" she choked out, her face white as a ghost.

"Violet."

He felt like he was having an out-of-body experience. Nothing seemed real. She was familiar—as familiar as his own image—yet also strange. Every bit as beautiful as he remembered, she had a depth, a maturity that was new.

"How did you find me?" Violet asked. Her expression was unreadable. Dylan couldn't tell if she was upset or just in shock.

"Well, there's this thing called Google."

"And it told you I was here?"

"There was a great article about the play you did, *Quilters*." The article had also mentioned that Violet was a recovering addict. That had hit him like a ton of bricks. What had she gone through? Why, oh why hadn't he been there to protect her?

"Oh, right," she said. "That was a while back."

"It sounds like you're doing really good work here," he said, hating how stiff and formal he sounded. Why were they talking like strangers when he wanted to pull her to him, hug her tight, and tell her how much he loved her and how he'd missed her every moment since they parted?

He looked at the woman Violet had been talking to, who was watching them with undisguised interest. "Um, is there somewhere we could go to, uh, catch up?" he asked Violet. "We're, uh, old friends," he explained to the eavesdropper.She gave them a knowing smile. Dylan figured she'd have to be blind, deaf, and dumb not to pick up on the electricity between them. Who did he think he was

235

kidding? Old friends?

"There's a courtyard out back," said Violet. "We can talk there."

"Take your time!" the woman called out as the door shut behind them.

Dylan followed Violet down the hall in silence. He hoped it was giving Violet an opportunity to collect herself. He knew his emotions were in shambles, and he'd had a chance to prepare; he couldn't imagine what she was going through, being completely blindsided like this.

When they got outside, Violet took a seat on one of the wooden benches. She looked down at her laced fingers. "So, um, it's been awhile."

"That's an understatement."

"So, what have you been up to?"

"Well, I'm working as an accountant. And I've finished some short stories that I'm hoping to get published."

"Oh, that sounds great," she said, but Dylan got the impression that she was focused elsewhere. She looked up at him shyly. "I heard you got married." Even though she tried to keep her tone casual, Dylan could hear the hurt underneath.

"That's a story. A long one."

"I've got time," she ventured slowly, shifting in her seat.

Dylan took a deep breath. *Where should I begin? How much should I tell?*

"Well, to back up a little, when I was overseas, it wasn't long before I realized I had made a big mistake in leaving you. I'd thought it was the right thing to do at the time, but it wasn't. I tried to find you, write you a letter."

"You did?"

236

"Yeah, I tried everything I could think of, but it was like you had fallen off the planet. No one knew where you were or how to reach you."

Violet bit her lip. "I'd stayed at a center in Arizona for fifteen months, and I didn't want to be found," she admitted. "I wasn't able to deal with what had happened, so I was trying to start over."

"I know the feeling," he said. "That's what the Peace Corps was for me too. Something *completely* different with people who didn't know anything about who I was or what had happened to me. But I never thought that meant walking away from you forever. When I couldn't get in touch with you, I just about went nuts! I even thought about leaving early, but I couldn't just abandon my post. Those people had become like family to me, and I really felt like I was doing some good there. So I waited it out and vowed that I would track you down as soon as I came home."

He paused. "And that's what I did. I got off the plane, bought a motorcycle, and took off to look for you. Just forgot about how crazy the LA traffic could be, I guess." He smiled ruefully. "I got into a crash . . . a pretty bad one."

"Oh no! That's terrible," she said. "I wish I'd known."

"It *was* terrible, but I survived. And I met someone," he said carefully. "My nurse, actually." Dylan considered how to approach the next part without throwing Tess under the bus. He didn't want Tess's duplicity to be the first thing Violet learned about her. He'd explain the entire story some other day. "There was a . . . misunderstanding at the hospital, and I thought you had actually been there while I was unconscious."

"W-what?"

Dylan shook his head, brushing off the question. "It was a mix-up. And I thought you'd visited and decided not to stay."

"But I never would have done that!" Violet said angrily.

"I know. I mean, I know that *now*. But at the time, I believed it. I was pretty devastated. And Tess—my nurse—was there to pick up the pieces. And since I thought you didn't want me anymore . . ." He shrugged. "It wasn't a love match, at least to begin with. In fact, I was on the verge of divorcing her when she got sick. Really sick with MS. I just couldn't leave her, not when she needed me so much."

"Oh Dylan!" she exclaimed.

Dylan put his hand up. He wasn't looking for pity. "I know it sounds bad, but the weird thing is, the more I cared for her as she got sicker, the more I grew to truly care about her. It wasn't a burden. It was . . . good."

Violet nodded, her eyes filled with compassion. He could tell she understood exactly what he meant. Just like she always did.

"I've even decided that's what I want to do with my life," he continued. "Tess and I had no kids, but she knew how much I love them. I joined the local Big Brothers program with Tess's support. I've given free tutoring in math and English for underprivileged boys during the weekends. Tess went with me on her good days. I'm taking some online counseling classes too. Hopefully, I can be a counselor for troubled kids when I have free time. I may consider cutting back my accounting job when the time comes."

"That's great," Violet said. "I can totally see you doing that. You've always been so good with people and kids."

Dylan smiled gratefully. Coming from Violet, who knew him so well, the validation meant a lot. "I had just started school when Tess developed recurrent infections. At first, it didn't seem to be too big of a deal, but then she suddenly went downhill fast. She passed away in the hospital from pneumonia."

Violet lurched forward in her seat. "What? Seriously? Dylan, are you okay?" She took his hand in hers. "I am so incredibly sorry to hear that."

"It's okay, Violet. I'm okay. Really. I'm sorry she's gone, of course, but I don't have any regrets. We had a good relationship there at the end. Actually, she really helped me move on."

Violet looked at him curiously.

Not to complicate the situation, Dylan only showed Violet the card from Tess.

I hope for you all the love and happiness you have given me.

He looked Violet right in the eye. The moment of truth had arrived.

"Violet, I love you. I never stopped. I miss you and wish things could have been different between us. I feel like a jackass coming to you when you're doing so well, but if nothing else, I had to meet with you again and see for myself that you were, in fact, okay. And damn it, I'm so proud of you."

Violet shifted her gaze to the far wall. Dylan realized he'd said something wrong.

When she looked back at him, there were tears in her eyes.

"Dylan, you know I was an addict, right?"

"Yes, it was mentioned in the article."

"Well, that's not all," she said. Suddenly she was shaking like a leaf. Dylan felt his chest constrict; his heartbeat started pounding in his ears.

"I was also a stripper." She blushed, but she didn't look away.

Dylan's world imploded. *Oh no! Not his beautiful, precious girl. God, hadn't she been through enough?* He felt like reaching out his arms to hug her tight.

Her manner became brisk, matter-of-fact. "I'd moved to LA to get into acting, but I ran out of money, and I wasn't about to ask anyone . . . ." She shrugged.

"Oh Violet!" he said, heartbroken. "Why didn't you come to me? I would have given you whatever you needed. I would *never* have let

239

you—"

Violet stiffened. He could see he'd wounded her pride. He realized she didn't want his pity any more than he wanted hers. His heart clenched even more at her valiant fighting spirit.

"It was a dumb thing to do," she admitted, "but I think maybe everything happens for a reason. This might all be part of God's plan for me. You know what you said about everything pointing you to be a big brother and counselor? Well, that's what it's been like for me too. I feel like everything I've gone through has been leading me to help people here. I've found my calling, my purpose. I'm . . . I'm actually ready to take my vows. I'm becoming a nun."

A nun? Dylan felt like he'd been punched in the gut. Only then did he realize how sure he had been, deep down, that Violet would be his again. He knew she still loved him, that their connection was as strong as ever.

Nevertheless, could it be that love wouldn't be enough? No earthly love could surpass theirs, of that he was sure. Yet, could he compete with *God*? Should he even try?

He looked at the woman he had loved for as long as he could remember, whose face had haunted his dreams and whose memory had given him hope, even in the darkest of times. He knew he couldn't walk away without telling her how he felt.

"Violet," he said slowly, "I love you. I've always loved you and always will. And that means I'll support you if you want to become a . . . a nun." He paused before continuing. "But I want to be with you, to marry you just like we planned. If there is any hope for us, and you have any inkling of giving it a go with me, I'll do whatever it takes. Every fiber of my being is telling me I belong to you. That God made me for you. Can you tell me that you're *that* sure of your calling?"

Violet looked deeply troubled. "I feel more and more certain every day that goes by," she said. "I've found such a sense of peace here that it seems like it's meant to be. This is the first time in a long time that I don't want to be someone else."

Dylan felt despair threatening to pull him under.

Then she continued. "But if I'm completely honest, I can't say I'm one hundred percent sure. I keep praying. Asking for a sign."

"And?"

"Nothing yet. Every time I think about taking my vows and everything I'll have to give up and what my life will be like, I feel really good, really peaceful. Then I get to the part where I have to take this off." Her hand went to her throat.

Dylan started in recognition.

The lovelock.

"I just can't imagine taking it off. I haven't taken it off since you put it on. Not once. It's the only thing that's been holding me back."

Dylan felt a sliver of hope cut through his despair.

The lovelock! She still wears the lovelock!

That had to mean something. He bit his lip. Saying the wrong thing could destroy his chances, just like last time.

"Violet," he said, choosing his words carefully, "did you ever think that might be your answer?"

She frowned. "What do you mean?"

"You said you prayed for a sign. Maybe that is the sign." His words came out in a rush.

"You asked for a sign, an answer. What if the answer is no?"

"I don't know," she said without conviction. "I was so sure this was my path . . . ."

"Violet, just because you feel called to help people doesn't mean you have to do it as a nun. I would never ask you to choose between God and me. But you don't have to!"

241

He stared at her with love and longing. All he knew at that moment was that he wanted to hold her face in his hands, kiss those lips he knew so well. Instead, he reached over and took her hand in his.

"I'm not naïve enough to think we can just jump back into a relationship like nothing happened. But I don't want to wonder *what if* anymore. Don't you think we owe it to ourselves to see if there's something still there, after all these years?"

Tears spilled from Violet's eyes. She let them trickle down her cheeks.

Then—she nodded. She nodded and squeezed his hand.

Epilogue

It was dawn in Los Angeles. Tendrils of fog slowly retreated past Santa Monica Bay, with a wan sun steadily brightening above the gray-blue waters. A morning that demanded a light jacket but had the promise of a warmer afternoon.

I-5's familiar stretch of scenery unfolded before them as they headed south. As Dylan drove, he reached out from time to time and gently touched Violet's thigh. Each time, she reached out to squeeze his hand in response.

Lana Del Rey's husky, haunting voice emanated from the speakers. The drive was quiet, reflective. It wasn't until the dark gate appeared that Dylan turned off the music and hit his blinker. They entered the cemetery, so green and serene, and looked out for the plot of land that they rarely visited but remembered far too well. The vehicle meandered through the vast expanse of green. The air was still crisp, but the steadily strengthening sunlight offered greater warmth. When they reached their destination, Violet shimmied out of her cardigan.

Dylan turned the motor off, and they sat for a moment. Violet looked at him and gave the smallest of smiles. He returned a reassuring look and ran his fingers through her hair, gently pulling her head toward him to kiss the top.

They exited the vehicle and walked toward the grave, hand in hand. A bird cawed in a nearby tree. They stopped, staring at the gravestone: WANDA LYNN SWANSON.

Eternally beside her on the left: AMBER CHRISTINE SWANSON.

Violet wordlessly laid a pair of yellow tulips on each grave. She dropped to her knees, her fingertips tracing Amber's name on the marble gravestone, pausing on the remarkably short span of years engraved upon it.

"Thank you," she whispered. "You were right; I was wrong. As always."

She kissed her fingertips and touched the gravestone again before turning to her mother's. She stared at her mother's grave for a beat before speaking. "I've forgiven you. It's been hard, but I've done it. I understand what you went through much better now. I've made some mistakes too, done things I'm not proud of. I'm sorry for everything you went through. I love you." She kissed her fingertips again and pressed them against the cool stone.

After a few somber minutes, she stood and brushed the grass off her knees, nodding to Dylan that she was ready to move on.

Dylan's mother and father were also side by side in their final resting place. Dylan had often been to his mother's grave with his father, but he hadn't visited on his own since his father was interred.

He stared at the graves. "I'm glad they're together now. Dad was lost without her," he said. "They really were soul mates, you know."

Violet nodded, wishing it didn't remind her of her own parents.

Just one more stop to make.

Several hours later they sat in the parking lot.

"You okay?" Dylan asked quietly. "Are you sure you want to do this alone? I can come with you."

Violet had a last-minute impulse to bolt. Nevertheless, she swallowed and shook her head instead. "No. I need to do this."

"Okay, I'll be right here waiting." Dylan leaned over, gave her a tight hug, and kissed her cheek as she prepared to exit the vehicle.

She mechanically walked toward the entrance. One month prior, Violet had gone to the California Department of Corrections and Rehabilitation's website to locate Aidan's prison, complete a questionnaire, and obtain approval for visitation. As anticipated, the inside was sterile and unwelcoming. The employees looked hardened and tough, but not unkind. A heavyset African-American woman pointed to a hallway to the left and instructed Violet.

"You'll need to go through procedures at the visitor's center first. That way."

There, a guard gave an overview of some obvious rules, emphasizing no prolonged physical contact, before leading her to a big room.

She headed toward a table at the far corner, took a seat, and waited. Violet could barely concentrate. Her eyes darted to the other visitors—mostly women, a few older children. A chill ran down her spine as she imagined seeing her father face-to-face. She hugged herself, staring at the gray cement floor as she suppressed the urge to leave.

"Here she is," a commanding male voice said, startling her.

Violet looked up. A uniformed guard escorted an old man in an orange jumpsuit. Violet's knees were too feeble to support her, so she didn't stand up.

The man used the edge of the table to brace himself and lowered himself onto the chair in a tentative motion, as if he expected someone to snatch it away mischievously. There he was, her father, sitting across from her at that very moment. The table was about twenty-four inches square and no more than eighteen inches high.

He rested his hands on the table and stared at them.

The hands of a killer, the hands of my father. Oh my God!

Violet had been mentally reciting various scripts for her visit. However, her throat went dry; no words seemed right at this moment.

She could hardly recognize the man in front of her. He had hollow cheeks, sunken eyes, and thin, white hair. He sat motionless, emotionless. Violet tried to avert her eyes, yet couldn't help but stare. It was as if time had frozen.

Abruptly, he looked up as he finally summoned all of his energy and gathered his strength. "Violet." The voice was weak, but it was undeniably her father's voice calling her name. The sound of it brought back a rush of childhood memories and with it, a flood of emotions.

"I'm sorry . . . ." The words barely escaped his lips. Tears rolled down his tortured face as he looked down again.

Without another thought, Violet's hand found its way to his. "Daddy, I've missed you."

Aidan buried his face in his hands and began to weep uncontrollably. Violet found herself scooting away from the table, rushing over to him, and wrapping her arms around his violently shaking body.

She hugged him tight, sobbing with him. Her father.

The guard dashed over to pull her away.

* * * * *

They cruised down highway CA-75 South, with the grandiose sight of the San Diego-Coronado Bridge emerging. The magnificent view of the blue sea cleansed their spirits, transporting them back to a day full of hope and young love. The scenery was all the same on the way there—the same route, the same sun, the same bay, and, as they reached their destination, the same splendor of the Hotel del Coronado.

Violet stared at the magnificent red spires of the luxury hotel towering above the horizon. If she closed her eyes for a moment, she could easily forget all of the insanity that had occurred since she and Dylan were last there as college students. They had not been engaged at that point, but it had been the beginning of their commitment to each other—the day Dylan had given her the lovelock.

While it was a familiar, beloved destination, Violet couldn't help but feel a thrill of anticipation, like she was going for the first time. In a sense, they were. The young, naïve teenagers of the past were gone.

Older, wiser, and more compassionate individuals replaced them.

We've been through hell. The thought was liberating. They had faced the worst the world had to offer and come out on the other side better and stronger—and still in love.

Violet gazed at Dylan's smiling face and his twinkling eyes as he gave her hand a squeeze. Everything was right at that moment.

The future? She didn't know. However, whatever it held, they would welcome it with open arms—together.

Other Books by

Eichin Chang-Lim

Love: A Tangled Knot

New Adult Romance

Goo.gl/Km6Jsr

Convicted Felon or Doctor...Who Would YOU Choose?

If love is true, how long should you wait?

How much pain should you endure before moving on?

With the Golden Gate Bridge in sight, the story begins.

Who is this stranger in Kayla's arms? She'd waited seven years for this? A quiet, brooding, empty shell of her high school sweetheart, Russ . . . Is it time to "just move on already" as her friends so often encouraged?

Doctor Nick Leon is ready for her to move on too —as a nurse in Chicago, with him at her side. Nick, with his magnetic blue eyes— the one who was always catching her when she fell.

"Convicted FELONS need not apply." Russ gets the message, loud and clear. But with no job and nothing to offer Kayla, how can he possibly win her back? And how can he compete with that fancy doctor, his expensive home and his perfectly manicured lawn? His Kayla is just a bit too cozy there, and Russ needs it to end now. He needs a Hail Mary pass—but will it be in time to save his love?

FLIPPING

An Uplifting Novel of Love

Goo.gl/8diT4f

Flipping is an award-winning romance novel that highlights the power of love to move us forward and the strength of the human spirit to overcome life's challenges.

Life can flip in the blink of an eye, but love and passion will find a way to make it right.

What Price Will She Pay for Her Freedom?

SuAnn Chen has it all . . . Beauty. Intelligence. A wealthy family. She has everything she could want—**except** the freedom to choose her own husband.

Her father, a wealthy surgeon, has plans for her: since she can't **be** a doctor, *she **must** marry one.*

JonSun Tang has known nothing but poverty and hard work, enduring hardships that would have **broken** most people. And because he has *no desire to be a doctor*, he can never be a serious contender for SuAnn's hand in marriage.

Does JonSun even stand a *chance* against the parade of new doctor graduates that SuAnn must choose from?

Will his sweet, courageous soulmate *give up everything* for him—**a young man who has nothing**—but has vowed *he will give her the world* someday?

<u>Pick up your copy </u>and find out! <u>Goo.gl/8diT4f</u>

This uplifting, three-part love story begins with two young college students, their destinies each predetermined by different cultures. Journey with them as they forge new paths through the customs and traditions of their ancestors.

Follow along as, a generation later, the cycle of custom-bound expectations is **still** at play. Witness the power of love in healing, compassion, and acceptance in this touching, thought-provoking story!

A Mother's Heart

Memoir of a Special-Needs Parent

goo.gl/zHjZoC

It can be lonely parenting a special-needs child, but you are not alone.

A Memoir / Self Help book by Dr. Eichin Chang-Lim.

"Don't Expect Him to Call You Mommy or Daddy…"

Only one year after little Teddy was born, Eichin's world was turned upside down. Oh, she'd *suspected* something wasn't right. A mother *knows*.

She just hadn't expected to hear words like "profoundly deaf" and "genetic disorder," as Teddy was born perfect in every way. Ten fingers, ten toes. Over eight pounds, with the most beautiful sky-blue eyes.

And yet, an audiologist had delivered the news, *telling Eichin all the things her son would never be able to do.*

But doctors aren't gods—and sometimes, they're **no match** for a mother wanting to give her precious bundle a fair chance at life. She would fight the good fight and not allow the doctor's words to seal Teddy's fate.

In this candid memoir, Eichin reveals the heartache, the frustration, and the loneliness of raising a special-needs child. She shares her mistakes as well as the joys along the way.

A tender, true story of hope and triumph, Teddy's journey will leave an imprint on the soul of anyone involved with special-needs parenting.

If you or someone you know is exhausted and lonely from the journey, you'll find this memoir uplifting and heartfelt. You'll find a few helpful resources as well.

Be inspired. Be encouraged. Find your joy in the process. Scroll up and pick up your copy of *A Mother's Heart* and start reading today. **You are not alone!**

Please be kind and leave a review

Goo.gl/Km6Jsr

Goo.gl/8diT4f

goo.gl/zHjZoC

Made in the USA
Monee, IL
30 March 2023

30843631R00152